633 SQUADRON

The briefing room was packed to capacity. Air Commodore Davies picked up a pointer and turned to the model of the Svartfjord.

"Here you are then. This is the job you've been training for. We're going to throw bombs at this mountain and destroy a building that has walls as thick as a U-boat pen. Inside, the Germans are working on something so secret I'm not allowed to talk about it."

So 633 Squadron set off on what was to be an almost suicidal mission. Caught between the attacking German aircraft and the grim mountain walls, they plunged on into the howling valley of death . . .

633
SQUADRON

BY
FREDERICK E. SMITH

BANTAM BOOKS · TORONTO · NEW YORK · LONDON

633 SQUADRON

A Bantam Book / published by arrangement with the author.

PRINTING HISTORY

First published in Great Britain by Hutchinson & Co. in 1956
Bantam edition / March 1979

*Bantam Books are published by Bantam Books, Inc. Its trade-
mark, consisting of the words "Bantam Books" and the por-
trayal of a bantam, is Registered in U.S. Patent and Trademark
Office and in other countries. Marca Registrada. Bantam
Books, Inc., 666 Fifth Avenue, New York, New York 10019.*

To DES and BOB
The other two "musketeers" of A Flight

With thanks to my good friends in
Norway for their assistance

"I always thought it one of the greatest stories of the war," the young American said, his eyes shining. "The way those boys went in, knowing what was coming to them. . . . Gee, what great guys they must have been!"

The innkeeper's eyes were growing reminiscent. "They were," he said, "Great guys."

"And every operation connected with the Black Fjord was carried out from here?"

"Yes; Sutton Craddock was made their base. They arrived in January '43, and began training for the job shortly afterwards."

"So you'd met the rest of the squadron—Gillibrand, Barrett, Bergman . . . all of them as well as Grenville himself?"

"Yes, I knew them all."

The American shook his head in envy. "Grenville has been my hero since I was a kid at school. I never thought that one day I'd be standing in the pub where he and his boys used to drink their beer."

His eyes wandered round the lounge. Like the rest of the Black Swan it was of great age, with panelled walls and a timbered ceiling blackened by the smoke of centuries. Polished brass ornaments were everywhere, some shining golden in the soft lights from the shaded lamps, others winking back the firelight from the stone hearth. The counter against which the American and his friend were leaning was a massive structure, scarred and weathered, and at one end of it a large bowl of daffodils glowed with startling brightness against the pitch-black wood. Behind it a huge stand of oak shelves obstructed the view into the bar which lay beyond.

But the outstanding feature of the room was its photographs. These were hanging in double tiers round its panelled walls. There were pictures of aircraft: of a

Boston, of a crashed Messerschmidt 110, of a graceful twin-engined plane with R.A.F. markings and cannon protruding from its sleek nose: there were photographs of airmen, some in flying-kit, others in uniform,
nearly all young and nearly all smiling. Among them,
seeming incongruous in their company, was the por-
trait of a tall, fair-headed naval lieutenant. In its way
the room was a hall of fame: the innkeeper's tribute
to courage, to the men he had known and loved.

The American drew in a deep breath and turned back
eagerly. "Tell us something about 'em, Pop. Tell us
all you know about the Black Fjord job."

"Haven't you read the war histories?" the innkeeper
asked.

The American's voice was contemptuous. "Of course,
but you know what they are. They're so cold-blooded
they give you the creeps. Folks want to hear the real
stuff—how those boys felt during their training, the
girls they had, what they let out when they were drunk,
how they felt on the last day. . . . The human stuff!
One day some guy's going to put it all down, and
what a story it's going to be."

There was an odd light in the innkeeper's eyes now.
"You mean a biography that tells the stories behind
the story."

"That's just what I mean, Pop. And you must know
a few of 'em yourself—a pub's a great place for hearing things. How about telling them to us?" The American motioned towards his companion, a young English pilot officer alongside him. "Me and Danny here
are pretty soft on 633 Squadron. We heard about your
place a few weeks back and made up our minds to
do a trip up here the first chance we got. We thought
if we came across soon after opening time you might
be able to spare us a few minutes. We're due back tomorrow, so don't let us down."

The innkeeper, heavy of build and short-sighted,
looked at each eager face in turn. Both men were
young, no more than twenty-two or three. The American, who had introduced himself as Malcolm Daly,
was slimly built with dark hair and humorous yet
thoughtful eyes. He was wearing the uniform of the

2

U.S.A.A.F. His friend in the R.A.F., Danny Johnson, was more stocky of build with sandy hair and a square, pleasant face. Both were still young enough to feel hero-worship, and the atmosphere of the room had brought its glow into their eyes. The innkeeper glanced at the clock, then nodded.

"All right," he said, "I was going to look after the bar until eight, when a friend who's staying with me is due back from Highgate. But I'll ask my girl to take over. She won't mind—we never do much business on a Monday, particularly in the lounge. Take your beers over to a table while I go and ask her."

The two pilots went over to a table by the fire. Two minutes later the innkeeper returned. He had a thick folder and a photograph album under his arm. He put them down on the table in front of the two men.

"There you are," he said to Daly. "There's your biography. And here are some more photographs."

Daly stared at him. "Biography!"

The innkeeper smiled. "Yes. I've already done what you said—written a biography of 633 Squadron's operation in the Black Fjord, or the Svartfjord as it's called in Norway."

The American was dumbfounded for a moment. He picked up the folder and stared at it. The English boy was the first to speak.

"Are you going to go through it with us?" he asked eagerly.

The innkeeper settled his heavy body into a chair beside them. "Yes; I've arranged it with Ivy. She's going to finish her tea in the bar and take care of both rooms. She'll manage all right—as I said, we get very few in on Monday night."

The eager mood of the two airmen had infected the innkeeper, and he was now as keen to talk as they were to listen. He opened the album and pointed to a photograph of two shell-torn aircraft. "That's how two of the planes looked after getting back from Bergen. They flew four hundred miles like that. . . ."

At that moment a car engine sounded on the drive outside. It revved up once as if in protest, then died sullenly away. After an appreciable pause a man entered the lounge. The innkeeper half-turned, saw Ivy bustling through from the bar, and turned his attention back to the airmen.

The newcomer, wearing a trilby hat and an old, belted mackintosh, hesitated in the doorway. The atmosphere of the room seemed to daze him with its impact, and the sight of the three men at the table to add further irresolution to his movements. He was turning back to the door when he shook his head almost angrily and approached Ivy at the counter. After a further glance at the engrossed innkeeper, he ordered a beer in a low, unfriendly voice.

Ivy, blonde, over-ripe, inquisitive in a good-natured way eyed him with interest. In his middle thirties, she'd say, and not at all bad-lookin'. . . . A commercial traveller was her guess, having drink to help him forget how badly things were going. . . . She watched him take his glass into the corner by the door, then shrugged and returned to the bar. The newcomer sat among the shadows, his head lowered, his eyes alternating between the photographs and the bespectacled innkeeper at the table.

The innkeeper closed the album and pushed it aside. The young American grinned. "That was just to whet our appetites, Pop, huh? Now for the story. I can't wait—this place has got me. . . ."

The innkeeper was suddenly aware himself how the atmosphere had grown. The past was very much alive tonight—an invisible force, tugging at the sutured veins of his memory and starting the living blood flowing again.

As he drew the folder towards him, he suddenly thought of the newcomer and peered back across the room. His short-sighted eyes detected the blurred, shadowy figure in the corner, and he wondered if he should invite him over. He finally decided against it: the war had not hit everyone alike. If he were interested he would surely come across without being asked. He would be able to hear what they were talking about clearly enough in the quiet room. . . .

As he turned back to the airmen, the light reflections from the framed photographs, distorted through

4

the lenses of his spectacles, surrounded the room with dozens of luminous shapes. His mind, conditioned by the atmosphere of the room, gave him an instant simile. Like ghosts, he thought—their ghosts, gathering in silent company around them. But why had they come tonight, and what was the strange eagerness among them . . . ?

Both amused and irritated by his imagination, the innkeeper turned to the American. "You're quite right about there being a great deal missed out of the war histories," he said. "Much of the truth could not be told at the time. In fact, it has taken me all these years to get permission to write this biography. Apart from the intelligence work and the organization behind the raid, it also tells the inside story of 633 Squadron— why they were nearly wiped out over Bergen, and the real reason for Grenville's attack on the building there. It might even explain why Gillibrand won himself a V.C. . . . Of course, no one can ever know the full workings of a man's mind in a battle crisis, but at least the facts help one to make some shrewd guesses. I think you'll find all those facts in here."

There was respect as well as eagerness on the faces of his listeners now. "You've got all that in?" Daly muttered.

"Yes; this is the complete story of the operation. It starts with 633 taking up their new base on the airfield opposite, and ends among the Focke-Wulfs and flak in the Black Fjord."

There was a hush in the room as the innkeeper opened the folder. The ghosts nudged one another and drew nearer. . . .

And this, in somewhat greater detail, is the story they heard.

633 Squadron took over its new airfield at Sutton Craddock on the 8th January, 1943. It was a bleak day
with a spot of drizzle and a raw wind from the east.
The deep, low humming of the aircraft grew louder
until the windows of the Black Swan were rattling with
the noise. A crow, perched high on the crab-apple tree
in the front garden, took fright and fled down the road
like a startled enemy bandit.

The first Boston appeared out of the cloud. It was
piloted by Grenville, and he brought it low, studying
the layout of the airfield. He caught sight of the lone
inn on the road alongside the field and wondered what
it was. A Cockney voice suddenly came over the intercom.

"Looks as if the natives are friendly, skipper. See that
girl down there, waving to us? Now ain't that nice . . .?"

That was Hopkinson, his observer. Hoppy had the
eyesight of a sparrow-hawk. Grenville's eyes, the only
part of his face visible above his mask, crinkled in a
brief smile as he wagged his wings in reply. Then Control came through again and once more his gaze became intent on the airfield. He completed a circuit, then
came down to land. With flaps down and engines
throttled back, the Boston swooped over the field and
landed as gracefully as a ballerina. The rest of the
squadron followed her down, scattering groups of
sparrows like dry leaves in a wind.

The Black Swan across the way was an old country
inn with thick, whitewashed walls and a grey slate roof.
Behind its front garden was the private porch that gave
access to the living quarters. Alongside it a gravel drive
led to its two public rooms, the bar and the lounge,
both of which were at the side of the inn.

On hearing the approaching engines, Maisie, the
barmaid, had run to the door of the bar. She was a
big, handsome girl with black hair, dark eyes, and bold

6

features. She stood on the steps, waving a duster at each plane as it roared by. She was joined a few seconds later by the innkeeper, Joe Kearns. Kearns was a man in his middle fifties, bespectacled, stout of build, with thinning white hair and a pleasant, ruddy face. He stood peering up into the drizzle until the last plane had gone by.

It was a Bombay, full of administration and other groundstaff officers. Its black hulk passed right over them, the air whining through its struts and over its airfoils. Then it had landed, and the sky resolved itself into a formless ceiling again, devoid of shape or colour or noise.

Maisie's eyes were still sparkling with excitement as she drew reluctantly back into the bar.

"They looked fine, didn't they, coming in low like that? Did you see 'em waggling their wings—they saw me wavin' to them." There was satisfaction in her strong, throaty voice.

A smile pulled at the corner of Joe Kearns' mouth. "Yes; they saw you all right."

There was an archness in Maisie's walk now as she stepped back to the bar. She flicked her duster reflectively over it.

"I wonder who they are. One of the guards we had last week said they were a crack squadron comin' here for special duties. The corporal with him gave him a nasty look, so there might be somethin' in it."

"We'll probably get to know soon enough," Kearns said, closing the door to keep out the drizzle.

Maisie's eyes turned dreamy. "Gee; just suppose they've got some of those aces among them, like those you read about in the papers! Wouldn't that be wonderful?" She looked eagerly at Kearns. "D'you think any of 'em will come over tonight?"

Kearns shook his head. "I don't know, lass. They'll have their own messes, don't forget. But we're bound to get some over eventually."

One of them, although not one of Maisie's aces, decided to go over that evening before dinner. He was Adams, the Station Intelligence Officer. Before leaving

7

his billet he hastily checked his appearance in a mirror. The S.W.O. was a terror for smartness—there had been more than one case of senior officers being reported to the adjutant for untidy dress. . . .

The mirror showed a man in his middle forties with short legs, a plump, round face, and spectacles. His service greatcoat added to his stoutness and the peaked cap made his face look owlish. Nothing could look less military and Adams turned away from the vision in distaste.

There had been no need to worry about his appearance, he thought, as he groped his way up to the camp entrance. The black-out was complete, he could have gone out in his shirt tails and no one would have known. Twice he wandered off the path into sticky mud, and once he stumbled heavily against a pile of stacked bricks. Nothing is more bleak or unhospitable than a newly laid airfield, and he breathed a sigh of relief when he passed by the sentry at the entrance and started down the road.

Adams was something of a complex character. He hated war, yet would have given his right arm or a leg to have been young and fit enough for flying duties. Temperamentally he was unsuited for Intelligence work because of the romantic streak in his nature which constantly rebelled at having to keep silent over the deeds of courage he heard almost daily. He was a keen observer, highly imaginative, self-critical to a fault, and utterly contemptuous of his rôle in the war, being quite certain that the crews he interrogated shared his contempt. His wife was a woman fifteen years younger than himself—another indication of his inherent romanticism—and it was because of her he was making his present call at the Black Swan.

He stood now in front of the black-out curtain of the lounge, staring round at the panelled walls with their glinting brass ornaments. Maisie, reading a thriller behind the counter, looked up and quickly preened herself. He wasn't exactly the film-star type, but still he was a squadron-leader and Maisie decided he deserved one of her Sunday-afternoon smiles.

"Good evenin', sir. What can I get you?"

Adams approached the counter. "Good evening. Is the landlord about? I'd like a word with him, please."

"The landlord, sir! That's Mr. Kearns. Half a mo', I'll give him a shout for you."

With another bright smile, Maisie swung off to the side door, her skirt swirling invitingly about her legs.

"Joe," she shouted. "There's a gentleman from the aerodrome to see you. A squadron-leader."

Kearns entered the bar, eyeing Adams curiously. "Good evening, sir. What can I do for you?"

"I'm looking for a place for my wife," Adams told him. "I've just arrived today and one of the workmen said you had rooms here. What's the position?"

Kearns shook his white head regretfully. "Sorry, sir; but I don't let rooms any more. I'm a widower and can't get the help to do the cookin' and that sort of thing. Help's hard to come by these days, you know."

Adams looked disappointed. "If it's only the cooking, I don't think my wife would mind doing her own."

"It isn't only that, sir. There's the washing and the cleaning-up. . . ."

"Mrs. Billan would help you out there," Maisie interrupted. "She said she'd give a hand if ever you were stuck." The grateful look on Adams' face encouraged Maisie to continue. "He'll never get a room in Highgate—it's full of evacuees. Go on—let him have one here. We'll manage."

Kearns shifted uncomfortably. He was a kind-hearted man who always found difficulty in refusing a request. Maisie, exploiting his weakness ruthlessly, went on: "It ain't right to keep a Service man away from his wife, not when you've got empty rooms. It ain't patriotic."

She winked at Adams who felt his face redden. Kearns scratched his head. "You think your wife wouldn't mind doing her own cooking, sir?"

"I'm sure she wouldn't," Adams said, who was not sure at all.

Kearns was still undecided. "I hadn't intended to let them," he muttered.

"Go on—let him look at them," Maisie said, "It's the least you can do for someone who's fightin' for us."

Adams felt himself flush again. Kearns gave way. "All

right, sir. Seeing how things are, I'll do it. You'd better come through and see what I've got."

"That's better," Maisie said cheerfully, opening the flap of the counter to let Adams through. "It's up to us all to do what we can for the Services."

Somewhat hastily Adams followed the landlord. He came back ten minutes later, looking pleased. He went round the counter, then approached Maisie, who leaned forward.

"Well; are you all fixed up?" she asked.

"Thanks to you, yes. What will you have to drink?"

"You don't have to buy me a drink for that."

"I want to buy you a drink," Adams said awkwardly. "What will you have?"

Maisie surrendered gracefully. "All right; if it'll make you feel better. I'll have a drop of gin—we managed to get a few bottles last week. Like a tot?"

"No; I'll have a pint of bitter, please."

Maisie poured the drinks, then leaned voluptuously against the counter. "Were you in one of the planes that passed over here this afternoon?"

Adams nodded. "Yes. I was in the Bombay, the big one that came in last."

"Did you see me wavin'?"

"Yes. We all saw you. I waved back, as a matter of fact."

Maisie was pleased and was going to say so when the blackout curtain parted and two airmen appeared. One was a thinly built L.A.C., an old sweat with a long, dismal face and a pointed nose. He was wearing a crumpled rag of a field service cap and a camouflaged ground-sheet as protection against the drizzle. His companion was a young A.C.2, very new-looking in his high-buttoned greatcoat. The strap of his gas-mask, running down from somewhere alongside his neck, appeared to be half-strangling him.

The A.C.2 was the first to notice the squadron-leader. He halted dead in his tracks like a rabbit seeing a stoat. The old sweat gave him a push.

"G'wan," he hissed. "This isn't Padgate. And it ain't out of bounds to airmen. Watcha afraid of . . . ?"

Then he saw Adams was looking at him and he made a vague up-and-down motion of his right hand. An enemy, wishing to discredit him, might have said it was a compromise salute.

"Evening, sir. Grim night, sir,"

"Good evening, McTyre," Adams said, his blue eyes twinkling behind his spectacles.

With another surreptitious push McTyre sent the A.C.2 stumbling across the room to a table in the far corner. Muttering his contempt of fireballers who toady to authority, he pulled off his wet ground-sheet, revealing a uniform almost as greasy as his cap. His gas-mask, black with oil, was slung over his left shoulder in officer fashion, and the top button of his tunic was open, revealing a black shoe-lace of tie struggling to hold together the frayed remains of a service shirt. Adams eyed him in fascination, thinking what unholy joy his appearance would bring to the S.W.O.

Still muttering, the old sweat dropped into a chair. Beside him the erk sat stiffly upright, his young, round face emerging hot and flushed from his buttoned-up collar. His eyes were glued on Adams.

Maisie had all the snobbishness of her kind for other ranks. "Did they all come in today as well?"

"Some of them," Adams said non-committally. Seeing she was making no move to serve them, he threw a half-crown on the counter.

"Take them a couple of beers, will you?" he said casually.

Maisie's eyes opened wide. "My, is that the way you treat your blokes? Do you tuck 'em in bed as well?"

She filled two glasses and went over to the airmen. Adams drained his glass and picked up his gloves from the counter. "See you later," he said as she came back. "And thank you again for your help."

Maisie showed her disappointment. "Are you goin' already? When's your wife coming?"

"Monday, I hope. I'm 'phoning her tonight and will drop in tomorrow to let you know."

Seeing the young A.C.2 was rising, obviously trying to pluck up the courage to thank him, Adams moved hastily to the blackout curtain. "Cheerio, and thank you again."

"Cheerio," Maisie sighed. She watched him go out, then turned to the two airmen. She gave a sarcastic laugh.

"No wonder you joined the Air Force!"

McTyre scowled, picked up his beer, and slouched forward. "Don't get any wrong ideas about us, kid. You know who we are?"

Maisie eyed him with both scorn and curiosity. "Haven't a clue."

"We're 633 Squadron. That's who we are."

"Names and numbers mean nothing to me," Maisie sniffed, inwardly impressed.

McTyre's face assumed the expression old sweats always assume before erks and civilians: a mixture of cynicism, bitterness and contempt.

"You ain't heard of 633? What's the matter with you? Ain't you English?"

"Don't get fresh with me," Maisie snapped.

The young A.C.2 wandered to the bar. His eyes had not yet recovered from his being treated to a beer by a squadron-leader. McTyre jerked a grimy thumb at him.

"Just posted to us. Don't know the time yet."

"I ain't surprised, with that clock of yours floating around in front of him," Maisie threw back. "What've you come to Sutton Craddock for, anyway?"

McTyre's face took on a secretive expression. He leaned forward. "Special job, kid. Big stuff. Must be, or they wouldn't have sent us."

"You ain't half got an opinion of yourself, haven't you? What's so wonderful about your squadron?"

McTyre's voice held all the bitterness of the unsung hero. "If you read th' papers, you'd know. I keep telling you—there ain't a squadron in Blighty like ours." He screwed up his long face for inspiration. It came—brilliantly. "We're like . . . we're like the Guards in the Army, kid. The best! Ain't you heard of Grenville's raids on Rotterdam? Or on Emden and Brest? What's the matter with you . . .?"

Maisie's eyes had suddenly rounded. "Did you say Grenville? Roy Grenville?"

"That's right," McTyre said, his expression triumphant now. "Roy Grenville. He's our Squadron Commander. See what I mean now, kid?"

3

Twelve hours later a small Norwegian fishing-boat drew alongside a jetty in a northern Scottish port. Except for a car, standing with dimmed lights, and two waiting men, the jetty was deserted. The boat's diesel engine went silent as she drifted slowly in, the wind soughing through her riggings. The two waiting men seized her mooring ropes, and a few seconds later the boat was firmly anchored to the quayside.

The two men on the jetty hurried back to their car, one settling behind the wheel, the other taking his seat in the back. The engine started up impatiently. A few seconds passed, then a man wearing a dark-blue fisherman's jersey leapt up from the boat and ran towards them. He was no sooner in the car than it pulled away, throwing him back into his seat. He felt his hand gripped tightly.

"Hello, my boy. How did it go this time?"

"Very well, sir." The newcomer had a faint Norwegian accent.

"No trouble?"

"No, sir. Nothing."

The darkness was giving way to the grey of the dawn, and both men could see the other's features. The Norwegian was a man in his late twenties, tall and broad, with an open, pleasant face and a shock of yellow hair. His questioner was an elderly man of soldierly appearance with iron-grey hair and a trim moustache. The epaulettes on his khaki greatcoat showed him to be a Brigadier.

He had a clipped, controlled voice. "Any more luck?" he asked quietly.

"Yes. A little more, anyway."

The Brigadier's hand gripped the younger man's arm. "Well done. We've had a bad week, wondering how things were going." He paused, then went on: "How are you feeling after the trip? Would you like a rest before the interrogation? We're all pretty keen to get started, of course, but I can arrange a rest if you need one."

"No; I'm all right, sir. Where are we going now?"

"We've got a place in the country—it's only fifteen minutes from here. Anyway, you can have a long rest tomorrow. In fact, you should have a fairly easy time for the next two or three weeks. This is what we have laid on for you. . . ."

The Brigadier spoke for over ten minutes. "You'll leave by train in two days' time," he finished. "When you get to Highgate, the Air Force will take you over. We've put an Air Commodore in the know, a chap called Davies, and he'll take you to the squadron's new base at Sutton Craddock. Once there, your job is to prevent curiosity. That could be a nuisance, so we've arranged for you to go as a naval lieutenant. The story will be circulated that you've been sent by the Admiralty as a liaison officer—to study Air Force procedure, and also to tip off the squadron about enemy naval movements and so on. Most bomber squadrons get one sooner or later, and we think it will cover you up nicely. Of course, you'll get more detailed instructions before you go, but is everything clear so far?"

"Quite clear. What squadron is it, sir?"

The Brigadier's voice expressed his satisfaction. "We've done well for you there, although Bomber Command didn't let them go without a fight. We've got 633 Squadron—Roy Grenville's boys. As you probably know they are one of Bomber Command's crack squadrons." His tone grew serious again. "They need to be, from what we hear."

The Norwegian was looking puzzled. "But Grenville's squadron uses Bostons, doesn't it? Surely they cannot carry heavy enough bombs for this job? And you say Sutton Craddock is down in North Yorkshire. Shouldn't they use a base in Scotland to cut down the range?"

Again the Brigadier lowered his voice. "Jerry might start getting suspicious if a new light bomber squadron moved up into Scotland. He'll be wondering about 633, of course, but for the very reason you mention he won't guess its purpose."

The doubt was still in the Norwegian's eyes. "But I still do not understand, sir. How can they do this job in Bostons?"

"They won't have to," the Brigadier told him. "There's something very special coming along. Don't worry—they'll have the planes to get there."

Back at Sutton Craddock that morning all the orderly disorder of a squadron on the move was at its height. An endless convoy of lorries was bringing in the stores. Thousands of gallons of high-octane fuel were being poured into the petrol dump; hundreds of tons of equipment was being stacked into the workshops, the hangars, and the Nissen huts. The bomb-store at the far end of the airfield was being filled with 2,000-lb. A.P.'s, 1,000-lb. and 500-lb. M.C.'s, 250-lb. incendiaries, fragmentation bombs, S.C.I.'s, 4-lb. incendiaries, and dozens of different types of fuses and detonators. In the station armoury were being stored the spare Browning guns, the gun-sights, the belt-filling machines, the Mk. IX bomb-sights, the spare bomb-carriers, the bomb-pistols: all the hundred and one ancillaries that go with the weapons of a modern squadron.

In the workshops men toiled, heaved and swore. Mechanics complained about their tool kits, lost in transit. Sweating N.C.O.'s dashed from officers to men and from men back to officers again. As fast as stores were removed, fresh piles took their places as the lorries rolled in. New postings from training units wandered rain-soaked and glassy-eyed through the chaos, too dazed to palpitate at the yells and curses from red-faced N.C.O.'s.

Everywhere it was the same. The Orderly Room looked as if a bomb had burst slap in the middle of the floor. Requisition forms, leave passes, ration slips: all the bumph so dear to Sergeant Whitton's heart was strewn in unbalanced heaps on desks, chairs and cupboards, and littered over the floor. Typewriters lay at odd, dejected angles, clearly without hope of being used again. Men moved like nightmare figures, moving paper from A to B, wincing as another pile thudded on A again.

Panics came thick and fast. The Station Equipment Officer found a packing-case of men's underpants was incredibly filled with Bloomers Blue, Style 7, a grave mutation indeed. The Armament Officer found his harmonizing gear a shattered mess of twisted tubes and pulverized glass. The Maintenance Officer found that one of his bowsers had been routed to Scotland; and the Signals Officer found his dachshund pup, Hans, was missing. For safety Hans had been put in the care of three wireless mechanics who were bringing the Signals Van to the airfield. A pub had proved his downfall. While the three airmen were inside, having a hasty pint, Hans had spied a comely bitch pattering prettily down the pavement outside. With a yelp and a howl Hans had gone out of the window and hotfoot down the street after her. Result—Hans A.W.O.L., and sparks twittering round the Signal Officer's lips.

But at last order began to emerge. The example was set by the Station Disciplinary Officer, W/O Bertram (known from the C.O. down to the lowest erk as Bert the Bastard). After allotting his hundreds of airmen their billets, he set about putting an end to this nonsense. Superbly indifferent to the chaos raging around him he lowered his massive frame down on a packing-case and made out his first duty roster. The sight of those D.R.O.'s was salutary. The guard-room rallied and made its first kill—an A.C.1 wearing a pair of civilian shoes. The Maintenance Officer contacted his bowser heading for the Western Isles, and said a few succinct words to its driver. Hans was discovered by an M.P. howling outside a house of low repute and brought back a sadder and wiser pup. The Intelligence and Navigation Officers found their charts and maps and began getting their offices in order. The Squadron Office, the Flight Offices, the Messes, the Cook House, the Crew Rooms: all started receiving their equipment at last. The familiar yellow gas detectors began appearing in their usual places, at the entrance to the E.T. rooms and the latrines. . . .

In short, 633 Squadron was rapidly becoming itself again.

17

4

The station wagon drove into the gates of Sutton Craddock and halted. The M.P. on duty peered in, then stiffened to attention. A sergeant, already alerted, came out of the guard-house at the double, his boots clattering on the tarmac road. He skidded to a halt and saluted.

The driver, a pretty W.A.A.F. with a supercilious nose, leaned her forage cap and curls from the side window. "Station Headquarters—the C.O.'s office, please."

The sergeant pointed along the road to a long, low brick building on the left. "Second door, Miss, and take the first corridor to the right. . . ." Before he could finish the car shot away from him. He thought ponderously, then threw a discreet salute after it.

The Station Commander's office that morning was not its usual self. The rooms on either side of it had been emptied for the occasion and a security guard posted in the corridor and on the road outside the window, both men with instructions to look as inconspicuous as possible.

Barrett, the Station C.O., was standing restlessly at the window. Barrett was a heavily built man of forty-two, with thinning hair, rather melancholy brown eyes, and a moustache large enough to earn him the nickname of Wally from his men. He was a South African by birth, his parents having settled in England during his early teens. He had joined the R.A.F. as a regular, and an apprenticeship at Halton had been followed by a pre-war tour in both India and the Middle East. Although not imaginative, he was efficient, conscientious, and popular with his men. His ribbons included the A.F.C., and the D.F.C., the latter medal having been won over Kiel in the early days of the war when he had collected a chest wound that had grounded him for a long time. Because of it he was still under orders to fly as little as

18

possible—an order that irked him, for he was a very keen pilot.

As he stood at the window the distant roar of engines as a Boston was run up for testing came to him. Queer business, this posting, he reflected. Too much secrecy for his liking. Anyway, maybe something would come out of the bag today. He certainly hoped so.

The station wagon pulled up outside with a squeal of brakes, Barrett gave it one look, then strode quickly to the door, motioning the sentry towards him.

"They're coming now," he said gruffly. "Don't let 'em see you're on guard. But keep a close watch once they're inside."

He returned into his office and waited. A few seconds later he heard footsteps in the corridor, then a tap on the door.

Barrett knew the first of the two men who entered. It was Air Commodore Davies, an alert little man with a sharp, intelligent face and quick darting eyes. In certain moods he resembled a truculent cockrel. Temper or not, he was a man Barrett held in high esteem. He came forward now with characteristic quick strides, his hand outstretched. He had a sharp, somewhat high-pitched voice.

"Hello, Barrett. How's everything going? Seeing daylight yet?"

"We're nearly out of the wood, sir. We're getting the kites air-tested today."

"Good man. That's fine. Now I want you to meet Lieutenant Bergman. Lieutenant Bergman: this is Wing Commander Barrett, 633 Squadron's C.O."

The Norwegian, tall and broad-shouldered in his naval uniform, stepped forward. Barrett took a look at his firm mouth and steady blue-grey eyes and decided he looked a good type. He held out his hand.

"Glad to meet you, Lieutenant."

"I am very pleased to meet you, sir."

Barrett noticed the foreign accent and wondered whether it had any connection with the conference to follow. He saw Davies looking at him.

"Where's Grenville and your Intelligence Officer?"

"They're both in the S.I.O.'s room, sir. I thought

19

there might be something you wanted to tell me before they came in. I can get 'em here in half a minute."

Davies shook his head. "No; I don't think there's anything. Give them a call, will you?"

As Barrett spoke into his desk telephone, Bergman moved to the window, watching the airman who was sauntering up and down with the utmost unconcern before it. He caught Barrett's eye as the C.O. put the receiver down.

"One of your security men, sir?"

Barrett looked disappointed. "Why, yes, he is, as a matter of fact." He went resentfully to the window. "I told the damn fool to look as inconspicuous as possible."

Davies's bright eyes twinkled. "I shouldn't worry too much, Barrett. Lieutenant Bergman has a nose for them. He needs to have, in his job."

There was a tap on the door. "Come in," Barrett shouted. Bergman turned with him, watching with interest.

One of the men who entered was Adams, his eyes curious behind his spectacles at the sight of the naval officer. Bergman examined him, then turned his gaze on his companion. This one, he knew, would be Grenville.

Roy Grenville was twenty-six, slightly over medium height and compact of build. The force of his personality struck Bergman at once, that indefinable magnetism that makes a man a natural leader. Yet there was nothing about his appearance to conform with the popular conception of the ace pilot: he wore his uniform correctly and well. The same self-discipline showed in his expression and movements, indicating that here was a man who, after subjecting his mind and body to a hundred perils, had learned all their tricks, and now had both under rigid control. He looked an intelligent man who was applying all the power of his mind to the business of war with a ruthless disregard to its effects on himself. Below his pilot's brevet was an impressive row of ribbons, including the D.S.O. and D.F.C.

Introductions were made and Bergman found himself shaking hands with Grenville. The pilot's eyes stared

20

into his own, assessing him, coldly speculative on his rôle in the conference.

Davies, who knew Grenville, exchanged a few warm words with him, then took his place behind Barrett's desk. His quick, keen eyes flickered on each man in turn.

"The first thing I'm going to impress on you," he began, "is the need for absolute secrecy in everything you're going to hear. Not only Lieutenant Bergman's life, but the lives of hundreds of others could be lost by careless talk. In fact," and his voice was grim, "God knows just what isn't at stake in this show, so keep your mouths buttoned right up."

He threw a glance at Bergman, smiling now. "As you're going to find out in a moment, the Lieutenant here isn't quite all he seems. But as far as the rest of this squadron goes, he is a Norwegian Naval Officer who has come here to find out what makes the R.A.F. tick, and also to act as a liaison officer between you and naval affairs in northern waters. Most bomber squadrons get a naval officer sooner or later, and this is yours. Look after him and play up to him. That's something you *can* let out of the bag."

He stared briefly out of the window, then turned to them again, his voice lower now. "In actual fact Lieutenant Bergman is a liaison officer acting between the Norwegian Linge—that's their resistance movement—and our own Special Services. He used to spend most of his time over in Norway, tipping us off by wireless about shipping movements and that sort of thing. Now, however, he has handed those duties over to one of his assistants because he has made a discovery too important to be mentioned over the radio, even in code. During the last few months he has been nipping backwards and forwards, sometimes by sea, sometimes by air, to find out what more he can do about it, and also, of course, to keep his resistance men organized. Now it seems things have gone far enough for us to be called in to help.

"Now I can't tell you what the job is going to be, because I don't know myself yet. Frankly, I was only told this little bit three days ago and then, I suspect"—

21

and he threw a wry smile at Bergman—"only because the powers-that-be decided it would look less suspicious if your squadron orders came through Group in the ordinary way instead of direct from Special Services. But this much I can tell you. . . .

"You're going to operate with these Norwegian patriots. You're going to drop supplies to them when they need them, and you're going to make any attacks Lieutenant Bergman thinks necessary. I hope he finds plenty necessary because then it'll help to justify your existence to Bomber Command, who loaned you to Special Services with the greatest reluctance. They don't know what is behind all this, either. But, according to Lieutenant Bergman and a certain gentleman I cannot name, you're going to be given the biggest job you've ever tackled within the next few months, and you have to start training for it shortly. No, don't ask me what it is—I haven't a clue. All I'm told is that it's immensely important and that you'll need to be trained to perfection to carry it out. Now I'm going to let Lieutenant Bergman take over for a minute or two. He might enlighten you a little more—we'll see. Lieutenant Bergman. . . ."

All three men watched the fair-headed Norwegian intently as he rose to address them, and all felt disappointment when he gave a rueful shake of his head.

"I am very sorry, gentlemen, but the Air Commodore has covered everything that I am allowed to tell you at the moment. Of course, when training starts, you will have to be told more, but until then I have the strictest instructions to say nothing about this discovery. I can only assure you that its importance cannot be exaggerated."

He sat down apologetically. Davies shrugged his shoulders. "Well; there it is—very hush-hush indeed. Your guesses are as good as mine." He turned to Bergman. "All right, you can't talk about the big job. But what about the preliminary stuff leading up to it? What about that convoy you were talking about that has a bearing on it?"

"I'm waiting for news of it now. It should come through in the next day or two."

Davies gave his attention now to Barrett and Grenville. "From his contacts the Lieutenant has been tipped off that a fair-sized enemy convoy, anchored in a fjord to the north of Bergen, might be making a dash southwards in the next few days.

"There's no hope of getting it at anchor, but it'll be a different matter when it sails. It's obviously a job for us because, apart from the time factor, it will be at the wrong side of the minefields for the Navy. That's why I want you operational at the earliest opportunity; we must play safe. . . . Get your kites air-tested today and don't let your men wander far away. Lieutenant Bergman will give you all the details once I've gone so you'll be ready when the green light comes through. All right; any questions before I go?"

Grenville's face was expressionless, but Barrett was shuffling restlessly in his chair. Davies's keen eyes fixed on him.

"Any questions, Wing Commander?"

Barrett looked slightly uncomfortable. "I don't quite follow how the machinery of this is going to work," he said gruffly. "I don't mean regarding the big job— we'll hear about that later—I mean on the preliminary stuff—such as the dropping of supplies or this shipping strike. Does the Lieutenant give his orders to me, or do they come through from Group?"

A delicate diplomatic point. Bergman, in appearance at least, was a junior of rank to Barrett. Davies made it clear the point had not been overlooked.

"Orders will come through from Group, from me," he said without undue emphasis. "After I have given them, you can then approach the Lieutenant for the finer details. Sometimes—as in the case of this shipping strike—it may be necessary for him to attend the briefings. If so, I'll tell you. When that happens the crews must think he is there on Admiralty orders. Quite clear?"

Apparently it was. Barrett's moustache lost its temporary agitation as he sank back into his seat.

23

Adams spoke for the first time. "I take it arrangements will be made for a full range of photographs and maps to be sent me, sir?"

"You'll be getting a cartload," Davies told him. "They should be on their way now. Anything else?"

His eyes moved on to Grenville, but the Squadron Commander's expression did not change. There was silence in the room, every man knowing the futility of asking the questions he had in mind. Davies nodded and picked up his gloves.

"Right; then I'm off. They haven't finished with me back there—God knows what else they have brewing for us. Keep on your toes in the meantime; the green light for this shipping strike might come on at any time."

He paused at the door, his quick, bright eyes flickering from man to man. "And mind you look after your new naval officer! From what I can gather he's worth more than a division of men just now."

Barrett saw him out to his station wagon. As it pulled away down the tarmac road, an airman, coming out of the nearby Orderly Room, let out a wolf cry on seeing the pretty W.A.A.F. driver, only to freeze into horrified silence as Davies glanced out of the window. His consternation increased when he noticed Barrett not twenty yards away.

Barrett scowled and returned to his office. He put a call through to his Maintenance Officer, then turned to Grenville. "Townsend says all the kites will be ready for air-testing by 1500 except for M Mary. Some are ready now. You'd better go round and tip off your crews. No wait. . . . Maybe we'd better first have a chat with Lieutenant Bergman about this strike, so we know what we're in for. Then you can take him round with you and introduce him to the boys. Adams, I'll want to see you again this afternoon. Say at 1500 hours. . . ."

Half an hour later Bergman accompanied Grenville to the Flight Offices. He felt a certain diffidence while walking along the tarmac with him: Grenville was taciturn and the Norwegian's own training had done nothing to make idle talk come easily. As a result they walked most of the way in silence.

It was a bitter afternoon, the wind probing bleakly among the Nissen huts and sweeping unmolested over the scarred, cement-stained ground. Over to the east a dark bank of clouds was massing, waiting impatiently for the brief winter day to end. As they came in sight of the airfield Bergman saw the squadron's Bostons at their dispersal points, each surrounded by its attentive mechanics.

A Naafi girl was coming out of A Flight office carrying a trayful of tea mugs as they approached. Grenville held back the door, motioning for Bergman to enter. The Norwegian went in curiously. The air was thick with cigarette smoke. Groups of Flight crews were clustered round the room, some playing cards, others swapping yarns. The Flight Commander, "Teddy" Young, was sitting with his cap tipped over his eyes and feet up on his desk, miraculously dozing in spite of the blaring wireless and din around him. Young was an Australian who had worked his way over to England at the beginning of the war with the express purpose of joining the R.A.F. He was a powerfully built, ginger-headed man with a slow Australian drawl.

Somone shook him. He saw Grenville and rose at once. "Hello, skipper," he said, reaching out and turning off the wireless. "What can I do for you?"

The Flight crews eyed one another curiously, clearly puzzled by the presence of a naval officer. Someone let out a raspberry, quickly suppressed as Grenville stared around. A respectful silence followed.

"I want you to get your kites air-tested as soon as possible," Grenville said. "And then keep your men within call. No twenty-four-hour passes."

Young's expression was curious. "What's coming up, skipper?"

"You'll hear that later," Grenville said. "All you have to do now is get your kites tested and keep your men within reach."

Young shrugged but showed no resentment, a fact that told Bergman much about Grenville's popularity with his men.

25

"O.K., skipper. Fair enough. I'll keep 'em around."

Grenville motioned casually to Bergman. "By the way; this is Lieutenant Bergman. He's been sent to us by the Navy as a liaison officer. If you're nice to him he might get you some of those duty-free cigarettes."

Laughs came, easing the slight tension. After brief introductions, Grenville took Bergman out, leaving Young 'phoning up the N.C.O. in charge of Maintenance.

They crossed over to B Flight office. B Flight was commanded by Sam Milner, an American who had joined the R.A.F. in 1939. Milner looked more like a professional man than a pilot, being neat and meticulous of appearance. Townsend, the Maintenance Officer and one of the station wits, said that even in flying kit Milner could make a pair of dangling earphones look like a Doctor's stethoscope. Nevertheless, Milner was one of 633's top three pilots.

He nodded at Grenville's introduction and shook hands with Bergman. "We wouldn't be doing any shipping strikes, would we, Lieutenant?" he drawled.

There was a groan from the crews in the office. A buzz of speculation broke out after the Norwegian and Grenville left them and went outside.

"That should cover the security angle," Grenville said "Now we'd better see the adjutant about some quarters for you."

Ignoring Bergman's protests that he could arrange this himself, Grenville led him towards the Administration block. The path they were taking took them near a Boston that was going up for air-testing. As they approached, its pilot opened up his two Cyclone engines, sending a cloud of gravel rattling against the metal roof of a Nissen hut.

Watching it, Bergman became aware of a disturbing sense of responsibility. All these highly trained men to whom he had been introduced were to risk their lives on the strength of his information in the weeks to come. Mistakes would mean losses, perhaps losses of friends. Until his own time came to go back into action, he knew he would be happier if allowed to share some of the missions with them.

26

He put a hand on Grenville's arm and tried to speak but the bellow of the engines drowned his voice. Grenville waited until the Boston rolled away, his face expressionless.

"Can you arrange for me to come with you on this shipping raid?" Bergman asked. "There are men on the coast giving signals—it is something new and I would like to make certain it works satisfactorily."

Grenville's voice was by nature curt. It was doubly so now. "That's out of the question. Right out."

"Why?" the Norwegian asked.

"You can't go on a shipping strike! To begin with we've no room for you and in any case it's far too dicey."

"What do you mean by dicey? Dangerous?"

Understatement was Grenville's way. It was not easy now for him to give the facts. He pulled up the collar of his greatcoat, a gesture of irritation.

"Shipping strikes are always dicey. The flak is heavy and accurate, and you have to fly through it to get your target. That means losses, often heavy ones. It's quite obvious you couldn't be risked on a show like that."

"But my life is no more important than yours, or your men's!"

"Davies didn't say that! His last words were that we should look after you. Taking you on a shipping strike would hardly be doing that." Grenville looked down at his watch impatiently. "Let's get over to the adjutant, please. I'd like to get my kite air-tested before lunch."

Bergman checked him again. "I don't think you understand. I'm not under Air Commodore Davies's orders. If I wish to go, I am quite free to do so. And I would like to go."

Grenville, never patient of temper, was losing it now. "And I'm saying you can't go. We've no spare kites for passengers; can't you get that into your head? And you can't go in anyone's place. Operational flying isn't a game for amateurs. A passenger could cause the death of the whole crew." His voice became brutally frank. "You do your job, Bergman, and let me do mine. Tell me what to sink, and I'll try to sink it. But don't go wanting a place in the grandstand, for God's sake."

27

Bergman could also be stubborn. "Why can't I go as a gunner? I have used machine-guns before. And perhaps before we go I could have an hour or two's instruction on how to use the turret."

"Don't be a fool, man. You can't learn aerial gunnery in two hours."

Bergman was determined not to use his power to demand a passage until the last resort. "I know that, but it is not likely you will run into fighters on this raid, so that gunners will not be in action. And I might be needed to locate the convoy." Feeling he had won a point, he went on quickly: "Let me go, please. I would feel much happier sharing the raid with you. . . ."

Grenville did not miss the meaning or the sincerity of the Norwegian's last words. At that moment the Boston, which had been rolling down the runway, turned and began her take-off. A few seconds later she passed over them with a crackling roar. Grenville's eyes followed it, then dropped back on Bergman.

"I can see a point in your risking your neck to make sure the operation is a success," he said curtly, refusing to concede, even to himself, that sentiment had in any way influenced his change of mind. "If you think it will do that, then come along. I suppose we can manage somehow."

Bergman showed his pleasure. "Thank you. If you would introduce me to my pilot, perhaps I could go up with him on his tests this afternoon. . . ."

"If you go with anyone, you go with me," Grenville said. Ignoring the Norwegian's thanks he looked down again at his watch. "I think we'd better do an air-test now, and fix up your quarters after lunch. Come on, then. I'll take you to the stores and you can draw your flying kit."

Now that the affair was settled Grenville showed no resentment. Indeed his tone seemed more friendly, and Bergman ventured an unrelated question as they carried his flying kit and parachute towards the Squadron office.

"Do you know of any rooms to let in these parts? I have a sister I would like to get down here. We have not met for rather a long time."

"You've got a sister over here?" Grenville asked in surprise.

"Yes. We were both in England when the Germans invaded Norway. I was at university at the time."

"You'd better see Adams. He has just got his wife a room in an old pub opposite the airfield. As a matter of fact I believe she arrives today. He says there are other empty rooms. You should ask him to take you over."

"I will," Bergman nodded gratefully.

Grenville put a 'phone call through to his observer, the cheery, freckle-faced Hoppy, and then the two men changed into their flying clothes. Fifteen minutes later A Apple, the Boston with the distinctive red spinner caps, was thundering across the airfield and heading towards the distant clouds.

5

Just after lunch Adams made his way down the road to the Black Swan. The east wind was stirring the bare twigs of the hedges, and he was grateful for the warmer air that met him as he entered the lounge. Kearns came round from the bar to greet him.

"Good afternoon," Adams said. "Has my wife arrived yet?"

"Aye, sir; she got in about an hour ago. Do you want me to give her a call?"

"No; don't bother. I'll go up and see her."

"All right, sir. Come through this way."

Adams tapped on the upstairs bedroom door, then entered. A slim, fashionably dressed woman was sitting on the bed opposite him, smoking a cigarette. She was about thirty, with dark, well-groomed hair, and a narrow, elegant face. At her feet was an opened suitcase with half its contents strewn on the floor around her.

Adams closed the door and went over eagerly, bending down to kiss her. She let him touch her cheek, then turned away sharply. Adams' face dropped at once.

"Sorry I couldn't meet you in, darling," he muttered. "We had an urgent conference this morning—there wasn't a hope of getting away."

Her voice was waspish. "It took me over half an hour to get a taxi. I was frozen to the bone when I got here."

"I'm sorry, darling. . . ."

She gave a sudden, violent shudder. "I'm absolutely frozen. And this room's like an ice-box."

Adams looked around guiltily, noticing for the first time there was no fireplace. "I'll get you a paraffin heater," he said hastily.

"You'll have to get me something, or I'll never survive the winter."

"There is a private lounge downstairs you can use, you know. It has a fire."

"I've seen it. The landlord has shown me around."

There was a brief silence. Adams wandered dismally over to the rear window and stared out. It overlooked the garden and the field behind the inn.

"I took a rear room because the one at the front overlooks the airfield, I thought this one would be quieter. I remember your saying at the last place how the planes kept you awake."

She inhaled deeply on her cigarette, making no comment. Adams' eyes wandered round the room, taking in the old-fashioned marble-topped washstand, the ornate mahogany wardrobe and dressing-table, and the stiff-backed chairs. He looked back at his wife, Valerie. She had not moved, one slim leg was still crossed over the other, and her thin mouth was turned down at the corners. She was clearly in one of her moods.

Adams could not hide his disappointment. "I thought you might like it here," he muttered. "I know things are a bit old-fashioned, but they could be worse and——"

She broke in with a sarcastic laugh. "Old-fashioned? Have you seen the kitchen? It has a stone floor, bare walls, an old-type gas-stove that explodes in your face, and a sink that's fit for nothing but pig swill. And there are absolutely no facilities whatever for doing any washing."

Adams nodded heavily. "I know there are snags, but what could I do? Highgate is full of evacuees—it's hopeless even to look for a room there. Things are pretty difficult everywhere these days."

He realized he had said the wrong thing as soon as the words came out. "Don't tell me there's a war on," she snapped. "If you do, I'll scream."

Adams recognized all the signs of a first-class quarrel. He looked hastily at his watch. "I'll have to be getting back, I'm afraid. Barrett wants to see me again this afternoon."

Valerie showed a spark of interest. "Has it anything to do with your posting here?" When he nodded, she went on: "What's behind this move? Has Barrett told you anything yet?"

Adams looked uncomfortable and did not speak. She stared at him. "Well, what's the matter?"

"It's very hush-hush," Adams muttered, shifting uncomfortably.

"What about that? You've told me things before. Why the secrecy now?"

Adams moved despairingly towards the door. "Sorry, darling, but I can't talk about it. In any case I don't know very much. . . ."

"Things have gone pretty far when you can't trust your own wife, haven't they?"

For all his meekness Adams had a temper. It began to show now, in spite of himself. "I'm not to blame for the Official Secrets Act, you know."

Valerie's thin mouth curled. "There's no need to shout. We don't want everyone in the place to know we're quarrelling."

Adams took a deep breath, let it out slowly. "The last thing I want to do is quarrel. It's simply that I'm not allowed to breathe a word of this to anyone—it's supposed to be too big." He looked at his watch again. "I'll have to go. I'll be over this evening, all being well."

She rose. "What do you intend doing tonight? Are you going to bring a few of the boys over?"

"Why, no; I hadn't planned to," he muttered. "I thought as it was our first evening we'd have it alone."

She came nearer and stood beside him. Once more he found himself uncomfortably reminded that she was the taller of the two. She put a hand on his arm, her tone changing.

"I'd like a little company tonight, darling. It'll do me good. Bring one or two of the boys over, please."

Adams remembered the projected shipping strike. "There's a slight chance we may all be on duty tonight." Then, seeing her expression, he went on hastily: "Only a slight one. I think it'll be all right. Who would you like me to bring?"

"Oh, Jack Richardson. And what about Roy . . .?"

"Roy has no time for Richardson, you know. In any case I believe Richardson is Duty Officer tonight. I can ask Roy, but you know what it's like getting him to parties."

Valerie pouted. "I'm certain he'll come if you tell

him I've just arrived and feel like company. Try him, anyway. Now who else can you ask?"

Her change of mood made a split in Adams' mind, one half of it thanking God and becoming co-operative, the other half turning hurt and resentful. The co-operative half won.

"We've had a Norwegian naval officer called Bergman attached to us. He told me over lunch he wants to find a room for his sister. Perhaps if he came over tonight, he could meet the landlord at the same time. He seems a nice chap and if he comes Roy may come too. I've got the idea Roy likes him."

"Splendid, dear. That'll be lovely. You're really very sweet." She lifted a hand and touched his cheek. "I know I've been grumpy, but that long wait at the station was so upsetting. A little company tonight will put me right again." With that she put up her face for him to kiss.

Adams went downstairs with his emotions in a tangle. He ran into Kearns in the hall.

"Everything all right, sir?"

"Yes; everything's fine," Adams muttered, afraid the innkeeper's shrewd eyes were reading too much on his face.

"Don't you worry, sir," Kearns said unexpectedly. "We'll do our best to make her comfortable."

Adams wondered afterwards why he did not deny the inference that he was worrying about anything, and realized it was because the ring of sympathy in the innkeeper's voice had come at a moment of need. His only thought at the time was that he liked the elderly man and would like to buy him a drink.

"I'm sure you will," he said. At the door he turned back. "We must have a drink and a chat together one of these nights."

"Be glad to, sir," Kearns said, looking pleased. "Very glad to indeed."

Adams went out in the biting wind again. His only other clear reflection came at the camp entrance when the sentry presented arms. Irrelevantly but quite intensely, he realized he had never felt less worthy of a salute.

33

Probably because of the station order that prevented men going far afield, the public lounge was well-filled that night, and Valerie told Adams she preferred it to the quietness of the private sitting-room. Anyone without charity might have suspected that the number of unattached airmen sitting among the regular customers had some bearing on her choice. She was wearing a wine-coloured dress of light material with half-length sleeves, something totally inadequate for a winter evening, but the various admiring glances she received appeared to more than recompense her.

They had been in the lounge about fifteen minutes when Grenville and Bergman arrived. Valerie brightened up immediately on seeing Grenville.

"Hello, Roy. How nice to see you again."

Grenville's face was expressionless as he took her hand. "Hello, Val. You're looking well. This is Lieutenant Bergman, Mrs. Adams."

Valerie's eyes had already appraised Bergman and her tone suggested approval. "Delighted, Lieutenant. Please sit down, both of you. We're so glad you've come, aren't we, Frank? We were both bored to death. I'm afraid it's going to be very dull here."

"Don't tell the lieutenant that," Adams said, with a heavy laugh. "He's hoping to get his sister here."

"So I understand," Valerie said. "That'll be lovely. Where is your sister now?"

"In Scotland," Bergman told her.

Valerie lifted pencilled eyebrows. "Really! How nice for you. And you're going to get her a room here?"

"If I can, yes."

Valerie wondered what Bergman, a Norwegian naval officer, was doing at the airfield. She was also curious to know how he came to have a sister in the country. If Grenville hadn't been there she would have asked outright, but Grenville was tight on security matters, something she had learned to her cost. She decided to tackle Adams later, and contented herself with an indirect question.

"Does she speak English as well as you, Lieutenant?"

Bergman smiled. "Much better, I think."

"It'll be lovely meeting her. When are you hoping to get her down?"

"Once I find a room, she can come at once," Bergman told her. At that moment he noticed Kearns talking to Maisie behind the bar. "Is that the innkeeper? Perhaps I could go over now and speak to him. . . ."

Valerie put a hand on his arm. "We'll see everything is fixed up, don't worry. Have a drink with us first, and then one of us will take you over to him." She turned her eyes on Adams.

Adams rose hastily. "Yes, that's the idea. What will you all have?"

As Adams approached the bar, Maisie was in the last stages of an argument with Kearns. The innkeeper had brought a few bottles in to the lounge which he wanted displaying on the high shelves behind the counter. Knowing whoever put them up would have to stand on a chair and stretch upwards, he wanted to do the job himself, but Maisie would have none of it.

"I ain't got sciatica like you," she told him. As he still protested she went on: "Aw, let 'em look, if they want to. It ain't going to lose us the war, is it?"

Without further ado, she climbed on to a chair and motioned to him to pass the bottles up to her. As she reached upwards with the first one, displaying a generous length of leg, the blackout curtain was pulled aside and two Air Force warrant officers appeared. One saw Maisie and let out a howl.

"Hey, Jimmy. Take a look at this. We've found somethin' here, kid."

The hum of conversation stopped as every eye turned on the speaker. The airmen knew him well; the civilians were soon to have that pleasure. The first thing they noticed was a broad, craggy face, split open into an infectious grin, and topped by a mop of fair, unruly hair. It was Gillibrand of B Flight, one of Sam Milner's crack pilots. Everything about Gillibrand was big— big hands, feet, generosity, craziness, and courage. He stood grinning at Maisie now, his unbuttoned overcoat swinging back and revealing the D.F.M. beneath his pilot's brevet.

His companion, Jimmie Willcox, provided a contrast in types. Willcox was a slim, dark-haired boy who could have not weighed more than nine stone, with a pale, sensitive face and wistful eyes and mouth. He looked no more than eighteen although he was actually twenty-two. At the moment he was blushing.

"What a sight to greet a feller on a winter night," Gillibrand said.

Maisie turned, staring at him. "What's the matter with you, you big gorilla? Ain't you ever seen legs before?"

"Not like yours, baby," Gillibrand grinned, shouldering his way forward. "They're really something."

"What's the matter with all you Yanks? Don't they let you see women until you're twenty-one?"

"I'm not a Yank. I'm a cousin of yours, baby. I'm a Canadian."

Maisie sniffed her disgust. "Don't go calling yourself my cousin. I've got decent relations."

Gillibrand motioned to the bottles. "Go on, baby; don't stop. That was a great act."

Maisie stepped down from the chair with dignity. "I'll put the rest up when the wolves have gone," she told Kearns.

The hum of conversation returned at a higher level, the bewildered locals throwing glances over their shoulders at Gillibrand, who was now talking to his observer. Adams paid for his drinks, put them on a tray, and returned to his table.

"What do you think of our mad Canadian?" he asked Bergman as he handed him his glass.

The Norwegian was laughing. "He seems quite a character."

"He's a character, all right," Adams said, sitting down. "He's completely crazy and a flying fool. If he sees a gun firing at him, he wants to fly down the barrel to get at the gunner's throat. Roy here could tell you some yarns about him."

"Who is that with him?"

"That's his observer, Jimmie Willcox."

Back at the counter Gillibrand was nudging Jimmie

and pointing at Maisie, who was pretending to ingore him.

"It's always a good sign, kid, when they act toffee-nosed. Means you're all doing all right. Watch me." He approached Maisie. "Hey cousin! How 'bout having a drink with your relation from across the sea, huh?"

Maisie was very haughty. "I'm particular who I drink with," she said, nose in the air.

"What about my buddy here, then? He ain't done nothing to you."

Maisie eyed the blushing Jimmie and softened. "He's different. He's a gentleman."

Gillibrand let out a howl of delight and pushed Jimmie forward. "Kid, you're a success. Buy the girl a drink."

"Stop pushin' him about," Maisie snapped. "Can't you see you're embarrassin' him."

Gillibrand looked at Jimmie, then slapped him on the back. "Just my way, son. No harm meant. Come on; let's go over and sit with the natives. Nothing like a few hayseeds to liven things up."

He pulled his small companion across the room. As he saw Grenville, he flipped up a respectful hand. "Evenin', skipper. Nice dive they've got here."

Grenville nodded. The startled locals scattered as the Canadian went among them. Within a minute he had them all gaping as he plunged into a hair-raising story of the war.

Adams gave a laugh, the first relaxed sound he had made that evening. "What a character! Look at their faces! They can't keep their eyes off him."

Someone at the counter could not, either. Maisie caught Kearns looking at her and flushed: a rare thing for Maisie.

"Men who look at women like that shouldn't be allowed in decent pubs," she said. "It gives 'em a bad name."

Kearns smiled. "I don't think there's any harm in him, lass."

Maisie sniffed. "I wouldn't trust myself alone with him—not for five minutes, I wouldn't."

There was a twinkle in Kearns' shrewd eyes. "I'll bet you wouldn't, lass."

Maisie glanced at him suspiciously, but his face was bland and innocent again.

Four hundred miles away, in the cold and darkness of the Northern winter, the convoy that was 633's target lay at anchor off Innvik. Innvik, a port six miles up the Svartfjord north of Bergen, was an ideal wartime anchorage. It was guarded from the air by the long, precipitous mountains that flanked either side of the fjord, and protected from the sea by the rocky island of Utvik, a naval fortress lying four miles out from the coast. An additional protection was the winter darkness. From late November until February the sun did not rise high enough to clear the mountain tops, so leaving the water below in permanent gloom.

The convoy had been at Innvik for eight days. In that time it had discharged its cargo to a secret destination farther up the fjord, and replaced it by another. Except for one small hitch soon to be put right, all had gone well, and shortly the convoy would leave its haven and steal south down the long Norwegian coast, picking up other ships and an escort on the way. Its destination was Stettin in the Baltic, and in spite of the watchful British Navy and the probing planes of Coastal Command, the odds seemed greatly in favour of its reaching there safely. The long nights and the steep coastal mountains would offer it the protection they had given to so many ships before. And after delivering its valuable cargo of wood and metal ores in Stettin, it would return again to the Svartfjord with a cargo of even greater significance.

There seemed, then, every reason for enemy confidence and for the party which the Convoy Commander gave his officers before the serious business of briefing began. But he was not aware of what was taking place that very night only six miles away from his hotel.

Five hundred feet above the Svartfjord's dark and narrow mouth, a man was making his way through the snow towards a thick clump of dwarf birch that grew under a rock face. Reaching it he paused a moment to make certain he was not observed. Nothing moved in the snow around him, and satisfied he pushed his way into the trees.

"Olaf," he called softly. "Olaf; where are you?"

A deep voice at his elbow made him start with fear. "I'm here, Jan Ericson, checking up you aren't a German." A hearty laugh followed and Ericson felt his arm grasped. "Come on, Jan. Take your skis off and come inside."

Ericson was led through a thick camouflaged cover of conifer branches and foliage into a tent, in which both a paraffin lamp and a heater were burning. A camp-bed took up one side of the tent, a pile of provisions the other. Ericson knew that alongside this tent was another containing a battery-driven transmitter and receiver.

The paraffin lamp showed Ericson to be a slight man with quick, nervous eyes. He was warmly dressed in a thick ski-suit, but his face appeared pale and cold. The wireless operator, Olaf Johansen, was a thick-set man in his early forties, with bushy eyebrows, a weather-beaten face, and a shock of untidy brown hair. He was wearing serge trousers and a leather windbreaker. As he entered the tent he threw a .38 revolver on the camp-bed.

"I heard your skis and thought the devils might have started night search parties in the hope of spotting a light."

Ericson had a thin, breathless voice. "Be careful. They had a Storch up the other day trying to locate you."

Johansen grinned. "I know. And I decreased my signal strength as he flew nearer and sent him off in the other direction. Don't worry about me—this rock face is a big protection, anyway. What about the convoy?"

"Alvin managed to see me for a few minutes today. A railwayman tipped him off—apparently the last consignment of ore has been held up because of a landslide blocking the line. But they expect to get it through on Wednesday and will sail on Thursday."

The burly Johansen scratched his chin and grinned. "Thursday, eh! That's good. That leaves us plenty of time. I'll let Bergman know tonight. Anything else? Any news from farther up the fjord?"

Ericson shook his head. "No. Nothing yet."

Johansen's rugged face was grim now. "The moment you hear anything, let me know at once. You know how important it's supposed to be. Tell everyone to keep his ears open. Now, what about a hot drink? You look cold."

Ericson shook his head "No; I must get back. The devils have put me on early shifts this week."

"But you've plenty of time. Come on, man. Sit down and relax."

"No, Olaf; I must go."

Ericson was clearly nervous and Johansen made no further effort to detain him. He saw him out of the trees and watched his diminishing figure until it had vanished into the gloomy, snow-covered mountainside. Then he returned to his hide-out, and ten minutes later began tapping out his coded message to England.

On the surface nothing had changed. The mountains were as high, the darkness as unrevealing. Yet now the odds on the convoy reaching Stettin had appreciably dropped.

6

As Bergman had said, his sister did not take long in coming to Sutton Craddock once a room had been found for her. Bergman met her at the station and brought her to the Black Swan in a car Barrett had lent him.

They arrived just as Adams was stepping out of the front porch. With other members of the squadron that could be spared, Adams had been given a few hours' rest that morning in preparation for the long hours of duty that lay ahead. He was on his way back to camp when the car turned in on the drive. Although the glass was dropping fast, it was a clear morning with a pale blue sky and a wintry sun.

Bergman threw open the door and jumped out, waving a cheerful hand at Adams. "Hello. Come and meet my sister. She would like to thank you for helping her get a room."

At that moment a girl stepped out of the car, and Adams' romanticism made him draw in a sharp breath.

Hilde Bergman could not be taken for anything else but Scandinavian. She was bare-headed, and wore her mass of thick, blonde hair brushed up and over her ears. On many women it would have been too severe a style, on her it only served to reveal the perfect bone structure of her face, the foundation of lasting beauty. She had lovely, regular features, very composed for one so young, was tall and gracefully built, and was wearing a camel-hair coat with a light blue scarf at her throat. She came forward smiling, and as Adams took her hand he saw her eyes were a fine-grained tecture of blue and grey. Looking into them was like gazing to the bottom of a sunlit Norwegian lake.

"I am very pleased to meet you, Squadron-Leader, and must thank you for helping Finn to get me this room."

Adams had no sooner recovered his breath when he lost it again on hearing her voice. It had a mellow quality, it sang in his ears like a bronze bell, and her slight accent made it irresistible.

"I hope you like it here," he managed.

"I know I shall. I am looking forward very much to meeting your wife, too. Finn has told me about you both."

Adams began remembering things again. There was Valerie—yes, he ought to introduce them. He glanced at his watch, then nodded.

"Val's in her room at the moment. Let me help you upstairs with your things, and I'll introduce you to her. She'll be able to show you around today."

"You are certain you can spare the time?"

"Oh, yes. I'm a bit early; it's all right."

Valerie received the girl quite cordially, and without quite knowing why, Adams was relieved. In his gratitude it did not occur to him that Bergman's presence might have had some influence on Valerie's behaviour. In anyone other than his wife Adams was a good judge of character, but loyalty was inclined to bias his judgement of her. He stayed until Hilde and Bergman had returned to the girl's room, then took his leave. In spite of the long and anxious hours awaiting him, he felt an odd lightness of heart as he made his way to the airfield.

Back in the inn Bergman helped his sister to unlock her suitcases. It was clear from both their expressions that they were delighted to be together again. They had always been deeply attached to one another, and their exile in England had strengthened that attachment. Now he was alone with her. Bergman spoke in Norwegian.

"How do you like the inn?"

Her enthusiasm was spontaneous. "Oh, very much, Finn. It's a charming old place."

Bergman stared round at the heavy furniture and the old prints on the walls. "I hope it's not going to be damp."

"Oouf. . . ." She made a gesture of impatience. "You

42

worry about me too much, Finn. It is nice and I am going to be very comfortable here."

Bergman nodded and went to the window. He motioned her over. "Have you seen this?"

She followed his eyes and saw the airfield across the road with its hangars, Nissen huts, and beyond them the Bostons at their dispersal points.

"Just the place for an agent, isn't it?" Bergman said humorously. "Perhaps it's just as well you've taken it over."

"Have any other rooms the same view?"

"Only one. The innkeeper's bedroom—directly above you. But Security have checked on him: he's all right. And both he and his barmaid have been warned to keep their mouths closed on anything they see."

She watched his face closely as he was speaking. There was the faintest air of preoccupation about him —something she had noticed on first meeting him at the station. In one as trained in self-discipline as he, it usually meant only one thing.

"You're not going off again just as I have arrived here, are you?" she asked quietly.

He stared at her, then laughed. "No; of course I'm not. Why do you ask?"

She made a little fluttering movement of her right hand, a characteristic gesture. "I do not know, but if you are not going it does not matter. . . ." She motioned towards the airfield. "But I do not understand. Why have they attached you to the Air Force and why are you in naval uniform? Can you tell me, or is it something I should not know?"

He told her as much as Davies had told the others. "That's as far as I dare go at the moment," he finished. "And even that much is very secret indeed."

Her clear, steady eyes, the eyes Adams was still thinking about, were shining very brightly now. "But that is wonderful, Finn. It means you will be staying here—not going back. . . ."

He checked her quickly. "It means I shall be here for a few weeks. That is why I asked you to come."

"Only a few weeks. . . ."

43

He saw her disappointment and squeezed her arm. "That's longer than we've been together since 1940. Let's count ourselves lucky and make the best of it, shall we?"

She made herself smile immediately. "Of course we will. We will have a wonderful time. Tell me about everyone here. Have you made any friends yet?"

"Yes; I think so. There's Adams—I quite like him —and then there's Roy Grenville. I haven't told you, have I, that this is the famous 633 Squadron with Roy Grenville as Squadron Commander? You must have read about them in the newspapers."

She nodded. "Yes; I have. You say you and he have become friends?"

Bergman gave a rueful laugh. "I like to think so, although it's not easy to be certain with anyone as curt of nature as Grenville. He's a strange chap in many ways."

"What do you mean?"

"I don't know. . . . He gives me the impression of being a very intelligent man who has dedicated himself to this war. In peacetime I could imagine him as an explorer or an engineer—you know, the type that builds a bridge where no bridge has been built before. He has that sort of aggressiveness that every man needs to be a man. But, of course, aggressiveness can be used either way, to create or to destroy. The Nazis trained their youngsters to use it destructively. To defeat them we have to use ours the same way. I feel that is what Grenville has done—deliberately made himself into as efficient a fighting machine as a man can be."

"You make him sound soulless," she said.

Bergman shook his head. "On the contrary, I keep getting the impression he bitterly resents what he has had to do, and so takes it out of the Germans all the more. But I may be hopelessly wrong about him; he may really like war for war's sake. He's a most difficult man to understand."

"You seem to have tried hard enough," she smiled.

"I've been seeing a good deal of him these last few days, that's probably why. He has taken me up with him a few times."

She gave a start. "You don't mean on raids?"

"Heavens, no. Just round and about. I asked him to."

"Haven't you done enough flying?" she asked quietly.

Bergman shrugged. "I've never flown in Bostons before, and now I'm attached here I felt I ought to know something about them."

There was a disturbed look in her eyes now. She watched him closely and noticed how his gaze kept wandering towards the distant planes.

They chatted for another ten minutes, then Bergman picked up his cap regretfully. "I'm afraid I shall have to be getting back now."

"Will you come over tonight?"

His eyes wandered to the window again. He hesitated, then shook his head. "Things have worked out rather badly. I got some news through the other day that will keep us on duty tonight. It isn't quite definite yet—I shall get another message through later—but in any case we shall all be standing by. But I'll be over tomorrow at the first opportunity."

"Why are you going with them on this raid?" she asked, keeping her voice steady.

Even Bergman's training could not prevent his giving a slight start. "How did you know I was going?"

Hilde smiled faintly. "It wasn't difficult to guess—not after you told me you'd been up with Grenville. I should have known you wouldn't be content to sit back here while they went into danger." Her tone changed, became puzzled. "But why do they let you go? Your work is dangerous enough. Surely they do not need you once they have been given their target."

Bergman shifted uncomfortably. "There's nothing dangerous about this, particularly as I shall be flying with Grenville. Don't worry about it, please."

Her recollection of some of Grenville's exploits did nothing to allay her anxiety, but she knew the futility of argument.

"Promise me you will be careful," was all she said.

He reached out and pinched her cheek affectionately. "I will. Have a good night's sleep and don't worry. I'll be over tomorrow and will bring Grenville with me.

45

I'm hoping you'll like him. Bye-bye now. *Adjö da."*
"Adjö. Ta godt vare po deg selv."

She went to the window and looked out. A few seconds later he appeared on the road below, a tall figure in his naval greatcoat. He looked back and waved. She watched him until the corner of the inn hid him from sight, then raised her eyes to the airfield. The wintry sun had already disappeared; a dark mass of clouds had rolled in from the east and turned the light bleak. The distant Bostons looked forbidding now, and the wind, edging through the window frame, sent a shiver through her.

Once more the Bostons went through their series of complicated tests. Mechanics fussed around them; D.I.'s were filled in and signed. Crews left their warm, smoky offices and took their planes up for yet another flight trial. The last Boston, D Danny, belonging to Jack Archer of B Flight, came in just as the winter dusk, sprinkled with drizzle, was settling over the field. Archer taxied her over to his dispersal point, cut her engines, and climbed stiffly out, followed by his observer and air gunner. After a brief word with his maintenance N.C.O., he left the ground crew to make their final checks.

A petrol bowser came waddling alongside to top up D Danny's tanks. Armourers climbed into the nose and turret to arm the Browning guns with their long belts of ammunition. By 1650 the last instrument check had been made, the last panel screw pressed down and turned. Every hornet of 633 Squadron was now ready.

The air crews ate early that evening. Directly after dinner they were ordered to the Briefing Room where they were given their instructions. Bergman, in his rôle of naval officer, tried to give his contribution as nautical a flavour as possible. When the briefing was over the crews were ordered to stand by in the crew rooms for further orders.

The wait that followed was of that restless, stomach-tightening order that frays nerves and jags tempers. Some men played cards, others talked volubly, yet others sat silent, smoking cigarette after cigarette. Bergman was with Adams, Grenville, and Barrett in the Operations Room. New to operational flying, the Norwegian was finding it difficult to control his nerves as he waited for the crucial message to come through.

At 2000 hours a message came but it was not the one he wanted. The outcome was an order that all crews could stand down but must remain with instant call.

As always when an operation was delayed, the reaction on the crews was unfortunate. Keyed-up nerves had to slacken of their own accord and sometimes would not. The more experienced men went to their quarters where some managed to sleep. Others stayed in the crew rooms, playing cards, smoking, watching the clock. . . .

The hours dragged by to midnight, then into the cold winter morning. Incessant tension had now had its effect, and the squadron lay in an uneasy, exhausted sleep. At 0106 hours the Duty Sergeant was dreaming and turning restlessly over on his camp-bed. At that moment the bell of the teletype rang, bringing him awake with a start. He heard the clack-clack of the machine and the rustle of paper, and was on his feet and across the room in an instant.

633 Squadron swung into gear. The Duty Officer, making certain all outside communication was still cut, began making his 'phone calls. The Wing Commander, the Engineering Officer, the Station Armament Officer, the Navigation Officer . . . down the list he went, ticking each name in turn. Like a stone thrown into a pool, the initial alarm spread. Men awoke to the ringing of 'phones, cursed, and swung their feet to the ground. The chatter of voices grew. The Tannoy spluttered, barked, then blared forth triumphantly. "All air crews report to the Operations Room immediately. Repeat: All air crews report to the Operations Room immediately. . . ." It was followed by the harsh hoot of a siren.

Crews felt that familiar dryness in their throats as they grabbed their flying kit. Lorries started up in the darkness, their engines barking in the bitter wind.

The strike was on.

The patter of rain could be heard on the blacked-out window of the private sitting-room. Occasionally a few drops found their way down the chimney, making the fire splutter. Valerie put aside her magazine and yawned.

"What a night! I think I'll have a cigarette and turn in."

Hilde, reading a book in the armchair opposite, looked up with a smile. Valerie offered her a cigarette, then took one herself, putting it into a long holder before lighting it. She was an affected smoker and made something of a ritual over the operation. Inhaling deeply, she sank back into the armchair.

"They must be on a pretty important show or the weather would have cancelled it. You've no idea what time they are taking off, have you?"

Hilde shook her head.

"I suppose we'll just get off to sleep when they'll start up," Valerie said. Her voice turned curious. "Your brother won't be going with them, will he? As he is a Norwegian and in the Navy, I thought they might have been put on a shipping strike off the Norwegian coast."

Hilde gave a slight start on hearing Valerie's surmise about Bergman. She was careful to avoid any reference to his movements in her reply.

"I don't know what the raid is on, Mrs. Adams," she said truthfully. "My brother did not give me any details."

Valerie waved her cigarette-holder impatiently. "Don't be so formal, for heaven's sake. My name's Valerie." She had not missed the girl's faint start and eyed her now with some malice. "Oh, I know they don't like talking, but women usually find things out sooner or later. You needn't worry about talking to me, you know. After all, I am the Station Intelligence Officer's wife."

Valerie learned later that Hilde had the rare quality of frankness. She learned now that she was no idle gossip. The girl nodded her head but showed clearly she had no intention of discussing the subject any further. Valerie gave a brittle laugh and rose to her feet.

"Oh, well; if we don't feel like being sociable, I think I'll turn in. Good night."

"Good night," Hilde said quietly, and Valerie went out with a feeling of frustration.

The girl's eyes were troubled as she turned back to the fire, and the time slipped by unnoticed. A tap on the door made her start.

She turned to see Kearns standing in the doorway. He peered around the room, then entered. "You alone tonight, Miss?"

"Mrs. Adams has been with me, but she went to bed fifteen minutes ago."

"Your brother couldn't get over?"

"No. Not tonight."

Kearns motioned in the direction of the bar. "We haven't had a single airman in tonight. Do you think there's something on, Miss?"

She shook her head slowly. "They are not supposed to tell us, Mr. Kearns."

"Aye; and I've no business asking, for that matter," the innkeeper said quickly. "But I was in the last war myself and I can't help havin' an interest in the lads. They're as fine a crowd as I've seen anywhere. I like the look of that brother of yours too, Miss, if you don't mind my sayin' so."

She gave him a sudden, bright smile. "Thank you very much."

Kearns, in his own way as impressed with her as Adams was, moved awkwardly back to the door. "I'm goin' to make a cup of tea now—Maisie an' me always has a cup after closing time. Will you have one, Miss?"

"Thank you—if it is no trouble."

"No trouble at all, Miss. How do you like it? D'you drink it the same way as us, with milk and sugar?"

"Not with sugar, thank you. But otherwise the same."

"All right, Miss. I'll bring it through in a few minutes. Just you wait here by the fire."

He went back to the kitchen, to return five minutes later with a cup of tea and a plate of biscuits. He chatted a few minutes, then withdrew reluctantly to the door.

49

"If the planes ever keep you awake at nights, Miss, and you feel like a cup of tea or anything, don't be afraid of gettin' up and makin' one. You won't disturb any of us."

"You're very kind," she said softly.

"Not a bit, Miss. But I've got a son in the Army an' know how things can be. Good night, Miss."

"Good night, Mr. Kearns, and thank you."

Hilde realized he had the same thought as Valerie, that her brother might be flying with the squadron. She drank her tea, then went up to her room. The blackout curtain was not in position, so she undressed in the dark. The sheets felt icy as she slipped between them. Outside the restless wind kept tapping a tree branch against her window. She tossed about for a long time, but at last fell into a fitful sleep.

She awoke with a start, unable at once to identify the noise that had awakened her. It came again, a queer honk-honk like the sound of wild geese, only louder. Jumping from her bed she ran to the window. It was still dark outside and she had to strain her eyes to see the dim silhouettes of the Nissen huts. She realized now that the sound was that of a siren.

The morning was bitterly cold and the draughts from the window stung her bare arms. She tore a blanket from the bed, wrapped it round her shoulders, and ran back to the window. A few lights were appearing on the airfield now and she could hear the sounds of intense activity; the slam of doors, men yelling orders, trucks starting up. . . .

Storm lanterns appeared out at the dispersal points and the Bostons came into view, their wet wings and bodies glistening like huge insects. Men were all around them, pulling covers away and opening hatches. One by one their engines fired and they began moving clumsily forward, trundling away into the darkness at the right of the field.

Two minutes more and the flarepath lights clicked on, blinding Hilde for a moment. They were followed by the distant crackling snarl of two revved engines. The noise grew louder as the first Boston came into sight, picking up speed as it came down the runway.

It appeared sluggish at first, and three times its wheels lifted only to fall back on the glistening runway. It was moving at speed now, a black blue between the lights. Again its wheels broke free and this time with success. With a triumphant roar it cleared the distant fence and vanished into the darkness.

The others followed it. Hilde watched them all go, too fascinated to notice the cold. In the rectangle of lights they looked like darting fish with their shining, streamlined bodies. One by one they roared away until the last of them had vanished into the night. The flare-path went out like a candle being snuffed by a finger. All that was left was a deep drone of engines, and a minute later that too had gone, leaving nothing but silence and darkness behind.

7

633 Squadron refuelled and bombed-up at Sumburgh in the Shetlands. Sumburgh had been alerted and carried out the operation in record time. The aircraft lined up for take-off the moment the last trolley train pulled away. The weather had deteriorated and icy rain was falling.

Grenville swung A Apple into position, nose in line with the flarepath and waited for Control to release him. In the armoured nose compartment ahead was Hoppy, sitting with his navigational instruments and bombsight, and in the turret behind was Bergman with his Browning guns.

Bergman's excitement was growing. This was a new adventure for him and he was finding it hard to control his nerves. He peered out through his rain-splashed turret. The rest of the squadron were forming up behind them, their recognition lights glowing like watchful eyes.

A deep tremor ran through A Apple as her throttles were opened. The noise of her engines deafened Bergman and his stomach tightened as he felt the plane begin to move forward. This was it—the last take-off before the attack. Locked in his transparent cupola, watching the driving rain and the moving lights, he felt part of some fantastic nightmare.

In the pilot's compartment ahead, Grenville was holding A Apple in the centre of the runway. The Cyclones were gaining power now and the Boston was moving at speed, the lights on either side running into a blur. Sheets of water thrown up from the tarmac splattered against the perspex windscreen and hissed into spray against the driving propellers. The Boston was sluggish under her heavy load and Grenville felt her olco legs grunting with the strain. He held her down, waiting for her controls to lighten.

The runway shortened like a ribbon snipped by giant

shears. The Cyclones were screaming their hearts out now. Grenville's eyes were fixed ahead. There was a hill up in front there—he hoped the others would remember it. His lips moved as the Boston still held the runway. "Come on, come on! Get up, you bitch. . . ." The wheels smacked into a pool and sent a sheet of water over the windscreen, blinding him for a moment. He eased the stick back again, the Boston bounced, but more lightly this time. He held her down another five endless seconds, then tried again. She came up, dropped a couple of feet, then held steady. Another moment and the flarepath had fallen away and they were plunged in darkness.

Grenville grouped his squadron at 4,000 feet and led them out. No chance for low-level stuff—skimming the wave tops to avoid enemy detectors. Weather conditions were right against it, and would deteriorate the farther east they went. God knows what it would be like 200 miles farther out. . . .

Grenville had a word with Hoppy over the intercom, to check his course. Hoppy's voice came back, as cheery and efficient as usual. Satisfied, Grenville then spoke to Bergman.

"Everything all right back there, Finn?"

Bergman tried to keep his voice steady. "Everything fine, Roy, thank you."

They flew on in silence. The squadron was in battle formation, two flights of six planes, each flight in ranks of three, line abreast. All the planes had their recognition lights on, the chances of fighter interception in this weather were virtually nil, the chance of collision a far greater one. Twenty long minutes passed and then a white wall swept at them from out of the darkness. Aircraft huddled closer together, their red-eyed crews peering anxiously through the white hell of driving sleet and snow.

Another fifteen minutes and Parsons of B Flight was in trouble. Ice cut out his starboard engine. By a miracle he avoided collision in the tightly packed formation and slithered down towards the invisible sea below. Above him the squadron vanished into the snow. There was no way he could contact them—R/T silence was strictly enforced on the way out to avoid giving warning to the enemy's monitoring system. He jettisoned his bombs but was still dragged down by ice and his load of petrol. It looked like curtains when, at less than 300 feet over the sea, his faulty engine picked up again. Reluctantly he turned back to Sumburgh.

Grenville was forced down lower. Down to 3,000, down to 2,000. . . . Still no sign of a break. A Apple was feeling the effects of the blizzard now. Her controls were growing sluggish and Grenville had to keep moving them to prevent their icing-up. Ice was flying off the airscrew tips and smashing like bullets against the metal-skinned fuselage. The cold was growing more intense, soaking like icy water through flying clothes, numbing hands and feet. . . .

Grenville's face was grim. Another quarter-of-an-hour of this might mean the loss of half his aircraft. Apart from the danger of engine failure, there was the growing threat of collision. A Apple was slithering about now like a man losing his reflexes. All the kites would be in a similar state, some probably worse. . . . Grenville dropped lower, damning the white filth that was blinding him. Davies was relying on them to get this convoy. So was Bergman. A hell of a thing it would be if their first job for the Norwegian was a failure. It might reflect on him. Certainly Bomber Command would have something caustic to say. . . .

Grenville cursed his helplessness as his reddened eyes stared out into the opaque, driving blizzard. Again A Apple skidded, forcing Grenville to make a violent and exaggerated movement of his controls to bring her straight again. It was no good, he realized bitterly. Another few minutes of this might mean disaster. He switched over to R/T and lifted his face mask. . . .

At that moment they broke out of the storm. From a suffocating white nightmare they were suddenly projected over a seemingly bottomless blank void. With the ice breaking and shedding off their wings they swept on, once more a deadly threat to the unsuspecting convoy.

Each man expressed his relief according to his nature. Grenville had already accepted the good fortune and was now considering his battle plan afresh. Hoppy, completely confident in his pilot, began checking his instruments again. Bergman, who had forgotten his nervousness in his fear of losing the convoy, was now conscious of relief, and, paradoxically, nervousness again. Behind, in B Flight, Gillibrand's teeth clamped down on another wad of gum, his eyes glinting their pleasure at the fight to come. In front of him, Jimmie Willcox, alone in his hatch, was staring white-faced into the night, a nervous tremor racking his body.

Ten minutes more and according to Grenville's E.T.A. the Norwegian coast was approaching fast. Hitting snow again he led them up to 3,000. It proved only a squall and surprisingly they emerged into moonlight. Grenville quickly switched off his recognition lights, his pilots following his example. Then, taking advantage of the moon, he dropped down to ultra low-level, skimming low over the shimmering, icy waves. At this height the enemy could not pick them up with his detectors and Grenville was hoping for a surprise. Surprise was the essence of shipping strikes—the first attack to be made while the gunners were dozing or having a forbidden cigarette.

Another squall, sleet this time, then moonlight again. Bergman had a sense of unreality as he stared out at the dancing pathway of light along which they skimmed. This was a million miles from war: this was beautiful, ethereal, dreamlike. Moonlight touched the graceful aircraft behind him, frosting their wings and edging their propellers' arcs with silver.

The pilots, however, had no time to admire the beauty of the scene. Grenville had the aircraft tightly bunched like a school of fish. It was dangerous work, calling for intense concentration and quick reflexes. To fly into the slipstream of the aircraft ahead, even for a second, meant almost certain death. The sea below was hungry, for all its frosted moonlight.

Grenville peered ahead. According to Hoppy the Norwegian coast must be close now. And it was a murderous place for aircraft at night. High mountains falling sheer into the sea, often too steep to hold snow, black and deadly. They had already taken a high toll of planes in this war. With face mask in position, ready to shout a warning, Grenville stared into the darkness with aching eyes.

Hoppy came through on the intercom. "Three minutes past E.T.A., skipper." Three minutes, and still nothing! The moon was a curse now, dazzling the eyes and making the sky ahead appear darker by contrast. Would the mountain-tops reflect it and give warning? Grenville did not know. He had the impression that A Apple was travelling at twice her rated speed. The moonlit water below her was streaking by as if the plane were hurling itself to destruction.

Grenville cursed his imagination and stared again into the darkness. He thought he saw a faint light flash, far over past his starboard wingtip. He blinked quickly and looked again. Then Hoppy's excited voice came through.

"There's a light, skipper. Over at two o'clock."

Grenville led his pilots into a ninety-degree turn, a manoeuvre that only superbly trained pilots could have executed at that height. They headed south now; parallel to the still invisible coast. Grenville spoke to Bergman.

"Is that one of your men? Over there, at eleven o'clock?"

Owing to the position of his turret, Bergman had difficulty in seeing. Grenville swung farther over to starboard. Bergman saw the light now. It was flickering on and off, obviously signalling.

Bergman had an Aldis lamp in his turret and he sent a message back. The light went out, waited, then flickered again, falling astern as the Bostons droned on.

"Keep going," Bergman told Grenville. "The convoy passed here an hour ago. We'll get another message farther south."

Less than four minutes later another light flashed at them. This one was high above them, clearly from a mountain-top. It was bright and dangerously close. Bergman took its message and gave it to Grenville.

"Dead ahead, Roy. Minutes away."

Grenville took a quick look around. The moon was on his port quarter. Ideally he should attack into it—

it was always difficult for ship gunners to sight aircraft coming in against the moon. But that meant heading straight for the mountains. Too risky. He would attack on this course—if he remained lucky they would at least have the element of surprise with them.

They hit another snow squall. Grenville made a quick decision. He stayed low and switched on his landing lights so that they skipped over the heaving waters. His pilots followed his example, huddled together again for safety.

The snow thinned and fell away. They swept out into another moonlit gap and then they saw the convoy, dead ahead.

There were fifteen ships, perhaps more, lying like black beetles on the frosty water. Not a light shone among them. Unaware as yet of their peril they steamed on in the protection of the darkness, the mountains, and the mine-fields.

Behind them 633 Squadron prepared to attack. The small shapes ahead began to grow out of the moonlit waves, to become larger, darker, and more solid. There was still no sign of alarm among them. Another three seconds and Grenville snapped on his R/T.

"Crossbow leader calling. Line Apple take a ship apiece in rear rank. Line Betty take the next rank. B Flight attack survivors. B Flight will follow in sixty seconds. Repeat. . . ."

Every aircraft was now under full boost. Every man was ready, his fatigue forgotten. They all knew what was expected of them; Grenville had put them through the drill often enough. Come in below deck level and from the nose or stern to avoid as much light flak as possible. Wait until she's towering above you, then back on your stick and over. . . . Let your eggs go, down her funnels if you can, and then get down on the water again and stay down. Jink low among the ships so if they fire at you they may hit one another. Then pick yourself another target and do it again. . . .

A searchlight suddenly blazed out from a small ship on the starboard flank. It was followed by another, then by three more. Lights began signalling, frantically from the dark hulks. The first tracer came, red stuff, starting

57

slowly as tracer always appears to do, but getting faster until it was snapping by like a vicious steel whip. Other gunners took alarm and also opened fire. A curtain of tracer came up now—red, yellow, all colours, glowing like beads on a dozen strings. Searchlights frantically swept the sky.

Both guns and searchlights were as yet angled too high. Now the rear ships were within range and Line Apple opened up with its combined twelve guns. The ships loomed nearer, nearer, enormous now against the luminous sky. . . . A jerk of the stick, a blurred impression of masts, winking guns, a bridge, a derrick, a jerk as if the Boston had been kicked in the belly, and then down again, still alive, screaming over the sea, ruffling the waves with the slipstream, dodging between the hulks of frantic ships. . . .

Grenville had picked himself the freighter dead ahead. He dropped the bombs himself, letting two go as the dark funnels yawned beneath him. As he went over an alert gunner raked him with a 7 mm., drilling a line of neat holes in his port wing. As he jinked away he heard an excited yell through his intercom. from Bergman.

"Se der. You've got her! There she goes!"

The short time-delays had exploded and the red flash appeared to split the ship in two. The whole area was now a mad chaos of soaring tracer, exploding shells, and blazing ships. In the red light the Bostons looked like black-winged devils as they added to the havoc.

Grenville attacked a second ship with his remaining bombs. This attack was not successful; his bombs bounced and rolled off its heavily-timbered decks. He jinked away, passing near the small ship on the starboard flank of the convoy that had first sighted them. Flak and tracer was radiating from it like the quills of a porcupine. It turned its full fury on him, lashing the air with explosive and steel. Ugly red flashes burst all around, making A Apple shudder with the concussion.

Grenville swung violently out of range and the flak ship turned its attention on nearer aircraft. B Flight were coming in now and getting hell. Grenville, patrolling the perimeter of the action, saw that two other flak ships had closed in on the convoy. His earphones rang with a medley of shouts and curses. He made himself heard over the din.

"Crossbow leader here. No attacks to be made on enemy flak ships now joining convoy. Withdraw as soon as all bombs dropped and orbit three miles west. Repeat. No attacks to be made on enemy flak ships. . . ."

B Flight were having trouble. The tremendous barrage from the flak ships, helped by the now fully alerted gunners on the freighters, was driving them from their targets. A Boston was hit as it attacked a large freighter. From a streak of black lightning it turned into a cartwheel of fire as it received a direct hit in a fuel tank from a 37 mm. shell. It spun into the sea and vanished in a fountain of steam and spray.

Gillibrand's T Tommy was hit by the small flak ship as he made his run-in. A hole big enough to drop a football through suddenly appeared in his starboard wing. His big jaw clamped on his wad of gum, and he banked steeply over. To hell with orders—those bastards were asking for it. He came in low and at the stern of the floating gun platform. Everything on it opened up—quadruple automatic 20 mms., 37 mms., and its 7 mms. To Jimmie Willcox, staring down helplessly from his forward hatch, it was like flying into an exploding ammunition dump.

Gillibrand brought his stick back and howled over the erupting ship. He let his bombs go, then swung his controls hard over and skidded crazily to port, deceiving the gunners who were waiting for him to dip down astern. The port beam gunners were lining him up when both the bombs exploded. When the shattering glare had died down there was nothing on the sea but small pieces of wreckage and a pool of blazing oil. Gillibrand shifted his gum from one cheek to the other and grinned.

"Whaddya think of that, Jimmie boy? That fixed 'em, huh?"

The youngster's face was like a death mask. His teeth had bitten deeply into his lower lip and blood was

59

trickling down his chin. He could feel the frantic pounding of his heart in his head, his hands and his feet. His stomach turned over, making him retch. He tried to reply, but only a whimper came from his lips. The intercom was kind to him, distorting the sound.

Gillibrand addressed his gunner as well as Jimmie. "The R/T was u.s.! Don't forget it, you guys, or Grenville will take my hide off when we get back. Now what else is cookin' round these parts. . . ?"

From A Apple, circling the perimeter of the action, it was like looking down into hell. Gillibrand's T Tommy looked like a moth being pierced by a hundred white-hot needles as it attacked the flak ship, and its escape seemed a miracle. The flak ship exploded but the others were taking their toll. Another Boston of B Flight was hit when attacking a freighter. It went straight into the ship's beam, flaming petrol sweeping right over the deck above.

Grenville was swearing slowly and viciously. He gave a curt order to his crew. Hoppy's voice came back immediately. "O.K., skipper. I'm ready."

In the dark turret, lit only by the flare of bursting shells and burning ships, Bergman's voice failed him. His whole body was aching from nervous strain; and his underclothes were soaked with perspiration and clinging coldly to his body. He thought of the warning Grenville had given him earlier, and managed a rueful grin in the darkness. This certainly did take some getting used to. . . .

Grenville's voice came again, as sharp as a whip. "Are you ready, Finn? Do you understand what you have to do?"

Bergman managed it this time. "Yes, Roy; I understand. I'm ready."

"All right. Hang on then."

A Apple echelonned away and plunged down into the centre of the convoy.

8

The Bostons returned to Sutton Craddock just after noon. Hilde was up in her room when she heard them. She ran downstairs and out on to the gravel drive. Maisie and Kearns were already there, having come out from the bar.

The hum grew louder, a deep throbbing note like that given by an organ with the lower stops out. There was nothing to see yet, low thick clouds effectively blanketed the sky. But as the hum grew louder irregularities in it could be heard as if some of the engines were missing. Over on the airfield a siren was wailing and ambulance and truck engines were starting up.

The noise was deafening now, a heavy roar that beat down on their temples. The first Boston came out of the clouds like a wraith. As it banked carefully over the road, they saw daylight through a jagged hole in its wing. It slid slowly out of sight behind the wooden fence, its engines coughing and the wind whining over its airfoils.

Another damaged plane followed it. Shrapnel scars showed on its fuselage and tail unit. One engine was missing alarmingly and sending out a thin stream of black smoke. It lowered itself as gingerly as a cat down a sloping roof, and vanished in turn behind the fence.

One by one the rest came in. Kearns stole a glance at Hilde. Her face was very pale and her eyes enormous as they followed the planes down. For all her natural composure she looked very young and vulnerable at that moment.

At last the sky was empty of sound again. Maisie, who had not spoken a word during this time, turned to Hilde. Her voice had a high-pitched, brittle ring.

"How many went out—d'you know? I didn't wake up until half of 'em had gone."

"Twelve," Hilde said.

Maisie's voice was suddenly hushed. "Twelve! But only eight landed just now!"

Hilde nodded, then turned and went inside. Maisie stared at Kearns. "That doesn't mean four have gone west, does it?"

Kearns shook his head heavily. "I don't know, lass. We'll have to wait and see."

The telephone in the hall rang fifteen minutes later. Kearns answered it, turning to Hilde, who had appeared at the door of the sitting-room. His voice was relieved. "It's for you, Miss. I think it's your brother."

With a murmur of thanks she took the receiver from him. She spoke in Norwegian, her voice low and a little unsteady. Kearns moved off to the door that led into the public rooms. Maisie was standing there and he took her arm.

"Come on," he murmured. "Give the girl a bit of privacy."

"There's something I want to ask her," Maisie said. Ignoring his protests she drew closer to Hilde, hesitated, then reached out and touched her arm.

"Sorry to interrupt, Miss, but do me a favour, will you? Ask your brother if the big Canadian is all right. . . ."

Bergman came over to the inn just after three o'clock that afternoon. To his relief he found Hilde alone in the sitting-room. She came over to him at once, gripping his arm tightly for a moment.

He put a hand on her hair and ruffled it affectionately. *"Hallo, kjaere.* How is my favourite girl-friend today?"

She pressed his arm. "Very pleased to see you. So pleased she'll forgive you for neglecting her for so long."

He saw how pale she was and offered her a cigarette. She accepted the light, inhaled deeply, then turned to him. "What was it like?" she asked quietly. "Can you tell me or is it a secret?"

Bergman shook his head. "No. As far as I'm concerned it isn't a secret any longer. The Censor will pass on the news to the papers just as if it had been a normal raid. To keep it hushed up would make things suspicious. It was an attack on a convoy off the Norwegian coast—what the Air Force call a shipping strike."

Valerie's guess had been remarkably accurate, Hilde thought. She led Bergman over to one of the armchairs. "Sit down and tell me all about it."

Her eyes never left his face as he gave her brief details of the strike. He was sitting near the window and the bleak daylight showed up all his weariness. He finished his short account on a humorous note, telling her about Gillibrand.

"There was a tremendous row when they landed. Grenville was going to have him arrested but he swore his wireless had been faulty and he hadn't picked up Grenville's orders. His wireless mechanic bore him out. Just the same, I thought Grenville was going to arrest them both."

"But why?"

Bergman laughed. "Apparently this has happened before. Gillibrand talks his mechanic into putting in an unserviceable report. It's a risky game, with Grenville the Squadron Commander."

For a moment the tension within Hilde eased. She laughed with him. "I shall have to meet Gillibrand."

"You'll find it difficult to miss him. He's a tremendous character."

"And what was it like flying with Grenville?" she asked. "So far you've made it sound as if all your plane did was fly about and let the others do the fighting."

Bergman's weary face became animated. "Grenville was magnificent. I can't think of anyone else who would have got his squadron through in such weather. And do you know what he did when he saw what the flak ships were doing to his planes?"

She shook her head, watching the enthusiasm glowing in his eyes.

"He ordered his planes to keep away, then kept flying near them himself to draw off their fire. And he kept it up until all his aircraft had dropped their bombs. I've never seen anything like it before."

Hilde sat motionless a moment, then said quietly: "Don't fly with him again, Finn. If you must go out with them, go with someone else. Please."

Bergman read her thoughts and shook his head. "He's not reckless, Hilde. He did that to save lives, not to risk them."

"Your life was risked," she reminded him.

Bergman shrugged impatiently. "That wasn't his fault."

She gave a quick, hopeless shake of her head. A burning coal fell on to the hearth. She picked it up with the tongs and threw it back into the fire.

"You lost four planes, didn't you?" she asked.

"Two. One lost contact with us and returned earlier, and another was pretty badly shot-up but got back to Sumburgh. We left it there to get repairs."

"How many men is that?"

Bergman moved restlessly. "Don't start getting morbid, please."

"Please tell me," she asked quietly.

He threw his cigarette into the fire, lit a fresh one. "Six. And two gunners wounded and in hospital."

She realized he was feeling the loss and changed the subject at once. "Will you be coming over tonight? And are you bringing Grenville with you?"

"I would have liked to do so but he has a great deal of work to do. And then there is this party afterwards. . . ."

Her eyes widened. "Party! What party?"

"They are having one in the Mess," Bergman explained. "It's a custom of Grenville's after a successful raid."

She showed her bewilderment. "But six of his men died today. Why does he want a party?"

Bergman shrugged. "They can't afford to brood over those that have gone—they'd go crazy if they did. Grenville knows what he is doing."

Hilde did not argue with him. "Will you be going to this party too?" she asked, her voice low.

He nodded. "I said I'd go over about eight. I must go, out of respect to Grenville if for nothing else. I'm sorry, particularly as I couldn't get over last night. But after this I should have a few free nights."

She had risen and was staring down into the fire. Bergman rose, putting a hand on her shoulder. "What's the matter?" he asked. "You seem very quiet. What's worrying you?"

She turned to him, her eyes uncertain. "I don't quite know. I think——" Her hand fluttered in the gesture he knew so well. "I think it is this friend of yours, Grenville. I believe I am a little afraid of him. . . ."

The naked bulb hanging from the ceiling gave off a harsh light that made Grenville's eyes ache. He was sitting at his desk reading a letter. He had almost finished it when he let out an exclamation and ripped it to pieces. Dropping his face into his hands he sat motionless for a moment, fingers pressed tightly into the thick dark hair over his temples. Then he picked up his pen and began writing again.

The letter took him over fifteen minutes to complete. He read it through again, shook his head, but this time folded it into an envelope which he put with five others that lay on his desk. Then he slumped back in his chair and lit a cigarette.

Thank God that was over. How he loathed the job, writing the same old platitudes, how they had died doing their duty, their courage in the face of enemy fire, and the rest of the bilge. What wife found any comfort in it when her children started asking where their father was? What mother gave a damn about courage as long as her son was alive and healthy? And that cant about them being remembered—that was a laugh. Who outside their own families was going to remember them after the war? Not a soul. No one liked being reminded of his debts, but there was one advantage in having them to the dead—you could forget 'em. . . .

Disjointed memories came to Grenville. The visiting journalist last year . . . puffed-up little man . . . announcing pretentiously that at least the bereaved would have the pride of knowing their boys had died under a famous command . . . his look of amazement when

Grenville had hit him . . . the fuss until Group had managed to hush it up. Pride! They'd damn him to hell for getting their boys killed, and who could blame them?

He swore viciously, jumping to his feet. It wasn't his fault, was it, if mothers had sons, and if men were damn fools enough to marry and have wives and children who could miss them. . . .?

Sweat trickled down his face, burning into the sores left by his face mask. He wiped a hand across his forehead, lowered it, and saw the sweat glistening on his fingers. He swore again, then glanced round the office in sudden alarm. Thank heaven he was alone.

The thought of others seeing him in this condition pulled him together. He was tired, that was all it was. He had ordered his crews to bed on their return: he should have gone himself. But he'd had to get in touch with Sumburgh about the wounded, Davies had wanted to talk with him, Adams had wanted to know how many damned rivets there'd been in the ships they'd sunk, these letters had had to be written—how the hell could a man sleep?

And now there was this party. He glanced down at his watch. Eight-thirty—it would be well on its way now. A party—on top of this! A couple of drinks and he'd want to puke his guts out. But it was his idea, wasn't it? The tough Grenville touch. . . .

He wondered where Bergman was. Probably still with his sister—he had said he might be a little late for the party. Quite a man, that Norwegian. He didn't like sitting back while others went into danger, although if all Davies said was true, he'd earned himself a rest. He must have been scared to death when they went in —that low-level stuff was hell for anyone green. But he'd taken it well, particularly at the end when they'd pin-pricked the flak ships. Not that he'd have hit anything with those guns of his except wave-tops, but he'd given it a bang. No one could do more than that.

Grenville wondered about his sister. She must know what his game was—it must be nerve-racking for her when he was over on the other side. He wondered what she was like. If she had half Bergman's courage, she'd be quite a girl. He looked at his watch again—there was still time to run over and meet her. Bergman would appreciate it, he knew that. They could have a quick drink, then he and Bergman could go to the Mess together. . . .

As always when he had made a decision Grenville acted promptly. He threw on his greatcoat, picked up the six letters, and gave them to the aircraftsman on duty in the Orderly Room. Then he made his way towards the camp entrance.

A bleak drizzle was blowing in from the east, and it was as black as the inside of a hat. He swore as his feet squelched in a patch of glutinous mud. As he passed the Mess he heard the muffled sounds of laughter and singing. The party was getting under way—in another two hours it would be a free-for-all as the boys worked off their tension. He walked quickly, trying to lose the ache in his back and legs. The guard at the gate recognized him and snapped to attention. He saluted back and turned right down the road outside. It was quiet here and he could hear the moisture dripping off the trees and soaking into the wet earth.

His eyes were accustomed to the darkness now and he saw the black silhouette of the inn looming up ahead of him. He had his hand on the door of the lounge when he paused. Why the devil had he chosen this of all nights to come over? He was in a filthy mood and couldn't be sociable if he tried! He took his hand off the latch, then swore again. Never turn back if you can help it, there's no easier habit to acquire . . . ! Get inside, say hello to her, then take Bergman over to the Mess! The party was the right idea after all—a few drinks would take away this tension and soften the edge on things. . . . Without giving himself time for further hesitation, Grenville pushed open the door and entered.

9

Maisie was washing glasses behind the lounge bar when she heard the crash of metal. The half-dozen locals, yawning over their beers, jerked awake at the noise and followed her as she ducked under the counter and ran outside.

A small car was lurched up against the wall of the inn. Two figures were silhouetted against its lights, one huge, the other small. A rich Canadian voice sounded as Maisie approached the car.

"Aw; we'll leave it there, kid. The steering's gone for a burton. I'll get Chiefy to have a look at it tomorrow."

"Hey, what's going on?" Maisie asked indignantly. "You can't come busting up your car on our drive."

Gillibrand swung round. A grin split his face from ear to ear. "Waal, waal! If it ain't my little dream girl. Hiya, honey! How're those big black eyes tonight? Shining bright for your cousin, huh?"

He slid his arm round her waist. Maisie backed hurriedly away. "Don't you touch me. You're drunk."

Gillibrand grinned again. "Kid; you do yourself an injustice. I ain't gotta be drunk to make a pass at you. C'mon, Jimmie boy. Let's sink a couple here before joinin' the party, huh?"

The locals scattered as the burly Canadian entered the lounge, his arm around his small companion. They approached the bar behind which Maisie had taken refuge. She eyed Gillibrand cautiously.

"Now take it easy, see. We don't want no trouble here. This is a respectable place."

Gillibrand draped himself over a stool, winking at his observer. "What are you talkin' about, kid? Jimmie an' me have come to say hello and to have a little chat. Now what's wrong with that?"

"Just keep it that way, that's all," Maisie sniffed. "And don't try to be fresh again."

Gillibrand's elbows shifted farther across the counter. "Say, you look real pretty when you're mad." He turned to Jimmie. "Don't she, kid?"

The boy nodded, trying hard to smile. A lock of hair was hanging dismally over his eyes and his face had an unhealthy pallor. He looked as if he had had too much to drink and now wanted to be sick.

"Give us two beers, will you, honey?" Gillibrand said, "and be matey and have a drink yourself."

Maisie poured them two pints, then, after some hesitation, gave herself a small gin. Gillibrand winked at her. "This is more like it, honey. This is nice." He turned again to Jimmie. "Bit different from this morning, ain't it, kid?"

The boy's lips moved in a caricature of a smile. "A bit, yes." He had a thin, shy voice.

Gillibrand grinned. "You never thought we'd make it when we went for that flak ship, did you?"

Jimmie gave a cracked laugh. "I didn't. I thought we'd bought it."

The Canadian laughed and slapped him on the shoulder. "Aw; you leave it to your Uncle Gillie—he'll always get you through. We showed 'em, and we'll show 'em again the next time they take a poke at us."

Maisie was all curiosity now. "What happened this morning? Can you tell me somethin' about it?"

Gillibrand winked. "Waal, maybe a bit here and there—if you keep your mouth shut afterwards."

"I won't say anythin'," Maisie promised. "Honest, I won't. What did you raid?"

"Shipping off the Norwegian coast. An' we gave 'em hell. Jimmie'll tell you."

Maisie threw a glance at the boy, who jerked his head nervously. "Did you hit anything?" she asked.

Gillibrand let out a laugh. "Did we hit anythin' . . .! Hitler's one flak ship short tonight, baby. It took a crack at us and put a hole in my starboard wing, so I turned on the heat. The pieces are still comin' down."

Maisie's black eyes were round and excited. "Was that you who came in with a big hole in one wing?"

Gillibrand grinned. "You were watchin', huh? Yeah,

that was me. And that wasn't the only hole we got—Jimmie'll tell you. This is how it happened, kid . . ."

When he had finished the story Maisie's mouth was a round O. "Gee," she managed. "Just imagine that!"

Gillibrand waved a big hand. "Aw, that's nothin'. I could tell you a hundred stories better than that. An' maybe I will some time. . . . Hey, what's the matter, kid? Where're you going?"

Jimmie had suddenly stumbled off towards the door. Gillibrand jumped from his stool and followed him. He returned alone two minutes later, shaking his head.

"Funny kid—wouldn't let me stay with him. Says he'll come back when he feels better."

"You shouldn't let him drink so much," Maisie said critically. "He's only a kid, and doesn't look very strong."

Gillibrand frowned. "What can you do? He's gotta learn. This is a tough game—you gotta be tough to keep in it."

"You won't toughen him up this way. I think this business this morning upset him. His eyes were like marbles when you were tellin' me about it."

The Canadian's jaw suddenly tightened. "Now wait a minute! That kid ain't afraid of anything, and don't you forget it. He's a good boy—see!"

"All right, all right," Maisie said to pacify him. "Then he's feeling queer because he missed a night's sleep and has had beer on top of it. Missing sleep does affect some people that way."

Gillibrand's face cleared. "That's different. That's sensible." He stared at Maisie, then grinned again. "You're all right, kid. How about you and me havin' a date one of these nights, huh?"

Maisie was surprised at her own caution. "Ain't you got a wife or a girl friend?"

"I got a girl, sure. . . . Everybody's got a girl. But she ain't here, that's the thing. She's down in London."

Maisie tossed her head. "I'm not the sort who plays second fiddle."

"You won't be second fiddle, baby. Here you'll be my very best girl. An' I've got a car—we can have some nice long rides together. Won't that be somethin'?"

70

Maisie jerked a sarcastic thumb at the wall. "You mean you had a car, don't you?"

"Don't worry; it'll patch up." Gillibrand lifted his glass. "Here's to them long summer nights we're goin' to spend together, baby."

"Evenings," Maisie said cautiously.

Gillibrand grinned. "All right, honey. Here's to the evenings."

Jimmie returned at that moment. His white face had a clammy appearance and his hand was trembling as he picked up his glass. Gillibrand reached over and took it from him.

"Leave that belly-wash alone, kid. Have somethin' to settle your stomach." The Canadian turned to Maisie. "What've you got for him, honey? Somethin' from under the counter, huh?"

Maisie half-filled a glass with brandy and slipped it to the boy. "That'll make you feel better," she said.

Jimmie thanked her and sipped at the neat spirit. The colour returned slowly to his cheeks. Maisie noticed the concern on the Canadian's face as he watched the youngster.

"That's better, kid?"

Jimmie nodded. "Yes, thanks. I don't know what went wrong. . . . It must have been the car ride on top of the beer."

"Yeah; that and the night's sleep you missed. Aw, it can happen to anybody. But, you know, you ought to relax a bit. It ain't good to be tensed up all the time."

Jimmie flushed. "I'm not tensed up. There's nothing wrong with me."

There was a shrill edge to his voice. Gillibrand waved a hand in good-natured protest. "You don't have to tell me there's nothin' wrong with you. I know that, don't I? You've got me wrong. I'm advisin' you to enjoy yourself more. You want to get yourself a girl. . . . Now there's somethin'. Girls make you feel good, slacken off your nerves." He looked at Maisie. "Don't they, honey?"

"Do they? Don't ask me."

" 'Course they do. An' heck, think how a guy would feel if he'd never had a girl and got the chopper.

71

Why, he'd be up there, all bright an' shiny, pluckin' those strings and wishin' like hell all the time he hadn't missed out. It's waste, kid, that's what it is. Criminal waste."

"Stop talkin' rubbish," Maisie snapped, afraid that the boy would either break down again or take offence.

Jimmie appeared to have recovered, however, for he gave a wan smile. "You'd better shut up or I'll take Maisie out," he muttered. "What'll you have—another beer?"

Gillibrand, delighted with the boy's show of spirit, was as fussy as a collie dog wagging its tail. "Attaboy! That's better." He grinned at Maisie. "I'll have to watch him, hey, baby?"

" 'Couse you'll have to watch him," Maisie said, winking encouragingly at the boy. "I like 'em quiet and well-behaved."

The door latch clicked. Gillibrand turned around casually, then stiffened. Grenville was approaching the counter.

"Evenin', skipper."

Grenville nodded at him and Jimmie, then turned to Maisie. "I'd like to see Lieutenant Bergman and his sister. May I go through?"

Conscious of the authoritative ring in his voice, Maisie hurried along the counter. "Why, yes, sir. They're in the sitting-room, I think." She lifted the flap of the counter. "This way, sir. Through this door and across the hall. That door there, look, straight across. . . ."

Grenville nodded his thanks and crossed the hall. Maisie closed the door and returned to the others, her eyes eager with curiosity. "Who was that? You called him skipper. He ain't Grenville, is he?"

Gillibrand bit off a wad of gum and grinned. "That's the guy, honey. An' by the look of him he ain't exactly forgiven me for what happened this morning."

Maisie shook her dark head in awe. "That's Roy Grenville—and he ain't no older than my brother. Gee, can you believe it. . . .?"

Grenville knew at once she was Bergman's sister; there was a resemblance about her fine eyes and good

72

forehead. She gave him a questioning smile from her armchair.

"You'll be Miss Bergman," Grenville said, moving from the doorway. "Lieutenant Bergman's sister."

Her low-toned voice with its attractive accent gave him his assurance before she finished speaking. "Yes; I am Hilde Bergman. Are you looking for my brother?"

He nodded. "My name's Grenville. I thought your brother was over here."

An odd, indefinable expression came into her eyes as he gave his name. There was a perceptible pause before she spoke again.

"Good evening, Squadron-Leader. Please take off your coat. Is there anything I can order for you?"

Grenville shook his head. "No, thank you. Not now. And if you don't mind, I'll keep my coat on. I shan't be able to stay long."

"Just as you wish, of course." She motioned to the armchair opposite. "I'm sorry my brother is not here, but he left for the camp a quarter of an hour ago. He said there was a party he had to attend." Her eyes examined his face. "I understood him to say you were giving it."

In some indefinable way Grenville imagined her tone had changed slightly on hearing his name. He dropped into the chair, feeling his way cautiously.

"Yes; there is a bit of a party. That's why I can't stay. But I had a few minutes and thought I'd like to run over and meet you, and then perhaps take your brother back with me." He changed the subject. "Do you know this part of England at all?"

"No, I have never been in Yorkshire before."

He motioned to the panelled walls. "Do you like this inn? Are you comfortable?"

"Oh yes. It is a lovely old place. I like it very much."

For the first few minutes Grenville felt ill at ease, and his analytical mind, incessantly self-critical, gave him a reason. Before the war he would have enjoyed the company of such a girl. Now he felt gauche, out of place. It was the war, he told himself. Three years of it had coarsened him, both in his own eyes and the eyes of others. Now he was fit for nothing but Service life where rank so often took the place of culture and embarrassment for one's shortcomings could be kept at bay by the shouting of an order.

Gradually, however, the atmosphere of the room, with its old-world furniture, darkened wood, and gleaming brass, began to soak into him, relaxing his tight nerves. The warmth of the fire also had its effect, making his eyelids heavy. He studied the girl opposite him. She was beautiful! Her mass of hair was as bright as that of a child's. And her voice—if only he could lie back with closed eyes and listen to it! He was tired, and it was as soothing as a moonlit sky after a barrage of flak. With an effort he forced his eyes open, made himself talk.

"You haven't seen any ghosts in here yet?" he asked. "Cavaliers, Roundheads, and that sort of thing?"

Hilde laughed. "No, not yet. But I have not given up hope."

"Do you usually travel about with your brother?"

She understood the significance of the question. "When it is considered safe, yes."

Grenville nodded. She knew—it was safe to talk. "Then you'll have a pretty good idea why he has come here?"

"I know he is working with your squadron, but that is all."

He wondered if she had heard about the shipping strike. Her question made it appear she had read his thoughts.

"How did my brother manage this morning? I know that he flew with you."

There was no doubt about the sincerity of Grenville's reply. "He did a fine job. It wasn't a pleasant trip and he took it well."

She nodded. "He told me nothing of his part in it, but he did mention your efforts to draw the fire from your men. He thought that very brave of you."

Embarrassment immediately made Grenville's voice curt. "I think he exaggerated a little. The danger wasn't as great as he imagined."

She shook her head. "My brother has seen too much

74

danger to exaggerate it. He has had more than his share of it since the war started."

What was that undertone in her voice? In one as composed as she it was difficult to place. . . . Then Grenville recognized it and instantly the rest was clear to him.

"It was your brother who wanted to come along," he said, understanding now her apprehension. "He insisted on it."

He saw he had guessed correctly. He also saw that there was deep emotion in her, in spite of her natural gentleness.

She turned to face him. Her voice was still low in tone. "You know why, don't you? That was because my brother cannot sit back and send others into danger. But he has to face dangers that none of you can share —terrible dangers. It is not fair that he should share yours too."

Grenville shrugged. "I quite agree with you. But whose fault is it?"

"It is the fault of those in command," she said quietly. "No one should be allowed to take him with them. No one should offer to take him."

Excuses for himself never came easily to Grenville. "You should tell this to your brother. There's nothing we can do."

She turned her face away. "How can I talk to him? When a man has a sense of duty like that, there is nothing a woman can do."

Grenville's voice softened. "It's true—brave men can be stubborn. But I shouldn't worry too much about it. He'll be all right." He glanced down at his watch, then, surprised at his reluctance, rose to his feet. "I'm afraid I shall have to be getting along."

Hilde rose after him. There was a confused look in her eyes now. "You are not quite as I imagined you . . ." She paused, then went on hesitantly: "Will you explain something to me?"

There was almost a wistful note in her voice. Grenville turned back. "Yes, if I can. What is it?"

"I know that you lost six men today. Then why do

75

you hold a party tonight? It is something I do not understand. . . ."

There was a devil in Grenville that liked playing up to another's unfavourable opinion of him. As a boy it had earned him many an unwarranted thrashing, and, perversely, thrived on the punishment. As a man it was more under control but on certain moods could be as wicked as ever. Her question, touching him where he was hypersensitive, put him in such a mood now.

"Why? Because I like parties. I like getting drunk—it's a hobby of mine. What has losing six men got to do with that?"

The disappointment in her eyes goaded the devil in him further. "Don't worry about your brother," he said. "If he gets too drunk I'll see him to his bunk."

Her lovely, steady eyes met his own, and for a moment he had the odd sensation he was sinking down into their blue-grey depths. Down, sinking deeper, very cool, very tranquil, very forgiving. . . .

He turned away with a sharp exclamation. Five minutes later he pushed open the door of the Mess. A cheer went up, startling him. The haze of tobacco smoke made him think of a shifting curtain between two worlds. He pushed his way through it and reached the bar. Someone pushed a filled glass into his hand and he drank deeply. The liquor sank into his stomach, warming his aching back and legs. This was the world he had chosen: this was the only world left—until it blew up in flame and broken spars around him! He lifted his glass and drank again.

Adams found himself in the innkeeper's kitchen that night. Since his wife's arrival he had developed a habit of joining Kearns over a cup of tea after the bar closed. Kearns was a restful person with his pipe and slow, contemplative voice, and Adams was growing attached to him. His kitchen, with its two rocking-chairs and its singing kettle, was becoming a brief sanctuary from the mad world across the road and (although Adams did not realize it yet) from the unsympathetic woman who was his wife. Instinct told Adams the innkeeper could be trusted and in the weeks to come he was to tell him more than was always discreet. It was a lucky thing for Adams his instinct did not betray him.

This was the first night he went below the surface. The reason was not difficult to find: he was half-drunk. Losses always hit Adams hard, and this was no exception. He would have liked to go to the party, but dared not trust himself to conceal his feelings. In any case, it would have made him feel impossibly old and futile. . . . With all his friends in the Mess and Valerie unsuitable company for such an occasion, there had been nothing for it but to drink alone, which he had done in a pub in Highgate. On his way back to camp a sudden impulse had made him enter the inn through a back door. Unknown to Valerie, he had now been with the innkeeper for over a quarter of an hour.

The warm, quiet sympathy of the room was having its effect. Adams turned suddenly from the fire and faced the innkeeper.

"Did you notice the planes come back this afternoon?"

Kearns was packing his pipe. He paused. "Aye, lad; we saw 'em all right. Some were lost, I hear."

"Six men killed. I was sitting next to one of them at dinner last night. He was telling me what he was going to do when the war was over." The sound of his own thick voice filled Adams with a vague disgust.

Kearns shook his head slowly. "Aye; it's a terrible waste."

"That's how it goes, week after week, month after month, until you're never quite sure who's alive and who's dead. Your memory starts playing tricks with you—you get the ghosts mixed up with the living."

"Aye. War is a wicked thing, lad. A wicked thing."

Adams found his emotions were in a tangle again. He leaned forward abruptly, the firelight gleaming on his spectacles. "And yet, you know, I envy them. They do live before they die. They're not doing the same old job, growing old slowly, feeling old age coming on a bit more every winter. They get more out of life in a day than we get in a year."

Kearns shook his head stubbornly. "Don't say anything to make war sound better than it is, lad. War is a wicked thing. I know—I was in the last one."

Adams' half-drunken voice became suddenly resentful. "Oh; I know—I've been sitting on my backside too long listening to other people's exploits. I see the glamour because I'm an onlooker. . . . If I were in their flying boots I'd be scared to death. . . . All right, I agree with all that. But one thing I do know . . ."

"What's that, lad?" Kearns asked quietly.

"Just this. That those who come through will never find life the same again. Some won't know why, but I know. They'll never feel so strong, they'll never know blossom so white, they'll never find girls so lovely. And why? Because you never feel the real sweetness of life until you stand at the edge of death. . . . It's a paradox that makes me wonder if the whole business of living isn't one big, dirty joke."

10

Barrett stood by his office window, his blunt fingers drumming impatiently on the sill. He turned sharply at a tap on the door. "Come in," he shouted.

Grenville entered. Barrett waited until he had closed the door before speaking. "I've just had Davies on the blower. He's got a special job for us as soon as the weather's suitable."

"What is it this time? Another strike?"

"No, thank God. It's a single job, a recce." Barrett paused, his gruff voice dropping. "My guess is that it has to do with this big job everyone's so tight-lipped about. This is the gen I've got so far."

He took Grenville over to his desk on which lay a large-scale map of Norway. He pointed a blunt, tobac-co-stained finger at a point on the coast above the 61st Parallel.

"There's a fjord here called the Svartfjord. Apparently the convoy on which you dropped the hammer the other day sailed from it. It's very steep, is about twenty-five miles along, and at the back end there is a hydroelectric plant and a large camouflaged building. It's this building we have to photograph."

Grenville looked up from the map, his face curious. "You don't know what it is?"

Barrett grunted his disgust. "No. They're as tight as a bull's arse in fly time about it. But it's obviously impor-tant—they've got an elaborate plan worked out to kid Jerry we don't know it's there and are flying over that way by accident. Davies has had it all worked out, and gave it to Bergman yesterday. In a few minutes we'll go and have a talk with him—he's with Adams at the moment. I called you in to talk about the crew. Da-vies said he'd like you to go yourself—the job's that important. But I said I'd like a word with you first."

"Why?" Grenville asked.

Barrett looked slightly uncomfortable. "It seems a

rather dicey show to me. They don't want to send an escort for fear of making Jerry suspicious, and yet if it's that important he's bound to be on the alert. I don't fancy losing my Squadron Commander on some bloody mountain-top—not when I've got twenty-odd other pilots I can send."

"They aren't likely to keep a constant patrol at 30,000 feet," Grenville said.

"If you go, mind you stay up there," Barrett grunted. "If you can't see anything for shadows, never mind. Come back and let 'em organize something else. If you go lower they'll get you, as sure as hell." He paused, frowning heavily. "I asked Davies why they couldn't use a Spit for the job. He says they've tried twice, but drawn a blank each time. It seems this building is difficult to spot from the air unless you've someone with you who knows the landmarks. So we have to use old Popsy and take Bergman along as guide."

Grenville started at the Norwegian's name. "He's not going along, is he?"

Barrett nodded. "That's the point of the idea. He leads you over the building and tells the photographer when to press his button."

Grenville's face set. "To hell with it! I took him with me on the strike, I don't want him again. Particularly on a job like this."

Barrett stared at him. "But I thought you said he did all right on the strike."

"That was different. That was at night, in filthy weather. There wasn't a chance of fighter interception. But this will be in daylight. What happens if a patrol jumps us and I've no rear gunner?"

Barrett nodded his agreement. "You're right, of course." He stroked his moustaches thoughtfully. "You couldn't manage without Hopkinson, could you? Let Bergman go in his place and take your regular gunner along?"

Grenville's voice was uncompromisingly curt. "No; I couldn't. Let him keep out of this. We don't take staff-planning officers with us when we prang a target, do we? If we did we'd soon need Bombays instead of Bostons. Let Bergman do as the others do—give us the gen and then leave us alone. We'll get the photographs."

Barrett scratched his head. "I know how you feel, Roy. But I can't get round the orders. We haven't much of an argument, anyway. Two Spits have already failed on their own. We might do the same without Bergman."

"Then you can count me out," Grenville said abruptly. "I don't want Bergman with me."

Barrett nodded. "All right, that suits me. As far as I'm concerned you're down with a heavy cold. Right—now who do you suggest? Milner?"

Grenville was silent, his face moody. Barrett stared at him, repeating his question. Grenville shook his head. "Milner's down with the 'flu. I got word just before I came in."

"Who else, then? Young? Gillibrand?"

Grenville gave a harsh laugh. "Gillibrand! Are you trying to kill the bod? Gillibrand would probably go down and run his wheels over the bloody thing to see what it was made of."

Barrett was growing impatient. "What about one or two suggestions, then?"

Grenville made his reluctant decision. "All right; I'll go," he said abruptly. "But keep him grounded in the future. We're not a transport squadron."

In spite of his previous remarks, Barrett looked relieved. "I suppose it is just as well," he admitted. "There'd probably be a hell of an inquest if anything happened and they found you hadn't gone with him. O.K. then, that's settled. You go on the first favourable met. report. Now come on over to Adams and Bergman and get the gen."

Bergman and Adams were sitting over a pile of photographs and a map of Norway when Grenville and Barrett arrived. Adams had been fully briefed on the plan, and it was he who gave the details to Grenville.

He pointed to a cross on the map. "You hit the coast here at a point eight miles north of Utvik as near 10:15 as possible. The time factor is very important, as you'll see in a minute. You must be over 30,000 feet as you come in. . . ." His myopic eyes lifted to Grenville's set face. "That's one of the points I raised with the Air Commodore. Can you keep over 30,000 feet with a crew of three?"

Grenville shrugged. "Davies can't have it both ways. If I must carry passengers, I obviously can't get so high."

Bergman caught the black glance thrown his way and guessed its cause. He sat in uncomfortable silence. Barrett met Adams' eye and broke in hastily.

"I've told Townsend to take everything that's movable out of Popsy. We think she should make 30,000 feet, perhaps a bit more."

Adams nodded and looked down at his map again. "After crossing the coast you make straight for Hjelmestad, this small town here. The Germans have recently opened out an ordinance factory in Hjelmestad; we're hoping they'll assume this is the target for your reconnaissance. Allowing for your reduced airspeed we estimate it should take about five and a quarter minutes to reach it. You circle it once as if taking photographs, then start back south-west along this track," and his finger pointed at a pencilled line on the map. "That leads you right over and parallel to the Svartfjord which, as you'll notice, runs in a southwesterly direction before turning west to the sea.

"Your track will take you along its first eight miles," Adams went on. "The building is here—right at the end of the fjord—but they want as many photographs as they can get so go on taking them until the fjord turns away. To avoid suspicion, you don't follow it but keep straight on and hit the coast here."

"What are the Focke-Wulfs doing during this time?" Grenville asked.

Adams felt the embarrassment he always felt when discussing the ways another man should risk his life. He coughed to hide it. "That has all been considered in the time factor. We estimate you won't be over land more than fourteen minutes. Provided you aren't detected before you reach the coast, that gives you a fair escape margin. We know Jerry has got some of the very latest Fw 190 A-6's at Voss and Herdla, but even with them he can't reach 30,000 feet in that time. You should make it fairly comfortably."

"You haven't got any performance figures on these new Focke-Wulfs yet?" Grenville asked.

"No; but however good they are they can hardly get up to 30,000 feet in much under twenty-five minutes."

"It's cutting it pretty fine," Barrett said anxiously.

"It is and it isn't," Adams said. "Fourteen minutes over the coast is a fairly generous estimate—it may take even less time."

Grenville was studying the map and its detail. "Why is 10:15 so important? Couldn't we go in earlier?"

Adams shook his head. "There's a very special reason for that. At this time of the year, the sun never reaches to the bottom of the Svartfjord. But there is a large glacier covering one of the mountains that overlooks the building. Because of its angle, between 10:15 and 10:45 it reflects the sun downwards just like a large mirror. It should give sufficient light for a photograph."

Barrett's mouth had dropped open. "Who the heck thought of that one?"

Adams motioned to the silent Norwegian. "It's Lieutenant Bergman's idea. And one of his men over there has checked it for us. It works all right provided the weather is fine."

Barrett's face was full of admiration. "That's really smart. Lord, the brains that go into the business . . . ! O.K. Now let's all go over and see what Townsend is doing to old Popsy."

Two days later a favourable report was received by wireless from one of Bergman's operators in Norway. That night P Popsy, a Boston with more powerful engines, took off on the first leg of her journey. She refuelled at Sumburgh, where her crew had breakfast, and took off again in daylight. It was a bright winter morning with a cloudless sky. A day when war seemed an impossible nightmare.

Grenville did not force the Boston up and they were half-way across the North Sea before she reached her maximum ceiling. At 29,800 feet she did not yaw too badly—a better height than he had dared hope for. And he might squeeze another 1000 out of her before they reached the Norwegian coast—her fuel load would be lighter then. . . . To reach that height P Popsy had been stripped of everything not needed for the job in hand. All her armour had gone as well as her four front guns. Apart from the two Brownings in the rear turret, she was defenceless, relying on nothing but surprise and height to bring her safely through.

Alone in his turret, Bergman felt stunned by the immensity of the sky around him. He had never been at this height before and the experience was overwhelming. The congealed sea below looked like blue ice, without a wrinkle. The vast dome of sky was a cold pitiless blue and the sun brilliant, making his eyes ache in spite of his smoked glasses. The cold was intense, far worse than he had expected, and his hands and feet were in agony. Yet, in spite of the pain, he felt drowsy, lulled by the steady numbing roar of the engines and the gently swaying motion of the aircraft in the rarefied air. Behind him the exhaust gases of the engines were streaming out like the wake of a ship.

He remembered Grenville's warning and roused himself to keep watch below. If an enemy ship spotted them, it would wireless the coast for fighters, and if a patrol got up in time to meet them it would be curtains. But there was nothing below but the vast, empty sea.

In the pilot's seat Grenville was running over the plan of action. Provided they were not spotted on the way in, it seemed all right. You had to hand it to these people: they were thorough. That business of the glacier—that was clever. God—what a game it was. The tricks and the counter-tricks. . . .

He shut his eyes tightly, then opened them again. His dashboard seemed blurred. His artificial horizon, altimeter, air-speed indicator, pressure gauge, temperature gauge, oil gauge—rows and rows of indicators and gauges and all quivering and indistinct. . . . It was this intense cold, affecting his nerve centres. His legs had a bone-chilled ache that was spreading up his back—

he longed to stand up and stretch himself. He turned his oxygen full on for a moment and the instrument panel cleared.

He peered sidewards, looking down the immense void to the flat, formless sea below. Weather perfect so far. . . . There was a band of mist down there at ten o'clock but it didn't seem to stretch far. It had better not. Any mist in the fjord or a cloud haze above it and they'd had it, glacier or no glacier. . . .

Hoppy's voice came through the intercom, as cheery as always. "A couple of degrees off course, skipper."

Grenville swore. These damned navigators—they should try flying a kite dead on course. He checked with his compass, saw Hoppy was right, and swung the Boston gently to port. They droned on, a speck of dust in an immense blue void. . . .

At first it looked like a low-lying cloud, clinging to the edge of the sea. Five minutes later it became a snow-covered jagged coastline, looking like the outflung leg of a sea monster from their height. Grenville checked his course, swung slightly to port, then spoke to Bergman, with whom he had not exchanged a dozen words since leaving Sumburgh.

"That's your bay, isn't it, dead ahead? We go over it and straight on to Hjelmestad, right?"

Bergman checked the landmarks. "That's right, Roy. Straight ahead on this course."

"Keep your eyes open," Grenville warned him. "Particularly in the sun."

Bergman stared about him until his eyes watered, but they seemed alone in the enormous void. The sunken mountains drew nearer, painfully slowly from that height, until at last they crossed the coast. Bergman experienced all the bitterness of the exile as he stared down. Below was his homeland, and yet for him to set foot on it was a desperate venture. His bitterness against the Nazis served his body like fuel, steeling it against the crippling cold.

The alert would have sounded now and German fighters would be leaping off from their snow-covered airfields. Yet the mountains of the Antarctic could not have looked more desolate than those that passed slowly under their wings as they approached Hjelme-stad.

Bergman was tense in his turret, timing their flight from the coast to the town. It was just five minutes and eighteen seconds when Grenville spoke to him again.

"I'm starting to circle it now. O.K.?"

"O.K., Roy."

The town was partly camouflaged under its covering of snow. From their height it looked little more than a hamlet squatting between two mountain ranges. They took a wide circle over it, their condensation trails and exhaust gases forming a gigantic ring. They had been flying so long now that the roar of the engines had faded into a neutral background. Bergman felt he had lost all contact with the earth and was floating bodiless in the vast, silent stratosphere.

Grenville's voice brought him back to reality. "I'm turning off now for your fjord. Let Hoppy know when he can get cracking."

Behind him Bergman saw the distant coastline tilt and wheel round as the Boston banked on to her new course. Mountain range after range slid below them, the fjords looking like pieces of bent silver wire threaded through them. Checking the landmarks was not easy for Bergman: they looked vastly different from this height than from the ground. But with the aid of a map he and Adams had studied earlier he saw they were now approaching the upper reaches of the Svart-fjord.

He gave rapid instructions to both Grenville and Hoppy. Almost imperceptibly the Boston swung a few degrees to starboard. Bergman craned his neck side-wards. Two parallel mountain ranges, separated by a thread of silver were sliding towards them. One moun-tain-peak was shining with a brilliance that made it stand out even from the surrounding snow. Bergman grabbed his mask.

"There it is! Straight ahead. If you watch you'll see the sun shining on the glacier. See it! If we're correct, it should be reflecting enough light downwards for us to take the photographs. The building is right below it."

86

Grenville was silent. From his cockpit ahead of the mainplane, he could see something the Norwegian had missed—a thin film of strato-cirrus that was drifting slowly in over the fjord. It was no more than two miles wide and tenuous enough for the ground to be seen hazily through it. But it was more than enough to fog the camera plates. Hoppy confirmed this a moment later.

"That cloud's going to ball things up, skipper. Can't we drop under it?"

Grenville cursed. Hardly a wisp of cloud all the way from the Shetlands, and yet there had to be one drifting right across their target. He eyed the strato-cirrus, making rapid calculations. It looked at about 24,000 feet —6,000 feet below them. Not far, but it was those last few thousand feet that counted. Fighters would be swarming up now like tiger fish from the sea-bed. They would reach 20,000 feet quickly but from then on their power curve would begin to fall away. If he dropped lower he was playing right into their hands.

He spoke sharply to Bergman. "Now look! Forget the security stuff for a moment. We can go under that cloud, but it's going to be a gamble. We might make it, but so might the fighters. And if they get above us, it'll be curtains. Can this job wait for another day? Does it matter so much if a kite comes here under escort."

"We want to avoid that if possible, Roy. It'll give too much away."

"Then this thing is important enough for us all to risk our necks?"

"It's terribly important, Roy."

"So you'd like me to go down and chance it."

"I'd like you to, yes."

Without another word Grenville pushed the nose of the Boston down. He did not dive steeply, they were still a mile or two from the end of the fjord and he did not want to make his descent conspicuous. The altimeter needle swung slowly round the dial—29,000 feet . . . 27,000 . . . 25,000. . . . Grenville's teeth were clenched and his hands sweating. The Focke-Wulfs would think he had gone crazy. . . .

At 23,500 feet they reached the cloud, passing

87

through it in a second. It was useless for concealment, yet would silhouette them perfectly to the climbing planes. There was no flak, a favourable sign. Jerry was not suspicious of their intentions and did not want to disclose the importance of the building below. Grenville straightened out and, following Hoppy's instructions, began tracking over the target. A few seconds later Hoppy began taking his photographs. Grenville, certain now that the building below was their ultimate target, stared down curiously.

The mountains flanking the narrow Svartfjord were clearly of great height. On its western side, right at the end of the fjord, was a bulbous-topped mountain capped by the glacier Bergman had pointed out. The glacier was easily distinguishable by its mirror-like brilliance. Directly below it, at the bottom end of the enormous *cul-de-sac,* Grenville could just make out a dark building through his binoculars. Although dwarfed by his altitude it was clearly one of considerable size. Surrounded on three sides by precipitous mountains, with its only ingress the deep and narrow Svartfjord, it looked completely impregnable.

Grenville could make nothing of its purpose. Slowly it fell behind them as they droned on. Grenville lifted his eyes, stared ahead. Some eight miles from the building the fjord turned sharply at thirty degrees to head straight for the sea. At this point it was joined by a tributary from the east, a deep gorge that split the flanking mountains and poured a stream of fresh water into the salt water of the Svartfjord. Trained in observation, Grenville studied the gorge almost unconsciously as it passed beneath them.

The Svartfjord angled away from them now as they continued on their undeviating course. Hoppy's voice came through. "O.K., skipper. Photographs taken. . . ."

Before he had finished speaking Grenville had put the Boston's nose up, fighting to regain the altitude they had lost. They were still within their time-limit but God knows what 7,000 feet was worth to the Focke-Wulfs. . . .

His eyes, sore with the strain, searched the sky incessantly. The strato-cirrus had been wider than he had thought and was still visible behind. As he turned his head, his heart gave an explosive thud. A brilliant spot flashed for a second on one side of the cloud, then darkened underneath it. . . .

They were here and had altitude on him. Only one thing to do—go down. As he slammed his stick forward, his brain was racing like the screaming engines in either wing. He snapped his orders to Bergman.

"Listen! They've made it—they'll be down on us in a minute or two. Switch on your reflector-sight and make sure your safety catches are off. Keep your head and don't fire until they're right on top of you. Try to remember all I told you about deflection. Don't panic, and keep telling me which side they're attacking from. I'll help you as we go along. O.K.?"

Bergman's mouth was suddenly dry. "O.K., Roy."

The Boston's nose dropped more steeply. Bergman's stomach lifted, making him feel short of breath. The noise was deafening, pressing into his ears like brutal fingers. He switched on his hooded reflector-sight and its orange ring glowed ominously before his eyes.

Grenville's voice again. "Watch the sun!"

Bergman peered upwards through his smoked glasses. He thought he saw three black dots silhouetted against the blinding glare. The Boston was howling earthwards now, its wings and body trembling with the speed. To Bergman, looking back along the fuselage, it seemed the shuddering tail unit would break off at any moment.

Then he saw the Focke-Wulfs clearly for the first time. One was close, already within a thousand yards, the other two more distant. He shouted to Grenville:

"Three of them—closing in on our tail. . . ."

Instantly Grenville pulled out of the headlong dive. A hand seemed to be clawing Bergman's entrails out and his spine felt crushed under the unnatural weight of his head. The Boston groaned in agony, rivets springing, paint cracking off its tortured wings, tailplanes whipped like the tail of a child's kite.

The Focke-Wulf was still there, twenty-odd degrees to starboard. Bergman stared with fascination at its short quivering wings, its long transparent hood, and its huge radial engine. The olive-green upper surfaces of its wings, with their huge black crosses, showed vividly as it swung into position. In the brilliant sunlight it glowed like some great insect, beautiful and evil.

Grenville's voice came over the intercom. "I'm turning to starboard to increase his curve of pursuit. He might black out. Watch him and when he shudders, fire."

The Boston heeled over steeply. Bergman, crouched behind his sight, saw the Focke-Wulf's wings tilt at a steeper angle as it tried to follow them. He understood Grenville's tactics now. At that speed a steep banking turn increased the *g,* particularly for the fighter which had to turn inside them to get the Boston in its fixed forward gunsight. Bergman felt the strain himself, the bone-crushing sensation in his spine again, the tearing at his eye sockets. The Focke-Wulf's wing tilted more steeply. Bergman could see its pilot clearly now, crouched forward under his long transparent hood. The Focke-Wulf was close—not more than three hundred yards away now. The Norwegian's spine cringed as he imagined his turret slowly sliding into the pilot's gunsight. At any moment he would open up with his cannon. . . .

Then the 190 faltered. Bergman saw the sudden blind flutter of its wings, the helpless drop of its nose. The pilot had greyed out for a moment; this was his chance. He put his sight on the radial engine and fired one quick burst. His G.6 tracer curled by the Focke-Wulf's starboard wing-tip. A quarter of ring relative speed. . . . He made the correction and fired a long four-second burst, twenty bullets a second hosing out from each of his Brownings. His tracer appeared to be striking but now the nose of the 190 was coming up, its pilot was recovering. . . . Bergman fired another frantic burst and this time a white stream of glycol began pouring from the fighter's exhausts. Its propeller stopped, it banked sharply away and began gliding earthwards.

Bergman let out an exultant yell as he fired another burst after it. "I got him, Roy. He's broken off. I hit him——"

Grenville's voice cut his words off in his throat. "Watch out, you fool. Watch out for the others."

Bergman glanced back and his stomach shrank in fear. The two remaining 190's had closed in and were less than four hundred yards away. As he stared at them bright flashes ran along their wings. He twisted his guns back but was too late. Before his eyes the perspex turret splintered into white stars, he heard two shattering explosions and felt himself hurled backwards. There was a moment of intense pain, then nothing but red-streaked darkness.

Grenville felt the Boston shudder under the hammer blows of the cannon shells. A second later a shell tore through his hood. Air shrieked through the hole, buffeting his head backwards. Tracer flashed by like incandescent hail.

He threw the Boston into a spin to simulate loss of control. As always, when near extinction, his brain became unnaturally lucid, gaining the ability to consider more than one problem at the same time. One half of it was thinking about Bergman. He didn't answer over the intercom; it looked as if he'd got the chopper. . . . Condemning faces flashed before his eyes—Davies, Barrett, Hilde. Hilde . . . God! The other half of his mind was searching for a means of escape. Searching, discarding, selecting, all at fantastic speed. . . .

There was one faint chance of survival. He leaned forward, his eyes searching the spinning, reeling mountains that were leaping upwards to crush them. For the moment the firing had ceased but he knew the 190's were following him down, ready to open up again if he pulled out. He watched his altimeter needle; 5,000 feet, 4,000, 3,500—already below the level of some of those mountain-tops. If he didn't pull out now they were finished. . . .

Groaning with the effort, the Boston came out of her spin. Instantly the Focke-Wulfs hurled themselves at her again. Explosive shells probed for her fuel tanks, for her engines, for the flesh of her crew.

Ignoring the fire, Grenville searched for his objective. He found it not a mile ahead. Again he put the Boston's nose down. The scream of air through his shattered windscreen almost pierced his eardrums. A sunlit, snow-covered mountain peak flashed under his starboard wing, falling away dizzily into a tremendous gorge. The Boston followed the drop down, plunging into it like a meteor.

Out of the sunlight now! Into the gorge, its towering walls fined smooth by the Boston's speed. Green water flashing below, foaming and cascading over the rocks. . . .

Grenville's jaw clenched with satisfaction. He had made it—he was flying inland up the narrow gorge that ran into the Svartfjord. Now he had a chance, even though the 190's were still behind him, line astern, crazed with the lust to kill. The tremendous roar of the engines thundered across the narrow gorge, bringing down avalanche after avalanche of snow.

The stressed-skin fuselage of the Boston shivered under the impact of two more shells. Grenville dropped lower. Focke-Wulf's guns set up at two degrees . . . German thoroughness . . . forced pilots to fly low and so avoid tail gunners. Use it against them now. . . . That's it . . . he can't get you now without going lower still! Fox him . . . draw him down . . . he'll be watching you, not the gorge ahead. Here's a waterfall coming . . . hold it . . . hold her down . . . bit longer . . . longer. . . . Now!

Like a leaping salmon the Boston hurled herself up and over the waterfall. The 190 following behind had no chance. Before its pilot's reflexes could respond, the high shelf of rock was upon him. The plane vanished in an explosion of flame and spray. The pilot of the second Focke-Wulf lost his nerve and pulled out into the sunlight above.

Grenville followed the gorge for its full length before emerging into a wide valley. There were no enemy aircraft in sight but he knew the hue and cry would be on. At zero height the Boston turned for the coast.

Hoppy's voice came hoarsely through the intercom.

"Lummy, skipper; I thought we'd bought it that time. I could've washed me dirty feet in that water. How's Bergman? Is he hit bad?"

"We'll try to find out in a minute," Grenville muttered.

Below the level of the tree-tops, taking all possible cover, P Popsy headed for home.

11

The private sitting-room was empty when Maisie showed Grenville into it. The black-out curtain had not yet been drawn and the winter dusk was filling the room with shadows. A bright fire was burning on the hearth.

"She's in her room, sir," Maisie said, touching her curls. "If you'll wait here, I'll give her a call."

Grenville nodded and went over to the window. The dusk was robbing both the earth and sky of colour. He could see nothing of the airfield for the high fence, the boundary between a peaceful Britain and a Britain at war. On this side human life was of the highest value, a thing above price. On the other side it was freely bartered away for destruction. And only a wooden fence separated the two. . . .

Grenville turned back and glanced round the room. The fire, sharpened by the cold, was making the brass ornaments wink cheerily. He stood motionless, listening to the silence of the old inn. It had the profound peaceful quality of old age.

Then he heard her footsteps outside, and felt his pulses quicken. She came in, recognized him, and drew slowly nearer. He gave himself no time for hesitation.

"I have some distressing news for you, Miss Bergman. Your brother has been wounded. . . . Not seriously," he went on quickly as she lifted a hand sharply to her throat. "But he will be in hospital for two or three weeks."

She was a thoroughbred. She fought and conquered the tremor in her voice. "What has happened?" She came forward again, making a fluttering movement with one hand. "Please sit down."

Grenville remained standing. "It happened this morning. We were out on a photo reconnaissance. Three Focke-Wulfs jumped us and your brother was hit. Not seriously, but he was wounded in the right shoulder and suffered concussion. He'll be all right in a week or two."

"Where is he now?"

"I had to leave him in the Shetlands. They made arrangements to get him to hospital. I made certain he was all right before I left."

"What did you do this time?" she asked quietly.

"I beg your pardon."

Hilde looked him full in the face. There was a fine silt of resentment in her blue-grey eyes. "I am sorry but I cannot help feeling bitter. My brother has had to fly many times since 1940 but his pilots, knowing the dangers he had to face on landing, have at least taken care of him in the air. With you he has had only two flights—on the first one you deliberately risked his life, on the second you come back with him wounded. I told you when we met that it was not fair he should share your dangers too, but it seems you took no notice."

The tension of the fight had not yet worked out of Grenville. He was like a coiled spring, dangerous to handle. His hands tightened as he tried to control his temper.

"You don't think I tried to get him wounded, do you? This was his operation. My orders were that he should come on it, and this is the result."

"What was the operation?"

"Ask your brother, not me," Grenville said curtly. "I was only the taxi-driver."

Hilde moved over to the fireplace. With one arm on the mantelpiece, she stared down. The firelight seemed eager to touch her, running its glow over her slim body, limning its contours in shadows. A welter of emotions suddenly surged up inside Grenville. None was defined, but all seemed to gear up with his tension, inciting him to some act that would explode it away and bring him relief.

Hardly aware of the movement, he drew closer to her. She looked up and saw how near he was standing. The firelight, growing in strength as the room darkened, shone full on his face, betraying much that the dusk had kept hidden. She saw the intense weariness in the shadows under his eyes, the resolution in the lines of his cheeks and jaw, the bitterness and strain round his mouth. She looked into his eyes, where the fire-glow was hot, and saw tiny miniatures of herself framed there.

She frowned slightly, shaking her head. "I'm sorry. That was not fair of me. I should not say such things until I know more of what happened. . . ."

It was this retraction of hers that triggered off Grenville's impulse. That, and something which sprang without authority into her eyes on seeing the desire in his own.

He caught hold of her, jerking her towards him. Her mouth was parting in protest as he kissed her, and his lips imprisoned her words. He held her like this for a long moment, neither knowing nor caring whether she was struggling or not. His lips moved to her eyes, her forehead, her shining hair. She was lax now, her eyes closed and cheeks pale. She was crying something softly in Norwegian.

The light was suddenly switched on. For a moment Grenville did not know what had happened. Then he turned his bloodshot eyes on the door.

Valerie, in hat and coat, was standing there. Her voice was cold, spiteful. "I'm sorry. I'd no idea what was happening, of course. . . ."

Hilde tore away, supporting herself against the mantelpiece. Grenville's face was murderous. Valerie thought he was about to strike her and drew back in sudden alarm. He hesitated, cursed, then made for the hall. Two seconds later the front door slammed shut. There was no quality of peace now in the silence that returned to the inn.

Bergman returned from hospital sixteen days later. It was a grey blustery day early in February when he entered Grenville's squadron office, his left hand outstretched. His right arm was held up in a sling under his naval mackintosh. A severely bruised cheek, still discoloured, gave a lop-sided effect to his smile.

"Hello, Roy. It's good to see you again."

Grenville was on his feet, his own hand outstretched.

For a moment, mixed with gladness, there had been a faint measure of uncertainty in his eyes. Now he was smiling, a rare smile that made him look almost boyish.

"Hello, Finn. I didn't expect you out quite so soon. Sit down and tell me all about it. Here, have a cigarette."

Grenville's cordiality, unusual in one so taciturn, gave Bergman an assurance he had not felt before. Now he knew he had made a friend of Grenville, and his smile was an expression of his delight.

"It's good to be back. I've missed you all. Honestly, I really have."

Grenville laughed. "We haven't missed you quite so much. We've had a holiday from those crazy jobs of yours."

Bergman was curious. "Have you really had a rest? I know nothing has come through from my end, but I understood Bomber Command had borrowed you back in the meantime."

Grenville gave a rueful nod. "They did. We had to do a couple of Low Country jobs for them."

"What were they like? Very tough?"

Grenville's face turned expressionless for a moment. "So-so. They could have been worse." He shrugged, then his voice lightened. "Well; what are you bringing us? More trouble?"

"Later, perhaps. But at the moment I'm bringing you something good. I heard they were coming this morning, and persuaded the doctors to let me out. I wanted to see them arrive. You'll have heard, I suppose?"

Grenville nodded. "Yes; Davies told us last week." He looked down at his watch. "You've timed it well. They're due here any minute." He lifted his eyes to the Norwegian's pleasant face. "Will we be getting any more gen now?"

"Yes. The Air Commodore is going to come down, possibly tomorrow. He is going to tell you about the training he wants doing. It's pretty technical, of course —right outside my province."

Grenville nodded, not labouring the point. He

watched Bergman keenly. "Have you seen your sister yet?"

"Yes; I called over on the way here."

"Did she go to see you in hospital?"

Bergman looked surprised. "Didn't you know? Haven't you been across?"

Grenville was toying with a ruler on his desk. "I don't seem to have had much time. . . . But I saw she was kept informed about you."

"Hilde told me. It was very decent of you, especially to arrange a trip for her. Anyway; I hope you'll be able to get over more now." Bergman looked away, speaking with some diffidence. "I'd like the two of you to get to know one another. She hasn't any real friends over here—that worries me in case something should go wrong on one of these trips of mine. I know you'd see she was all right." He turned back anxiously. "You don't mind my saying that? I've no right to, of course. . . ."

"I shouldn't worry about her," Grenville said abruptly. There was a short, awkward silence. The sound of distant engines brought them both relief. Grenville jumped to his feet. "This sounds like them now. Let's go out and take a look, shall we?"

They stood on the tarmac path, staring up at the grey, windswept sky. The sound of the engines was approaching fast, coming from the west. Grenville pointed over the hump-backed roofs of the Nissen huts.

"There they are!"

Two graceful shapes emerged from the low ceiling of cloud. They were long and slender with a high tailfin and shapely, tapering wings. Their engines had a sweet, powerful note. They circled the airfield, banking steeply to follow its perimeter. One pilot feathered an engine and deliberately did a slow roll not a hundred feet above the wet grass.

"What a lovely job," Grenville breathed.

The two planes drifted in to land, as light as thistledown. They braked, then taxied towards the Control Tower. Grenville nudged Bergman's arm.

"This looks like the job we've been waiting three years for. Let's go and have a closer look at her."

They were not the only ones showing interest. Men were running towards the planes from all directions. The experts showed unqualified approval. The Maintenance Officer was running a hand dreamily along one of the 12-cylinder underslung Merlins like a man caressing a woman's smooth shoulder. The Armament officer could have been staring upwards into paradise when he was given a glimpse into the huge bomb bay. Rumour after rumour spread among the air crews and mechanics. One rumour came to stay. This was the kite that eight days ago, on the 30th January, had bombed Berlin in daylight for the first time. . . . Air crews nudged one another, holding their breaths in prayer.

The A.T.A. pilot broke the wonderful news. Yes; this was the kite, and 633 were going to be re-equipped with her. They were lucky all right—she was a beauty. Her name? She was called the Mosquito. . . .

The 'phone call came for Grenville in the late afternoon. He had just taken up one of the Mosquitoes, and his eyes were still bright from her performance. He lifted the receiver, gave his name, then froze. Her voice was low, but even the interference on the line could not destroy its melody.

"I want to apologize for the things I said to you that afternoon. . . . I did not know, but now Finn has told me and I am very ashamed. Will you please forgive me?"

Grenville had to speak carefully: his voice was eager to betray him. "I know how you felt. I'm the one to apologize. I was tensed up and very tired. . . ."

Her interruption was like a soft hand being placed over his mouth. "There is nothing to forgive. Will you come over with Finn so that I know you have forgiven me?"

His mouth was dry. "Yes. Yes, I will. As soon as possible."

"Thank you. Then good-bye . . . for the moment."

"Good-bye."

Grenville lowered the receiver. He noticed with no surprise that his hand was trembling.

12

Davies arrived the following morning, holding the same audience in Barrett's office as on the previous occasion. All his listeners noticed the change in him. He seemed less spry, to have lost something of his quicksilver. It seemed certain he had been told the purpose of the building in the Svartfjord, and was finding the knowledge a heavy burden. The implication made a deep impression on his audience. They listened in silence to his high-pitched voice.

"Well, gentlemen; you've got the first of your new aircraft." His eyes travelled from Barrett to Grenville. "As some of you have already found out, she's a beauty. In another week you'll be fully equipped. You won't be able to complain then that you haven't the tools to do the job because you'll have the finest light bomber in the skies today. First I want to say a few words about her.

"As you know, she recently did a daylight raid on Berlin. She was unarmed, relying successfully on her speed to bring her back safely. Wonderful job though she is, however, we've finally decided an unarmed kite, however fast, is a bit risky for the kind of jobs you might have to do. We next had a look at the fighter-bomber version, but the snag there is that the cannon breeches extend back into the bomb bay, so cutting down the bomb load considerably, and your bays, as you'll have noticed, have been converted to carry the maximum load of 4,000 lb. So we had a chat with the makers and they did a fine compromise job for us. To get the cannon in, they used two of the short-barrelled type and extended them in front of the nose. That gives room inside for the breeches. Of course, they couldn't give you four—with a full bomb load you'd be overweight—but they made up with two Brownings for good measure. Naturally, when you've got a full bomb load you won't get the same performance as the unarmed version, but you've got the satisfaction of knowing that once your bombs have gone, you've got a kite that can match any fighter Jerry can put up. Any questions so far?"

Everyone who had seen the new bomber had noticed one conspicuous thing about her. Grenville commented on it now.

"I noticed there is no hatch in the nose. How does the observer use his bombsight?"

"The answer to that one is that he doesn't," Davies said. "For the job you're going to do, a bombsight won't be any use. A damn good thing, because the makers needed a solid nose for the cannon." Seeing the puzzled frowns on three of his listeners' faces, he waved a hand. "Don't worry about it—I'll explain everything later on. I've other things to talk about now.

"First, your conversion. I want it done quickly, because I want special squadron training to start in less than two weeks. It's going to mean a lot of work and a lot of reorganization—I know that. Your gunners, for example, are going to become redundant. They'll be posted. Your remaining pilots and observers are going to have a lot to learn—and they've got to learn it faster than anything has been learned in the Service before. Time is running short, and believe me, time is precious. This thing is bigger than I'd realized. Too damn big."

There was a strained look in Davies's darting eyes as he continued. "Once you are crewed up and have got your kites, we're sending you up on a daily trip to Scotland. A couple of routes are worked out for you which you'll always use to make things easier for the Observer Corps. Up there we have a deep valley with a special target site waiting for you. As near as possible it will resemble the target you're being trained to prang."

His voice dropped, his eyes moving in turn from Grenville to Barrett and Adams. "You've probably guessed by this time what that target is. I'm not allowed to tell you its purpose—I may never be allowed to—but I can say that you're out to destroy that building at the upper end of the Svartfjord. But"—and

101

Davies paused expressively—"no one else must know. Your crews are going to get curious when the training starts—when they do, tell them to belt up. No man outside you three must know the target. I can't stress enough the importance of secrecy. Any man breathing a word of this will be court martialled at once."

He paused to let that sink in, then smiled wryly. "Sorry to sound so tough, but that's the way it is. Now a few words about the training:

"This valley in Scotland is meant to represent the Svartfjord. Of course, it's nothing like so deep, but it's the nearest thing we've got like it in this country. At one end of it a target site is marked out. Not, as you would expect, at the bottom of the valley, but instead in a corrie in the mountainside, under an overhanging clump of trees. That's where you will practise dropping your bombs. The idea is to fly along the mountainside, bank steeply over, pull away, and as you go—release your bomb. Centrifugal force will then sling it at the target. You can see now how useless a bombsight would be. It's an entirely new technique and will take a hell of a lot of experiment and practice. But we think it can be done—in fact it must be done." Davies's voice dropped even lower. "Those of you who have seen the target and know how difficult pranging it in the ordinary way would be, might guess the idea behind this. If you do, keep it to yourselves. I'm not allowed to let the cat out of the bag until the final briefing.

"Right. In a few minutes we'll go into Adams' office and run over all the technical snags. In any case, I shall be going up to Scotland with you and will help out with the early experiments. But now I want to run quickly through the combined operation as Special Services and Lieutenant Bergman have planned it. Here is the general scheme."

There was an expectant stir from the three hushed officers. Their eyes flickered for a moment on the fair-headed Bergman who was leaning in his chair, supporting his bandaged arm on his knee. His head was bent diffidently forward, his eyes staring down at the floor. They looked back at the small, serious-faced Air Commodore.

"If you haven't all seen the real thing, you've seen photographs of the target. It's at the bottom end of a hellishly deep fjord that is over twenty miles long. We know that Jerry doesn't believe we have a kite that can make a worthwhile attack on such a target, and until the Mossy came along he was right. However, he hasn't taken any chances—the target is too important. He knows that if an attack does come, the attacking force must fly inside the fjord for a considerable distance—probably from its mouth at the coast. No kite could prang the building from above and equally no kite could dive down on it—the mountains make both impossible. So Jerry has built flak posts all along the fjord sides. Lieutenant Bergman says he has everything lined up there—88, 37, and 20 mm., the whole bag of tricks. If you've read your Tennyson, this is the Valley of Death. And if you flew down it as things are at the moment you'd end up in far worse shape than the Light Brigade. . . .

"Jerry, then, has been thorough. But our Special Services and Lieutenant Bergman haven't been sleeping either. The Norwegian patriots over there have been organized and are waiting. They know their job, all they want now are the tools to help them do it. And this is one of your next operations. . . ."

Again the stir of expectancy. The tension could be felt. Davies pointed a finger at the lowered head of Bergman. "On a certain date in April, the Lieutenant will be dropped in Norway again. There he will contact the patriots and make certain everything is ready. He'll send a message through to us, and on receipt of it you will go out one night on a supply-dropping job. Among other things, the equipment you put down will consist of light machine-guns, ammunition and grenades. . . ." Davies gave a smile at the look on Grenville's face. "I see some of you are beginning to fit the pieces together.

"Right. So far so good. The patriots have got tools and will make themselves ready. So will you. At a given date a week or two later, when everything has been checked and re-checked until it's as perfect as anything can be in this imperfect world, you'll go out before dawn—bombed up and ready. For weeks before this date you'll have been going out at the same time, so that no one around will take particular notice of you. But this will be the real thing. You'll be going out to smash that building in the Svartfjord.

"In the meantime Lieutenant Bergman and his men will be doing their stuff on the other side. They'll attack these gun outposts and overcome their crews in a surprise dawn attack. This will actually take place while you are airborne—the timing is most important. There's no chance of the patriots being able to hold these posts once reinforcements arrive, and the building is so important Jerry will move heaven and earth to get them back once he is alerted. Fortunately these outposts are in isolated places, mostly on high mountain slopes, so however fast Jerry moves he can't recapture them under an hour or two. And in that hour, gentlemen, you'll be batting down that fjord in those new Mossies of yours, heading straight for that building. You'll drop your special eggs in a special way—and then get out smartly. If all goes well, the building will be destroyed and the patriots will get away before the reinforcements arrive. That's the scheme and it has to succeed. No one must even consider failure—the alternatives are too grave."

In the silence that followed, Barrett's asthmatic breathing could be heard clearly. Satisfied that he had made the impression he desired, Davies ended on a lighter note.

"We'll prang it all right, don't worry about that. And afterwards we'll throw a party that'll go down in history."

During the next two weeks 633 Squadron's conversion from Bostons to Mosquitoes went on apace. The air gunners were posted and their billets taken by a reserve of four pilots and four observers. Davies had these men sent as a precautionary measure. An emergency might arise, the squadron might be called on to fulfil some earlier mission, and if losses were sustained, they might find themselves short of trained men for the big occasion. A surplus of four crews, trained with the rest of the squadron, should cover all foreseeable emergencies. The wisdom of this move was to be apparent later.

By the 18th of February the crews were considered proficient enough to enter the second phase of their training. During this time Grenville, Adams, and Barrett had all been up to Scotland to take a look at the valley from the ground, and during the last five days, with either Barrett or Davies as passenger, Grenville had made innumerable dummy attacks on the target.

At first it had appeared impossible even to fly close to the target, much less to throw a bomb on it, and it would have been impossible in any plane less manoeuvrable than the Mosquito. The target lay in a depression on the otherwise steep hillside and was overhung by a tree-covered ridge. The difficulty was not so much in making the run-in as in avoiding collision with the steep hill at the end of the valley. At first Grenville practised without bombs, trying to discover the correct approach and maximum safety air speed at which an attack could be made. After he had given near heart attacks to the watchers below, the outcome was an air speed of 280 m.p.h., a run-in over the last 200 yards with vertical wings, a right 90 degree starboard turn to hurl the bomb outwards, then full throttle and a mad climb up and out of the valley.

The next problem was to find the precise moment to release a bomb. The pilot had to do this, and as things stood it was pure guess work. On the third day Grenville had an idea. He lined up various points on his port engine nacelle with the target and dropped 11½ lb. practice bombs until he thought he had found a sighting spot. When he returned to Sutton Craddock that day, he had a mechanic paint a red mark on the nacelle. The next day, as he swung the Mosquito over and pulled her back, he waited until the red spot was in line with the target before giving Davies the signal. He learned afterwards from the two spotting quadrant huts that his smoke puff had landed in the middle of the target area.

That was good enough. Davies had already told him that in the Svartfjord a bomb within fifty yards of the target would be close enough. He ordered similar marks to be painted on the rest of the Mosquitoes. Later on, others would have to take their place when heavier bombs with a different trajectory were used, but the principle and application would remain the same.

With this experience and knowledge behind him, he was able to give his crews a detailed briefing on the morning of the 18th. After telling them what would be expected of them in the training weeks ahead, he went on:

"None of you will take any practice bombs today. We'll spend the afternoon going in and coming out of the valley. You'll find that quite difficult enough to start with—particularly the coming out! Make your first run-in at 250 m.p.h.—we'll work up speed later. Get fairly close to the target before banking away, but take it easy at first. We want bombs on the target, not bodies.

"Keep in touch with me all the time on your R/T, but don't talk unless you're the one going in. I don't want the channel blocked by a lot of chattering old women. And while on the subject of silence get this into your heads. This training and everything about it is hush-hush. I don't want a word spoken about it, either by mouth or letter. The first man caught talking won't know what has hit him. . . ."

The same instructions on security were issued to the ground staff and the training began. As Grenville had expected, it was hair-raising. The first planes to enter the valley went in confidently enough, only to come shooting out a few seconds later like nervous corks from bottles. His earphones were filled with mutters and curses as pilots strove desperately to avoid the hill at the end of the valley. In the two-hour practice that afternoon only Sam Milner and Gillibrand flew near enough the target to have successfully bombed it, and that at the cost of two trees from the ledge above. Gillibrand's T Tommy eventually limped home on one engine, a severed pine branch sticking aggressively out from the Coolant radiator in its starboard wing.

The next day went better. More pilots caught the knack of pulling their Mosquitoes round at the right time, and soon Grenville had them coming in at higher speeds. On the fourth day mechanics fitted light-series carriers and they went out with sixteen 11½ lb. practice bombs apiece. All went well that day, although few bombs went near the target. The following day brought tragedy. Dawson of A Flight, who, like Gillibrand, had been delaying his turn more and more for the sake of accuracy, did it once too often and went slap into the cliff. The blazing remains of his Mosquito went tumbling down to the moss-covered rocks below. Although the accident happened towards the end of the training session, Grenville made every pilot do one more run-in before returning home.

The Mess was quiet that night. Both Dawson and his observer had been popular and their deaths introduced a grimness into the training, something that had been lacking before among the light-hearted crews.

Inevitably there was an offender against the security regulations. Not three days after the training started a letter was brought to Grenville by the Station Censoring Officer. It was from an A.C.1 Atkins to his girl-friend, Ruby Sampson. After preliminary endearments, it read: *We've got some new kites now (what a job they are, ducks, you ought to see them) and now we've been put on some training stunt up in Scotland....*

Grenville did not bother to read on. The ruthless streak in him came to the surface at once. He ordered a full squadron parade and had the offender marched up and down the ranks. On his front and back he wore a placard bearing the words "Take a good look at me. I am the B.F. who can't keep his mouth shut." The unfortunate A.C.1 Atkins broke into tears before more than half his ordeal was over.

Drastic though the punishment, its effects was salutary. The letters that followed, from all ranks, were so austere in content they must have brought tears to many a neglected girl. But there was no stopping the rumours that circulated among the men inside the field.

One of the most startling, voiced by no other than Gillibrand himself, was that they were training to bomb Hitler's Eagle's Nest in Bavaria.

"Stands out a mile," Gillibrand said, winking at Jimmie. "Can't be bombed from above, so we're gonna put 'em through the windows when he and Musso are having a girl party. Clear as the dew-drops on my Aunt Sally's nose."

In this atmosphere of rumours and rising tension, the training went on.

13

The battered saloon with the multi-coloured bonnet squealed to a halt outside the inn, its radiator-cap giving out a hapless wisp of steam. Gillibrand turned and thrust his wristlet watch under Maisie's nose.

"There y' are, honey. Twenty minutes early. What did I tell ya?"

Maisie shifted gingerly on the broken springs of her seat. "I thought we were comin' back by car, not flyin'! Don't you ever drive like that again when I'm with you, d'you hear? I ain't been so scared in years."

Gillibrand slapped her shoulder. "Aw, you enjoyed it. I saw your eyes flashin' as we came round them corners. You were lovin' it, kid."

Maisie eased herself off the seat. "And I'm not going out with you again until you do something to this thing I'm sitting on. It ain't fit for a decent girl—the way it nips and pinches."

Gillibrand grinned. "I'll fix it. You won't know it when I get back from leave."

Maisie took offence at once. "Oh, sure. Now you're going off to see your girl-friend, you'll get it fixed. But it's been good enough for me all these weeks, hasn't it?"

"Now don't get all jealous, kid. You knew I was goin' down to see her on my leave. I ain't been holding out on you."

Maisie sniffed, but inwardly had to admit the truth of what he said. She fell moodily silent. Gillibrand pushed a cigarette into her hand. "Have a fag before you go, kid. An' cheer up. It'll soon pass—seven days ain't no time at all. Then we can start where we left off, huh?"

Maisie's eyes flashed. "You've got a nerve. I'm supposed to sit around here for a week twiddlin' my fingers while you're necking a girl down in London. What do you think I am, a mug?"

Gillibrand pulled her towards him, nuzzling his nose against her cheek. "You're a swell kid, that's what you are. Aw, hell; a guy can like two women, can't he? Some of those Eastern guys like hundreds. Give me a kiss, honey. That's better. . . ."

She returned his kiss fiercely. There was bitterness in her hot, dark eyes as she drew back and stared at him.

"I'm a fool," she said thickly.

"Aw; stop talkin' like that." He tried to pull her towards him again but this time she resisted.

"That's enough," she muttered. "Leave me alone now." She motioned towards the airfield. "How is it you're able to get leave? I thought you were pretty busy right now."

Gillibrand grinned. "So we are. But I'm takin' my kite in and out of cracks in the ground better than anyone else around here. That's the only reason they're givin' me leave. But seven days—hell, I'm due for a month!"

"What's Jimmie going to do while you're away?"

The grin left his face. He turned to her, frowning slightly. "Matter of fact, that's one of the things I wanted to talk to you about. He might be a bit lonely at nights—he's too shy to make friends. How 'bout you looking after him—mothering him a bit, huh?"

She gave a harsh laugh. "Me? A fine mother I'd make."

"I dunno. I reckon you'd make a good 'un, kid. How 'bout trying it on Jimmie, anyway?"

Her cheeks reddened at his words. She took her resentment out on the boy. "You talk as if he were a baby. What's the matter with him? He's only a couple of years younger than we are."

Gillibrand shook his head. "I ain't good at words, so it ain't easy to say. But that boy hasn't grown up somehow."

"He's shy—I know that."

"He's more than that, honey. He ain't faced life the way we have. He's kinda afraid of it. That's the way I see it, anyway."

Maisie was staring at him. "Go on," she said.

He rubbed his big chin with his hand, then shrugged. "That's all, I guess. There ain't any more."

"You're lying," she said. "His nerve's gone, hasn't it?"

His face turned grim. "I wouldn't let anyone else say that, kid."

"I know you wouldn't. But that doesn't alter things. He's cracking up, and you know it."

He scowled out through the windscreen into the dusk for a long moment, then nodded abruptly. "Yeah; it's true. I've been tryin' to kid myself, but it ain't any use. He cracked up on our last op."

"What happened?"

"Aw, we were sent out on a low-level prang over Holland. At that height you gotta watch the coast defences. If you don't pick your way through gaps in 'em carefully, they get you as sure as hell. We got in all right, but over Eindhoven there was a lot of flak and the kid folded up. He couldn't plot a course back, couldn't do nothin' at all. . . . So I had to bring the kite back on my own. I hadn't a hope of finding a gap, and we nearly got the hammer breakin' out. It was a close thing."

Maisie's eyes were big, frightened. "But didn't they ground him after that?"

Gillibrand's bushy eyebrows drew together. "You don't think I reported him, d'ya? What d' you think I am, kid? A heel?"

"But what if he cracks again? You can't risk your life like that. . . ."

For a moment Gillibrand's grin returned. "Now don't get scared, honey. I ain't going to get killed." His expression changed, showing wonder. "Gee; what that kid went through that night! I ain't seen anythin' like it before. He cried—honest he did! He sobbed for his ma! The poor little bastard!"

Maisie's eyelashes were wet. "But you can't keep him flying if he feels like that. It isn't fair to either of you. You're both going to get killed."

Gillibrand frowned. "You don't understand. He don't want to go L.M.F. Nobody wants that. He's more scared of that than anything."

111

"But what are you going to do, then?"

He stared gloomily out into the early spring dusk. "I don't know, honey. I've given it plenty of thought but ain't got nowhere. I can see why he's like this, but that ain't much help."

"What do you mean?"

"Aw; it seems his mother died when he was a kid and he was put to live with an old aunt. She was the type with tight corsets—you know, wouldn't let him go to the movies, wouldn't let him play with the kids next door, kept him away from girls. . . . The poor little bastard had never been further than the front room until this war came along. And then he ends up with people like me. It ain't fair!"

"Is that why you've kept pushing him around, encouraging him to drink and that sort of thing?"

Gillibrand nodded. "Yeah; I see it this way—it's a tough war and you gotta be tough to last the pace. I thought that if I could pack enough confidence into the kid, he might be able to see it through. That's why I said he should get himself a girl, give her a kiss or two, make himself feel a man. . . . Aw, maybe I was wrong —I must have been wrong because he's cracked up anyway. But that was the general idea."

Her eyes wandered over his craggy face. "You're pretty fond of him, aren't you?"

He made a clumsy gesture with one huge hand. "You know how it is. . . . You always get kinda attached to someone you bunk and fly with. Makes you feel responsible for 'em, somehow."

It was growing dark inside the car now and her face was almost hidden in the shadows. "You say you'd like me to look after him while you're on leave. What do you want me to do?"

He turned eagerly towards her. "I don't like to think of the kid frettin' in his bunk in the evenings. If he came over here maybe you could talk to him and kid him up a bit—you know—make him feel somebody. And you must know a few girls round these parts. Couldn't you date him up with one? See what you can do, kid."

"All right," she said slowly, "I'll see what I can do."

He reached out, pulling her towards him. "Gee, kid, you're really something. If it was anyone else but Joyce I'd take my leave here with you, I mean it, kid. You're a real honey."

She returned his kisses with a fervour that startled him. Then, as suddenly, she pulled away and jumped from the car. Her voice sounded hoarse, indistinct.

"I'm late. I'll see you when you come back."

Gillibrand leaned across the seat and waved to her. "O.K., kid. Take care of yourself. Be seein' you, honey."

She did not wait for the car to turn but ran quickly down the gravel drive to the inn. She was crying.

The first of the Anson's engines fired, scattering a flock of sparrows that had landed alongside its starboard wing-tip. Bergman, wearing a flying-suit, helmet, and parachute harness, turned to Grenville and held out his hand.

"Well, this is it, I suppose. Up to Scotland, wait for a good weather report, then off we go." His accent sounded more pronounced than usual. "Good-bye, Roy, and the best of luck."

As always when under the stress of emotion, Grenville's tone was brusque. "You need the luck, not us. Hang on to it and don't take any chances."

Bergman smiled. "I don't intend to get caught if I can help it."

"Mind you don't," Grenville said curtly.

The mechanics were having trouble with the port engine of the Anson. Twice it fired and then cut out. Both of the waiting men turned towards it. The moment was a painful one and they were glad of the diversion.

The engine fired again and this time its steady roar merged into that of its companion. Bergman turned his blue eyes back to Grenville.

"You won't forget about Hilde? You'll explain why I did not go over?"

Grenville nodded. "I'll tell her. And don't worry about her. She'll be all right."

Bergman smiled. "I'm not worrying, Roy—not this time." He gripped Grenville's hand again. "Good-bye, Roy."

"Cheerio," Grenville said.

Their eyes held a moment, then Bergman turned for the plane. Grenville watched him enter it and did not move until the Anson had taken off and was climbing steadily over the distant trees. He returned to his office, sat in thought for a few minutes, then went to see Barrett.

"Will you want me this afternoon?" he asked.

"No, Roy, I don't think so. Take a couple of hours off if you like."

"May I borrow your car?"

Although it was the first time Grenville had made the request for himself, he had no doubt of the answer. Barrett's generosity with his car was proverbial.

"You know where it is, Roy. Help yourself."

Grenville returned to his office and 'phoned Hilde. "Would you care to come out with me for a drive? I've got a couple of hours, and it's a fine day."

Her low voice expressed her pleasure. "I would like that very much, Roy. What time will you be coming over . . . ?"

Grenville picked her up at the inn fifteen minutes later. He felt a disturbing sensation of gladness as she approached the car. She was bare-headed and wearing a dove-grey coat thrown loosely round her shoulders. Her face was flushed with pleasure as she slid into the seat alongside him.

"This is a nice surprise, Roy."

"I felt like getting away for a few hours," he told her as he drove away. "Is there anywhere particular you'd like to go?"

"No. Please go wherever you wish. I shall be quite happy."

Grenville was aware of an odd lightness of heart. It was irrational because Bergman had gone and he thought a good deal of the Norwegian. Yet the feeling persisted, growing even stronger as the airfield fell back out of sight.

114

It was the day, he told himself. The May blossom was already out and lay sprinkled among the green hedgerows like powdered snow. The clouds had lost their winter gauntness, and the sun was shining with a richer gold. Spring was everywhere, in the white daisies, the nesting birds, in the wind stinging his cheeks. . . . But he could not deny that the catalyst that made him respond to its magic was by his side. She could have been the very repository of spring, with her peach-smooth cheeks, lustrous hair, and clear, shining eyes.

They chatted lightly for a while, then fell into a long companionable silence in which words seemed unnecessary. They were driving over the moors with the sea a blue haze in the distance when she spoke to him again.

"You are looking happier today than I have seen you look for a long time, Roy. What has happened?"

Grenville's sense of guilt returned, particularly when he had realized he had not given her the news. He kept his eyes on the twisting road ahead. "Nothing," he said. "It must be the day—it's good to see the last of winter."

She laughed. "I thought you must have been given some nice dangerous raid to look forward to."

The lightness of his mood, already threatened by the stinging memory of Bergman's departure, suddenly vanished. On an impulse he pulled up the car and turned towards her.

"Why do you say that?"

The happiness on her face faded at his expression. "I'm sorry. Have I said something wrong?"

"You think I like war, don't you?"

He had already learned that she always spoke the truth, whatever the situation. She did now.

"Yes. I have thought so."

"Why?"

His tone puzzled her, making her low voice uncertain. "I'm not quite sure. Perhaps it is because you seem to spend so much time at the squadron, or perhaps it is because of what the others say."

115

"What do they say?"

"That you are always thinking of war and working out new tactics. . . ."

"That's my job," he said curtly.

Hilde hesitated again. "Yes, I know. But none of the others work as hard as you. . . ." She put a hand on his arm. "Please forget what I said. You were looking so happy a moment ago. Please smile again—it makes you look so young."

His eyes pulled away from her, following the cloud shadows that were scurrying over the undulating moors. He was resentful that she had the power to make him deny what he preferred others to believe, and his voice held that resentment.

"How can you think I enjoy this job—taking kids out to their deaths and then writing about it to their mothers afterwards?" He stared at her bitterly. "What do you think I am?"

In spite of his words her eyes were shining. "Please go on," she breathed. He saw her expression and his tone changed abruptly.

"What does it matter? If you want to believe it, don't let me stop you."

"You know I don't want to believe it," she whispered. "Please go on. There is so much about you I don't know. Tell me what you feel. . . . Tell me everything."

His eyes were brooding on the distant sea. "I hate war. But I also hate bullies—I always have. It's the one hate I've never been ashamed of. And just before the war I had a holiday over in Germany and saw what the Nazis were doing. When I got back I joined the Volunteer Reserve. A few months later the war broke out and that gave the Nazis a few more million people to beat up with their rubber truncheons. Somehow after that, everything else in life—marriage, a career—everything became unimportant until they were beaten and the whole filthy business was over." His voice turned bitter again. "I like to think there is a subtle difference between that and liking war."

"Don't be angry with me," she said quietly. "I had

116

no way of knowing this. You make everyone believe the reverse. Why do you do that, Roy?"

He could not have answered her if he had tried. Instead he told her about Bergman. As he had expected, she took the news without flinching, although the loss showed deep in her eyes. She gave a slight, protesting shake of her head.

"I know he went this way thinking it would be easier for me, but I would have preferred him to say goodbye. I have a strange feeling about him; I have had it some time now. I feel he is going into great danger."

"He'll be back in a few weeks," Grenville told her.

She looked away, her eyes following the dipping flight of a sparrow. "Well, he has gone, so there is nothing we can do," she said quietly after a pause. "I suppose it had to come, sooner or later."

Courage was a quality Grenville could appreciate. He watched her in silence. She turned back to him abruptly, making herself smile again. "We were talking about you, Roy. You said that to do your best in the war it is necessary to deny yourself everything else. Is that true? Would not some things make it a little easier to bear—perhaps even help you a little?"

"What things? A girl, a wife?" As soon as the words left his mouth Grenville realized how they had betrayed him.

Sadness tinged her faint smile. "Perhaps even they might be of some help."

He shook his head abruptly. "No! I don't want any woman biting her nails over me every time I go out on a raid. I've enough to worry about as it is. A man's a fool to get mixed up with sentiment in war-time."

"Can you prevent people being sentimental and biting their nails?" she asked softly.

Fear of his own emotions made Grenville unnecessarily harsh. "You can if you prevent them getting any damn fool ideas. I've seen too many sobbing girl-friends and bereaved wives to want to give the world any more."

She turned quickly away again, hiding her face. His next words, following the others like an echo, startled

117

him. "After the war it may be different, but no one can look that far ahead."

She turned back to him immediately. Her voice had a soft, singing note. "Some people can," she said. "Some people can wait a long time."

Once again Grenville had the odd sensation he was sinking into the blue-grey depths of her eyes. It was very hushed in the car, with the sunlit moors the only witness to a promise she had dared make no clearer. It was, Grenville suddenly realized, a moment he would never forget.

14

The hut was unbearably quiet. The naked electric bulb above, swinging on its flex in the draughts, shone down on Gillibrand's empty bed, with his pile of folded blankets. Jimmie's eyes moved to the wall above it where the Canadian displayed his pin-ups. In his imagination they were staring back at him in contempt. they knew him: they were only displaying their charms to taunt him and bring him to ridicule. . . .

He turned away from their mocking gaze. The harsh light shone on his thin face. His skin was a muddy, unhealthy colour and his brown eyes were constantly moving, shifting at the slightest sound. There was something in his expression of a lost child who had strayed from his parents and suddenly found himself in an incomprehensibly vast and perilous world. Once his lower lip began quivering and he dug his teeth punishingly into it. When he released it again there were two white dents that slowly turned an angry red.

It wasn't so bad as this when Gillie was here. Gillie didn't give you time to think. He was always pushing you about, making you do this and that, never leaving you alone. Sometimes it was irritating but it did help to take your mind off things. . . . What a wonderful thing to be like Gillie . . . afraid of nothing . . . doing anything you wanted to do without first thinking of the consequences.

Mind you, there had been times when he had hated Gillie. He had hated him when he attacked that flak ship. For weeks he had dreamed of that murderous flak, of steel cutting upwards through his body. . . . He jerked now at the memory and sweat formed inside his clenched hands. That hadn't been fair of Gillie. And it wasn't fair of him to take the chances he was taking up in Scotland. The way their kite had lurched when they hit that tree. . . . And a couple of days later . . . Dawson and Taylor . . . dying in flames for doing the same thing. . . .

Yet, on the other hand, you couldn't help feeling confidence in him. He gave it to you with that big laugh of his. He was so tough and sure of himself that he seemed indestructible.

But no one was indestructible! He'd kill them both sooner or later. And even if he wasn't so reckless, how long could you last in this game? At their last station, when they'd been operating on maximum and sustained effort for weeks on end, their losses in crews every two months had equalled their entire complement. So even if you were one of the lucky ones, like Gillie or Grenville, how long could you hope to last?

And now there was this new job coming up. From all the fuss and training it looked as if it might be one of those suicide raids.

Panic swept over the boy, bringing first a hot sweat, then a cold one. He couldn't go on; he couldn't stand the flak any longer. That raid on Eindhoven had finished him. If it hadn't been for Gillie all the squadron would have heard of it by now. But they all knew he was on the way out—you could tell it by the way they avoided his eyes and the way they bought him drinks. They knew all right.

And soon the M.O. would know. And then he would be grounded and disgraced. The dreaded letters L.M.F. would appear for all time on his documents. Grounded for Lack of Moral Fibre—a denounced coward, an object of derision for any safe clerk or aircraftman. And it would not end there. Knowing himself, he knew that that final proof of his cowardice would torment him for the rest of his life.

His body, tortured by his thoughts, rocked backwards and forwards in his chair. Tears stung his eyes. It wasn't fair! It wasn't fair that other men were never expected to face enemy fire while he, who had already done twenty operations, could have L.M.F. put on his documents. It wasn't fair that some men grew up like Gillie and others like himself. His tear-stained, resentful eyes lifted to the pin-ups again. Gillie got everything out of life. Girls brightened up immediately on seeing Gillie but never showed a spark of interest in him. They knew; they could recognize a failure better than men. And they were less forgiving, particularly over cowardice.

He'd go crazy if he stayed in here much longer, and yet he couldn't face the Mess. He remembered what Gillie had said, that if he felt like company he should go over and have a chat with Maisie in the pub. . . . He'd like that—Maisie was very pretty—but how would she treat him? She'd always been friendly, but that might have been for Gillie's sake—she was crazy on him.

Jimmie was a good quarter-of-an-hour before making up his mind to go. After all, he finally argued, if she wasn't glad to see him he could always come straight back. . . .

There were no more than half a dozen customers in the lounge and he felt very conspicuous as he approached Maisie at the counter. But she gave him a bright smile.

"Hello, dear; I was wondering when you were coming to see me." She motioned to one of the stools alongside the bar. "Here, sit down and talk to me. What are you going to have—a beer?"

They boy nodded. "Yes, please." He hesitated, then went on with a rush, "Will you have a drink with me?"

Maisie's dark eyebrows lifted in good-natured surprise. "Say, you're getting the idea! 'Course I will, dear."

She was pleased the boy had come over. Humming cheerfully she drew his beer, then bent forward and helped herself to a bottle underneath the counter.

She was wearing a black satin dress with a plunging neckline. As she bent forward Jimmie could see the deep cleft between her generous breasts. He found his eyes drawn down in guilty fascination.

"You'll be missing the big boy, I suppose."

He realized with a shock that she was looking up at him and could see where his eyes were fixed. His face burned with colour.

"I'm sorry. . . . I mean yes. . . . Yes, I am. Very much."

She threw a quick glance downwards and saw where his stare had rested. For a moment her dark eyes were amused.

"I'll bet you're missing him. What are you doing with yourself at nights?"

"Nothing, really," the boy muttered. "I haven't been out since Saturday."

Maisie tut-tutted her disapproval. "You could have come over to see me. I ain't far away."

Jimmie's face was still flushed. His efforts to keep his eyes from her while he sipped at his beer were almost painful. Maisie did her best to put him at ease.

"You ought to go to the Trocadero in Highgate one of these nights," she told him. "That's where all the boys go. You can get a drink there, and there are plenty of girls."

He looked surprised. "Do the girls go alone?"

" 'Course they do. They go lookin' for men like you. A warrant officer and an observer at that—you couldn't go wrong."

The look of longing faded from his eyes. "It'd be no use my going there. I can't dance, and anyway I'm too shy with girls."

Maisie gave a snort of disgust. "You probably act the gentleman with 'em too much. You want to push 'em about a bit. Girls like a man to be a bit on the bossy side. . . ."

At that moment four locals entered the lounge. Maisie eyed them with dislike. "Here they are—they'll probably start comin' in now you and me are havin' a nice chat. Don't go away, now! We've got plenty more to talk about."

But after its deceptively quiet start, the evening proved a busy one and Maisie found little time to talk to the boy. Before closing time, however, she made him promise to come over on the following evening.

To her surprise he came early, and she was delighted to find his shyness with her a little less pronounced. She had the opportunity of a long talk with him before the lounge filled, and managed to get him talking a little about his life before the war. She discovered Gillibrand was right; he had lived an unnaturally protected childhood. He promised to come again and she imagined he was looking more confident when he said good-bye that night.

To Jimmie this was a novel and exciting experience, so much so that his sensitive nature began to exaggerate it. He began to question whether he was playing fair to Gillibrand in seeing so much of Maisie while the Canadian was away. The thought worried him and on the Thursday night he decided to ask Maisie's opinion. But at first his shyness proved too much and he drank more than usual to give himself false courage. By nine o'clock the floodgates of his mind were down and his eyes followed Maisie with both longing and devotion. Yet he was still worrying about his loyalty to Gillibrand and as soon as the opportunity came he put the question to her.

At first she was highly amused that the boy could see himself a serious rival to the big Canadian. Then she realized the question was confirmation that her campaign was succeeding. She had to be careful: his sensitive eyes were on her. . . . She used the amusement in her voice to advantage.

"Anything's fair in love and war," she said. "Why, that's one of the Big Boy's own sayings." In spite of herself, bitterness crept into her voice. "Heck; he ain't got any cause for jealousy, he's gone down to London to see his girl friend. I'm only someone he passes his spare time with. Don't be so silly."

Loyalty to Gillibrand and resentment at the Canadian's conduct made a confusion of the boy's mind. "I hadn't tought of it like that," he muttered. "Then you think it's all right?"

" 'Course it is. You come here and see me whenever you like, whether he's here or not."

The thought of himself competing against Gillibrand made the eagerness in Jimmie's eyes fade. Seeing his dejection, Maisie's voice rose. "What's the matter with you? You take the same chances that he takes, don't you? You're doing just as important a job. . . ."

As she spoke a nightmare vision returned to her.

123

Gillie lost over enemy territory, struggling to find a course home as flak and fighters closed in, and this boy helpless with fear beside him. As her eyes cleared she saw tears quivering under Jimmie's lashes and realized that at any moment he was going to confess to his cracking nerves. Instinct told her it was the best thing he could do, but not here in the lounge. There was that cow Valerie Adams over in the corner. Her eyes had been on 'em all night. She wouldn't miss a thing. . . .

Maisie laid a hand on the boy's sleeve. "Listen, dear. I've got to wash these glasses now, but we'll have another chat later on when we can be nice and private. You stick around until closing time and meet me outside near the front door. I'm finishing early tonight."

Jimmie's face flushed, then went deathly white. Maisie's black eyes held his faltering gaze, her voice full and comforting.

"You needn't be afraid of me, dear. I'll take good care of you."

The room was quiet after the boy's sobs. His tears had soaked through the front of her dress, wetting the smooth skin beneath. Now, with his agony spent, he was resting his head where his eyes had rested earlier. Her body had a warm smell, both stimulating and relaxing, and he shifted his face, trying to get even closer to her.

Maisie's voice was rich, confident. "It feels better now, doesn't it?"

She had to strain her ears to catch his reply. "Yes. Much better. . . ."

She had left the bedroom dark to make it easier for the boy to talk and to weep. Now she stroked his damp hair gently, like a mother soothing a child. Her fingers wandered down his face, touching his eyes and wiping away the last of his tears. His body jerked once, spasmodically, then quietened again as she drew his head closer to her breast.

"You must think me an awful coward," he muttered.

"No; I don't. You're tired, that's all. You wanted

124

someone to talk to, and now it's all right again. Isn't it?"

His face, a white blur in the darkness, lifted up to her own. "I do feel better . . . much better. I'm awfully grateful. . . . Do you want me to go now?"

Instinct told her as sure as words the last thing needed of her. Her black eyes were unfathomable in the darkness. "No. I want you to stay."

He gave a gasp, almost one of protest. His body began trembling violently, yet she was conscious of a new strength rising into its weakness. She felt like a mother with a child at her breast, giving it strength from her strength. She bent over him, conscious of nothing but the ecstasy of sacrifice.

"There's nothing to be afraid of," she said. "Nothing at all." And her full, firm mouth pressed against his lips, checking their trembling.

15

The training of 633 Squadron went on right throughout April, but with two important changes. The first concerned their bomb load. Towards the end of March they had started dropping 1,000 lb. dummy bombs; now each Mosquito was loaded up daily with a single 4,000 lb. monster (the plane's maximum bomb load) and sent out to fling it into the target area. Twice a week lorries brought the specially-constructed dummies back from Scotland to be used again.

The second change concerned their time of take-off. Until now they had done the exercise in the middle of the day. Now they were ordered to be airborne at 0430 hours every morning. To crews already heartily sick of the valley and all it stood for, this was a most unpopular change. To make matters worse (and more incomprehensible) such an early take-off meant they had to stooge over the valley for over an hour before there was enough light to commence the exercise. On the surface the order was received with stoical resignation, but in the privacy of billets the comment from both air crews and ground personnel was lurid and descriptive.

There was one notable exception to this routine in the days that followed. It came on the 23rd April. When the Form D came through, rumours blazed round the airfield. This must be it! The Big Show was on! For hours the whole station sizzled like the fat in a frying-pan. Even the sight of the Supply Dropping Containers that the armourers were loading on to the Mosquitoes did not quell the excitement, although it considerably modified it. It all depended what was inside 'em. . . . Must be something important or there wouldn't be all those Redcaps hanging about.

The rumour was finally dispelled at the briefing of the crews that afternoon. It was not the Big Show. But it *was* an operation whose importance could not be exaggerated and one that had to be carried out with the utmost attention to detail.

The briefing was certainly detailed, for it lasted over two hours. Take-off was at 0025 hours as it was to be a night operation. Prompt to the minute the occupants of the inn opposite heard the roar of the Mosquitoes' Merlins as one by one the planes climbed into the darkness. The long night hours dragged slowly by and dawn was breaking before the low, deep hum of the planes was heard again. Anxious eyes counted them as they dropped over the boundary fence to sink from sight. . . .

But all were back. The operation had been an outstanding success. No enemy opposition had been encountered and all S.D. containers had been dropped inside the target area. Crews dropped out of their Mosquitoes, almost disappointed by the anti-climax. If the Big Show was going to be as easy as this, what was all the fuss about, anyhow?

There was no suggestion of disappointment, however, in a country house not far from Sutton Craddock. When the news came through a certain Brigadier and Davies gave vent to their relief in ways characteristic of their temperaments. The Brigadier smiled, coughed, then wiped his neat moustache with fastidious care. Davies jumped up like a puppet on a string, spun jubilantly round, then sat down with some haste. The Brigadier, however, showed no contempt for such behavior.

"Well done," he said instead. "If anything had gone wrong in that operation, the whole thing might have fallen through. Congratulations."

"If anything ever does go wrong it won't be 633's fault," Davies said, his eyes shining with pride of his Service. "Particularly with Grenville taking 'em out."

The Brigadier nodded. "So it seems. In fact, I think we should keep him on the ground now until the Big Show comes off—unless something exceptional crops up, of course. We can't afford to lose him at this stage."

127

"I'll see to it," Davies agreed.

"I also think it's time he was told the full story," the Brigadier said. "Will you bring him down next Wednesday morning after ten?"

"I'll fix that up. Next Wednesday at ten. . . ."

The Brigadier nodded again. Only his hand, doodling with a pencil on a pad before him, betrayed his hidden excitement. "That operation last night got us over the last really big obstacle. All we need now is our fair share of luck. If we get that, it won't be long before the curtain goes up."

The lounge of the Black Swan was full on the following Tuesday night. Maisie was serving at the counter and Gillibrand was draped over a stool alongside it. The Canadian's efforts at conversation were being thwarted by the demands of trade, and his usually good-natured face was sullen. Twice in the same minute he was interrupted. Once Maisie broke away to serve a pint of mild to a thirsty airman, a moment later she turned her head to answer the banter of an old countryman, one of her regular customers.

Gillibrand scowled. "Say; what's the matter with you tonight? You know I ain't exactly been on top of the world lately. D'you have to talk to every other guy in the place?"

Maisie sniffed. "It ain't my fault if your girl left you for someone else. Don't expect me to cry about it."

Gillibrand stared at her moodily. "You know, that was a funny business. It ain't happened to me before."

"There's always a first time," Maisie said with satisfaction. "Maybe she found out what you were doin'. I don't blame her one bit."

The Canadian's face darkened. "I spent my leave lookin' for the guy she fell for. Gee; I'd have given a lot to have taken it out of his hide."

"You'd better cut down on the drinking," Maisie snapped, seeing the resentment flaring up in his muzzy eyes. Her voice turned curious. "Where did you say Jimmie had gone tonight?"

"He said he was goin' into Highgate. Wouldn't come

in here with me. I can't make out what's happened to that little guy. He ain't the same any more."

Maisie's hand fingered an empty glass. "What do you mean?"

"Aw; he seems to have more bounce an' cheek—he ain't so backward as he was."

"Aren't you glad?"

"Sure I'm glad. Maybe the rest we're havin' is doin' the kid good. Only he doesn't have to quit goin' out with me, does he?"

"Maybe he feels it's better for him to go out on his own now and then," Maisie suggested. "He might learn to stand on his own better that way. You don't want to let it worry you."

Gillibrand shook his head moodily. Then his face cleared. "Anyway, kid, there ain't nothin' between the two of us now, is there? We've got a straight road ahead of us now, honey, ain't we?"

The glass with which Maisie had been toying suddenly slipped from her hand and broke into fragments at her feet. She looked down, then swept the pieces under the counter. When she lifted her black eyes to Gillibrand's flushed face again, there was still a residue of bitterness left in them.

"Did y' hear what I said, kid?" Gillibrand went on, with all the persistence of the half-drunk.

Her full lips twisted. "I heard you. A straight road, you said."

"That's it. That's the way it's goin' to be from now on. Just you and me, honey. . . ."

At that moment Joe Kearns came through from the bar. Unlike the lounge, the bar was having a quiet night; and the innkeeper kept relieving Maisie so that she could take orders from the tables, a privilege Kearns liked to extend to his customers whenever possible. Maisie caught his eye and turned back to Gillibrand.

"I'm going round for orders now. You'd better get back to camp and get your head down. You've had too much already."

Gillibrand watched her morosely as she went round the counter into the lounge. She took orders from the more distant tables first and returned to them with a loaded tray. On her way she passed a table occupied by Valerie Adams. Valerie was having another of her intimate parties. Apart from Adams himself, there were two other officers present, one being the stocky, ginger-headed Equipment Officer, Jack Richardson. Adams did not care for Richardson, but Valerie expressed a liking for his somewhat carnal sense of humour. The knowledge he found her attractive might have been the real influence behind her taste. As things were Richardson had been drinking heavily, his hot eyes had been roving without opposition over Valerie, and he was in a self-assertive, pugnacious mood.

Seeing Maisie go by, he shouted at her to take an order. She waved a hand good-naturedly.

" 'Arf a mo', dear. One thing at a time. Won't be a minute!"

Valerie let out an exclamation of disgust. "That girl! I've had nothing else but trouble with her ever since I've been here. She's impossibly common and cheeky."

Adams shifted, then gave a conciliatory laugh. "She's all right, Val. She's just a bit high-spirited, that's all."

Valerie's small, hard eyes turned on him with instant hostility. "Sorry. I'd forgotten you like that type."

On her way back to them, Maisie was halted by two countrymen at an adjacent table. Richardson followed Valerie's eyes and scowled. He leaned sideways and tapped Maisie's arm.

"What about that order? How long do people have to wait in this place?"

Maisie turned. She saw Valerie's disagreeable eyes fixed on her, guessed the cause of Richardson's impatience, and lost her temper. "What's the matter with you?" she snapped. "I told you I was comin' over. You ain't Hitler, are you?"

Richardson's hand closed tightly around Maisie's arm. "Who the hell do you think you're talking to . . . ?"

A second later an arm like a descending pile-driver squashed him down in his chair. His bulging eyes stared upwards, to see Gillibrand's enraged face inches from his own.

"Touch that kid again, you earth-bound punk, and I'll ram your face through the table." Gillibrand meant every word of it.

Richardson lay paralysed in his chair for a few seconds, then tried to rise. Maisie pulled frantically at the big Canadian, who moved back reluctantly, his inflamed eyes still staring down.

"What d'you wanna do? Make somethin' of it?" he snarled.

Remembering Valerie's presence, Richardson half-rose from his chair, but pride succumbed to prudence at the look of unholy joy on the Canadian's face. He sat down again, trying to retrieve some dignity from the situation.

"I'm not brawling in here with you, Gillibrand. I'll have you arrested in a minute."

Gillibrand thrust a jaw like the prow of an ice-breaker into his face again. "Go ahead and do it, punk. See what happens. I'll bust you all over the airfield, just as I'll bust anyone else who touches this kid," and his eyes roved belligerently over the rest of the party.

The only one not intimidated was Valerie. She gave a sneering laugh. "What are you trying to do? Make a good girl out of her?"

"She is a good girl," Gillibrand scowled.

Valerie laughed. "You needn't worry about anyone here touching her. If you're afraid of that, you want to go a little nearer home."

Maisie's face suddenly went chalk-white. Valerie noticed her change of expression and nodded mockingly. "Yes, dear; I know all about it. My room's right under yours, you know. It's surprising how much one can hear."

Gillibrand's fuddled eyes were moving from one to the other of the women. "What're you gettin' at?" he growled. "What's been happenin'?"

Valerie turned on him triumphantly. "You should ask that little observer of yours. He'll be able to give you *all* the details."

"What are y' talkin' about?" Gillibrand snarled. "What's Jimmie got to do with it?"

Valerie pointed at Maisie. "Ask her. It didn't take her long to find consolation when you were on leave. I suppose your friend was the first man that came along."

Gillibrand's eyes blazed. He swung round on Maisie. "You . . . and the kid? It's a lie. . . . Ain't it?"

Maisie's expression told him the truth. For a moment it seemed he would strike her. Then he turned away, his face murderous. He flung the black-out curtain aside and lurched out into he darkness.

Adams, his face white and ashamed, rose without a word and left the lounge. Maisie ran after the Canadian. She caught up with him on the drive and grabbed his arm.

"It wasn't the kid's fault—honest to God it wasn't. It was me. I thought it would help him—I thought it would help you both. . . ."

He heard nothing but her confession, and threw her away from him savagely. She struck the wall of the inn, almost collapsing from the shock. He stood before her, a denser shadow in the darkness, his breathing hoarse and uneven. "Joyce . . . and you! And now the kid! What's happenin' to everybody? What's goin' on?"

Despair and terror made her plead with him. "It wasn't Jimmie's fault. . . . Don't take it out of him. D'you hear? The kid wasn't to blame."

Gillibrand turned and lurched away down the drive, his feet crunching pitilessly on the gravel. Her hands reached out mutely after him, then dropped to her sides. The bricks of the wall were cold and rough. She put her cheek against them and sobbed.

Grenville opened the door of the Mess and paused there a moment. There was a good deal of noise going on—Parsons of B Flight had got news through that day that he was the father of a 9lb. son and was throwing a party to wet the baby's ears. As Grenville turned to close the door there was a smash of glass, a howl, then a roar of laughter.

The piano was the centre of the party's activities at

the moment. As Grenville went forward, Parsons, a slim, fairheaded youngster of twenty-two with a wispy, insecure-looking moustache, was leaning unsteadily against it, giving a doleful rendering of "Nellie Dean" to the accompaniment of cheers, catcalls, and boos. Catching sight of Grenville, he broke off and straightened himself with difficulty.

"Evenin', sir. Nice of you to come—ver' nice indeed. What'll you have to drink, sir?"

The noise around subsided as Grenville shook his hand. "Nice work, Parsons. Congratulations. Let's hope the little chap doesn't turn out as big a toper as his pa, though. I'll have a whisky, thanks."

The songs began again but with less abandon now. In an effort to ease the slight tension Grenville joined in, but soon fell silent. It was not the first time he had felt this curious sense of apartness—in spite of his efforts to suppress it, he had been feeling it more and more frequently over the last twelve months. It was this damned reputation the newspapers had given him: it affected the new youngsters, put them in awe of him. And, in turn, their attitude embarrassed him, made him curt, and so the thing got worse. . . .

Even among the old sweats there was that slight feeling. It wasn't too bad with them, of course, but it all added up and he didn't want it to add up. This was the life he had put everything into: he didn't want to become a creature apart in it.

But there was no escaping the fact that the party had become more self-conscious since his arrival. He had one more drink, then made his excuses. It seemed to him the young uproarious voices took on an immediate tone of relief as he passed into the corridor outside, and the impression made him feel old.

He stood over the telephone a full fifteen seconds before picking it up. He was very conscious of the note of self-defence in his voice when he spoke to her.

"I thought I might come over for a few minutes if you weren't doing anything. But, of course, if you have any friends there. . . ."

Her low voice was full of understanding. "I have no

friends here, Roy. And the sitting-room is empty to-night—Valerie and her husband are in the lounge. Please come—as soon as you wish."

The outline of the Mess merged into the darkness behind Grenville. His mind flashed back to his first meeting with her, acutely aware of the reversal in the order of things. He allowed the irony, but the significance he refused to consider. To escape his thoughts he walked quickly towards the Black Swan.

16

Barrett frowned and gnawed at one end of his tobacco-stained moustache. He stared down again at the operation order on his desk. *Priority top secret stop . . . convoy anchored off Invik . . . believed to contain one Elbing class destroyer . . . unknown number of flak ships . . . one Mosquito to be provided immediately for photo reconnaissance. . . .*

Another similar job to the one Grenville and Bergman had carried out, he reflected. The convoy must have something to do with this building—probably bringing equipment to it. . . . Shouldn't be too difficult a job, but there was no mistaking the urgency and tone of the order. He had to send his best available men. . . . Well, neither Grenville nor Bergman was here this time. Bergman was already over on the other side and Grenville had gone with Davies to the conference. In any case, Roy was withdrawn from operations until further orders. . . . Who to send, then? Milner came to his mind at once and he was stretching his hand out to his telephone when he remembered. Milner's young English wife had been taken ill—the American had been given two days' compassionate leave to see her. So he was out. . . .

Another name automatically stepped into his mind. Wonderful pilot if it wasn't for that confounded temperament of his. . . . And yet there didn't seem much that could go wrong on this job. The met. report enclosed with the order was excellent, and in a Mossy it should be a piece of cake. Straight out, photographs, and straight back . . . they shouldn't even see an enemy kite. On the other hand, if there was trouble, he was the man to fight himself out of it. . . .

The last thought decided Barrett. He put a call through to B Flight office. "Send me Warrant Officer Gillibrand right away," he grunted. "And tell his observer, Willcox, to come along with him."

The mouth of the Svartfjord fell behind the high-flying Mosquito. Below it, the dark clusters of flak that disfigured the blue sky like some virulent pox drifted slowly away, sullen in defeat. The coastline, as jagged in outline as a shrapnel-torn wing, passed obliquely below the nose of the aircraft, giving way to the vast, congealed sea.

The operation had been a complete success and all the required photographs had been taken. The convoy had showed no hesitation in firing at the Mosquito—it would have looked suspicious if it had not—but most of the flak had burst below them and no fighter had made their altitude. Gillibrand, looking huge and menacing in his flying-suit and oxygen-mask, turned his eyes on the small, hunched figure of Jimmie alongside him and scowled. It had all been too damned easy. . . .

Freed from the necessity of concentrating, his mind began brooding again on what he had heard the previous night. It had been lucky for the kid that the booze had got him and that he'd passed out before the kid had got back to camp. . . . Maisie said it was her fault, and maybe most of it was, at that. . . . They were all the same—he was learnin' that fast enough. But hell, this kid had a mind of his own, hadn't he? He didn't have to do a lousy thing like that!

His thoughts goaded him and his hands tightened on the controls. He wasn't going to get away with it this easy! So the little punk thought he was a man, huh? All right, little tough guy. Let's take a look an' see just how tough you are. . . .

The Mosquito dipped its port wing with sudden purpose and veered round. The coastline, now far behind them, tilted until it was running parallel to their line of flight. The swinging compass steadied itself.

Gillibrand caught Jimmie's sidelong, startled glance. His lips drew back.

"You don't have to tell me we've gone off course, kid. You know what I'm going to do?"

The boy's eyes held a vague expression of alarm as he shook his head.

"I'm gonna pay you back, kid. I'm gonna see just

136

how tough you've become all of a sudden. We're gonna have some fun, you an' me."

Jimmie's voice was faint in the intercom. "Our orders said we had to return straight back with the photographs. They're supposed to be important."

Gillibrand laughed harshly. "'Gettin' yellow already, kid? The only one givin' orders up here is me. Just wait, kid. Wait until I've finished with you. You won't be so tough then. . . ."

The fury into which the Canadian had worked himself made no concession to caution or duty. He'd break this little punk if he had to fly the Mossy through the side of a battleship to do it. High in the infinite sky, the Mosquito droned southwards down the coast, a lone, angry wasp looking for trouble.

There was a hush in the room as the Brigadier stopped speaking and the caw of a nesting rook in the elms outside could be heard clearly. For a few seconds even Grenville's self-control could not prevent his looking shocked.

"You'll understand now the importance of all we've been doing," the Brigadier said quietly, offering both Davies and Grenville a cigarette. "That building must be destroyed—we can't even contemplate failure. Knowing its importance puts a heavy responsibility on you, Grenville, I realize that, but I felt you should be told. I'd like to take the opportunity to say we have the fullest confidence in you. Are there any questions you would like to ask?"

Grenville nodded. "When are you planning to send us in?"

"I'm not allowed to give you the exact date, but if everything goes well on the other side it will be less than a month. It has to be because——"

The Brigadier broke off abruptly. Grenville followed his eyes and saw that a red bulb over the door was flickering urgently.

The Brigadier rose to his feet. "That means a message has been sent through. Please excuse me while I see what it is."

He came back two minutes later looking a different man. His face was quite grey and his mouth and cheeks pinched with shock. But Grenville and Davies rose to their feet in alarm. The Brigadier motioned to the Air Commodore.

"Davies; will you come with me, please. I have some serious news for you."

Davies flung an anxious look at Grenville and followed the Brigadier from the room. On their return Davies looked as white as the elderly soldier. He addressed Grenville at once, his voice urgent.

"When do your kites get back from Scotland?"

Grenville glanced at his watch. "They should have been down eighty minutes ago."

"Tell me—didn't you once train your men to do skip bombing—you know, precision stuff with time delays."

Puzzled, Grenville nodded. "Yes. We were given that Groningen prison job three months ago. Of course, we haven't done any in these new planes . . ."

"That's good enough," Davies interrupted curtly. He nodded to the Brigadier and picked up the telephone. Ten seconds later he had Barrett on the line.

"Barrett! Davies here. I want your Mossies re-fuelled and armed in less than an hour. Yes, you can. Make 'em work like hell. The bombs are to be 500-lb. M.C.'s with eleven-second delays. Got it? Right. Get your crews alerted. We'll be over as fast as we can and will give you the rest of the gen later. Now put me over to Adams, will you?"

After giving instructions to Adams on the maps and photographs needed for the briefing, Davies slammed down the receiver and turned to Grenville.

"That order grounding you is off. You'll have to lead 'em in. The job is to prang a certain wooden building in Bergen. Don't ask me why because no one is going to be told. There isn't any time to lay an escort on—as you heard, it's a rush job and there isn't a minute to lose. But if you go in at low level, surprise and speed should get you through. And if the worst comes to the worst, you've got armament on those Mossies of yours to fight back, thank God."

At that moment a lieutenant entered the office, giving the Brigadier a dispatch-box. The Brigadier turned to Davies. "These photographs will help your briefing. We'd better get along now. The car's waiting outside."

"You're coming along too, are you, sir?"

"I must. Hurry, please."

Less than half-an-hour later the station wagon screeched to a halt at the gates of Sutton Craddock. The sentry on duty had barely time to glance inside before it jerked away, to sit up against its brakes outside the Station Headquarters. The Brigadier, stern and pale, was already striding down the path when Davies gave Grenville his dismissal. His voice was half peremptory, half apologetic.

"We'll ring your office the moment we want you. In the meantime you'd better be getting yourself togged up."

With that, Davies turned and ran after the Brigadier. Together they entered Barrett's office. Davies closed the door, quickly introduced the two men, then came to the point without preamble.

"Have you got everything moving?"

Barrett nodded. "Apart from the briefing we should be ready for take-off in under an hour."

Davies knew the magnitude of the task and nodded his appreciation. "We'll have to make the briefing as short as possible. I'm afraid we have some unpleasant news, and a filthy job for you. The Brigadier will give you the details."

When the Brigadier had finished speaking, Barrett's ruddy face was as shocked and pale as anyone's.

"Good lord!" he muttered. "Filthy isn't the word. Surely we don't have to carry things this far!"

Davies, highly strung, needed no more to set him off. "You don't think we'd give such an order unless it were absolutely necessary, do you? Don't be a fool man."

Barrett had a big man's slow but resentful temper. At another time he might have taken offence but he caught a glimpse of the Brigadier's face. There were lines of agony round the soldier's grey eyes and stern mouth. Barrett made his apology at once.

"Sorry," he muttered awkwardly. "It's just as bad for you, of course."

The Brigadier looked his full age as he stared through the window. "It is a very necessary order, I'm afraid. You know the Nazis as well as I; you can guess their reaction in a situation like this. They'll stop at nothing, and there's no doubt what is happening at this very moment—indeed, we know it's happening. That is why there isn't a second to lose."

He turned towards Barrett, his voice sympathetic. "I agree men shouldn't be asked to do such a thing. And they wouldn't be, if it weren't for devils like these Nazis. Your men are going out on an act of mercy, and that is the solemn truth."

Barrett stood silent, then nodded slowly. "At least the men won't know," he muttered. Then he started. "What about Grenville. You haven't told him, have you? Or doesn't he have to go?"

Davies answered the question. "He'll have to lead them in, but we haven't told him, nor shall we. He's waiting in his office for orders now."

"And what about Adams?"

Davies looked at the Brigadier, who nodded reluctantly. "I think we'll have to tell him. But he'll have to keep it quiet or the morale of your crews will drop to zero."

"That's what I'm afraid of," Barrett muttered. He shifted, then set his jaw resolutely. "I'd like to go on this show, sir, I think it's my duty to go."

Davies was sympathetic, but shook his head. "No. Particularly now that you know what the job is. Sorry, but I won't hear of it." Noticing the Brigadier was growing impatient, he went on quickly: "We'd better get over to Adams now. The Brigadier has some photographs we can use at the briefing."

Barrett roused himself, moving his heavy body like a man in a nightmare. "Yes, all right. He's standing by."

Fifteen minutes later Davies, Adams, and Barrett left to attend the briefing, which the Brigadier dared not attend for security reasons. As they went, his grey eyes fixed themselves almost beseechingly on Barrett.

"See that they make a good job of it, won't you? It would be terrible if it were only half-destroyed."

Barrett's heavy face was grim. "Don't worry, sir. We'll make it the devil's last party."

17

Gillibrand had flown south for over twenty minutes and was thirty miles due west of Bergen before he found himself a suitable target. The weather was less settled here, and heavy banks of cloud were throwing shadows on the sunlit sea below. He flew into a clear area and a tiny, dark object appeared to the right of his starboard spinner cap. He dropped lower and examined it through his binoculars. It was a minelayer, busy on the huge enemy minefields that protected the shipping lanes down the Norwegian coast. From this height the ship's wake, stretching out fanwise into the frozen sea, looked like the excrement of a caterpillar on some enormous leaf. The time was 1407 hours.

Without hesitation Gillibrand put the Mosquito's nose down. The altimeter needle fell away as the airspeed indicator rose. 320 . . . 370 . . . 400 m.p.h. The sea was beginning to take shape now—slowly at first, then more quickly, its swell resembling the folds in a rucked-up sheet of cloth. At 8,000 Gillibrand had to pull up the nose slightly as the engines began to race. The whole plane was shuddering violently under the tremendous stress of the dive.

The ship was leaping upwards now. From a speck of driftwood it became a towering hulk with armoured superstructure, a squat funnel, and raised gun platforms; an impregnable metal castle rising from the blue-green sea. Gillibrand levelled out just above the waves, switching on his gunsight and his fire-and-safe button. From the corner of his eye he saw Jimmie, helpess in the hands of his pilot, staring with rigid gaze at the approaching terror.

The ship was massive in Gillibrand's gunsight now, hurling itself at him. A sudden rapid staccato of flashes ran up and down its full length, and steel lashed the waves below the plane into a seething mist of spray. With teeth bared, Gillibrand pressed his gun button.

The two Hispano cannon, aided by the twin Brownings, kicked back viciously as they pumped a total of twenty shells a second into the camouflaged hull of the minelayer.

Incoherent pictures flashed before the terrified boy's eyes like snatches from some crazy film. Cannon shells exploding in the water . . . rising higher . . . raking the ship's superstructure and gun platforms . . . A man in a navy-blue jersey clutching his stomach in agony and toppling from one of the platforms to the deck below. . . . Two other men, crouching behind a pom-pom, being hurled backwards, a shambles of quivering flesh and spouting blood. . . . A lifeboat dropping away from its davits . . . a four-barrelled pom-pom hurling shells right at their wind-screen. . . .

Then the smoking, erupting nightmare vanished and only the shadowy blue-green sea lay ahead. But the shells followed them, stabbing vengefully through the fuselage and hammering into the armour protecting their backs. Jimmie's body was racked with a violent nervous tremor. His terrified eyes pleaded mutely with Gillibrand, but the Canadian only laughed. The sea before them swirled crazily, the centrifugal force crushed the boy back into his seat, and the terror was back again, dead ahead. . . .

The minelayer was sending out frantic calls to the coast defence for fighters. As the Mosquito came back the ship's gunners opened up with everything they had. Through his gunsight Gillibrand saw a wall of tracer hurling itself at him. A shell ricochetted off his hood, another smashed through the instrument panel and passed between himself and the cringing boy. Grinning his hate, he opened fire again. Once more the Mosquito shuddered under the violent recoil. Bullets and shells sliced among the superstructure and deck timbers, cutting down men as a scythe cuts down grass. The base of the transmitting wireless aerial came into Gillibrand's sights. His shells were searching it out when suddenly the Mosquito was flung upwards by a tremendous explosion under its fuselage.

The minelayer spun down out of sight in a whirling chaos of smoke, masts, and spitting guns. The Mosquito, completely out of control, snaked upwards like a damaged rocket. Fighting desperately, Gillibrand managed to straighten it out at 5,000 feet. The mine-layer was still snarling viciously at them, and he drew out of range to take stock of the damage.

Half his instruments were smashed. Those still intact began settling down nervously after the shock. His port engine was belching smoke alarmingly. As he watched it, a jet of flame appeared under its shattered cowling. Quickly he feathered the propeller and switched on the fire extinguisher. Dirty grey foam appeared, flying back in spume from the wing. With a grunt of relief he saw the flames die down and vanish. Then he turned towards Jimmie.

For a moment he thought the boy had fainted. He was lying limply against his straps. Gillibrand reached out and shook him roughly. The boy's face-mask slipped down and Gillibrand saw blood on his lips. Instantly the Canadian knew terror.

"Jimmie! What's happened, kid? Jimmie . . . !"

He shook the boy again. Jimmie stirred, tried to straighten up, and his face contorted in agony. His frightened eyes turned on Gillibrand—eyes as transparent as those of a child. He tried to speak, but the blood only flowed faster from his lips.

"Kid! For Christ's sake. What is it, boy?"

Jimmie's eyes moved mutely to the first-aid kit. Suddenly Gillibrand understood. Holding the stick with his knees, he undid the canvas pack and pulled out one of the tiny morphia hypodermic tubes. He pulled back the boy's sleeve and jabbed the needle into the flesh, squeezing until the tube was empty.

The boy's head slumped back in relief. Blood trickled from his chin to the collar of his flying-suit. Gillibrand leaned over him.

"Jimmie! Say somethin' to me. For God's sake say somethin' . . ."

The boy did not move or speak. With fear choking his throat, Gillibrand swung the crippled plane round and headed back for Stutton Craddock. He flew like a madman, his blue eyes glaring rigidly ahead. The time was 1412 hours.

The twelve closely-grouped Mosquitoes swept over the coastal town of Whitby like a tornado. A car halted, its four passengers staring upwards from its windows and waving excitedly. A man on a bicycle turned his head in fright, ran into the kerb, and tumbled in a heap on the pavement. The planes skimmed a cliff, leapt over a golden strip of beach, then were over the sea, glancing over the wave-tops like a shoal of flying fish.

Impressions registered themselves on the retina of Grenville's mind in spite of his preoccupation over the task ahead. The ruins of the Abbey, pointing to the sky with gentle, admonishing fingers. . . . A fishing boat rolling gently in the swell, probably crabbing. . . . A flock of seagulls clustered around some object, their turning wings white against the blue sea. They flashed by and then there was nothing but the sea—the sea that was like a barren plain, stretching to infinity.

To Grenville the operation was a complete mystery. He had been told no more than his crews had been told at the briefing—that a certain building in Bergen had to be destroyed and the ways of finding it. Nothing more except Barrett's few mumbled words before take-off. There had been an oddly apologetic look on his face.

"Sorry Davies won't let me come along, Roy. But do a good job, will you? Blow it right out of the ground. We don't want anything left standing. . . ."

Barrett had been apologetic. Why? Grenville felt his irritation rising. Surely, after all the Brigadier had told him that morning, he could know what was behind this job! What was all the secrecy about?

The Mosquitoes were in battle formation, two tight lines of six aircraft apiece. They were flying at economical cruising speed without boost, so low that their slipstreams were ruffling the wave-tops and leaving a wake behind them. Every pilot's eyes were fixed on the water ahead: a slip in concentration at that height meant certain death. The observers were kept busy switching on fuel cocks, keeping a watchful eye on gauges, and ceaselessly scanning the sea and sky around them.

Ninety minutes passed and they ran into an area

scattered with medium-level cloud. The waves were higher and it had grown cold—a reminder that even towards the end of April Norway was still in the grip of winter. As they passed under the clouds a sharp shower of rain brought their visibility down to a few yards. The planes drew closer, wingtip to wingtip, nose to tail, a phalanx of screaming engines and hurtling wings. Observers sat tensed, straining to pierce the grey curtain that pelted horizontally by them. The rain hid the distant minelayer that was limping back to port with seventeen casualties on board, and by the time they broke from it she had vanished hull down over the horizon.

A break in the clouds and a blue sky again. Their shadows returned to the sea, like pursuing sharks that had re-discovered their prey. Hoppy looked at his watch. It was 1417 hours.

"Eight minutes to E.T.A., skipper."

A distant snow-cap, shining in the sunlight, suspended over the horizon like a cloud. . . . Observers nudged their pilots, pointing. "There it is! Enemy coast ahead. . . ."

A chain of grey islands grew out of the sea and flashed by. The Oygarden group—leading straight to Bergen. Hoppy pinpointed the mountain ahead and gave Grenville a correction. The squadron turned four degrees to port. They leap-frogged the islands and hugged the channels between them. Four minutes . . . five . . . six. . . . Going down a wide channel now . . . houses among the rocks on either side . . . a glimpse of camouflaged oil tanks . . . a smoking chimney. . . . Mountains mushrooming upwards . . . forests springing up green from the sea. . . . Into a wide bay now . . . a forty-five degree turn to starboard . . . and ahead the skyline was laced with the masts of ships. Beyond the ships was a mass of buildings, sweeping nearer at breakneck speed.

Bergen, dead ahead. Grenville was crouched forward in his seat, his gunsight and camera-gun switched on, bombs fused. No time now to wonder on the purpose of the raid. Another half minute and they would be screaming over the interlaced streets of the city,

146

searching for one building out of the thousands that flashed by. . . .

A startled voice suddenly broke the R/T silence. "Bandits, skipper! In the sun! Break port . . ."

Grenville allowed himself one quick look around. Twenty plus Focke-Wulfs were diving out of the sun, their red spinner caps like mouths agape with anticipation. An ambush: God! He switched his eyes upwards. A filigree pattern of contrails was pointed ominously down at them. More up there . . . dozens of them . . . alerted and belting down. . . .

Only superb training saved the squadron from that initial attack. Not 300 feet over the city Grenville led them into a tight turn. His orders came snapping over the R/T.

"Swordfish leader calling . . . defensive circle . . . work back to cloud base. . . ."

The break to port had fouled the 190's surprise attack. Before they could press home a second, the Mosquitoes had formed a huge defensive circle, each plane covering the tail of the one ahead.

Grenville over the radio again. "Swordfish leader . . . jettison bombs."

There was no hope of getting through to the target. The sky was full of enemy fighters, converging from all directions. A hail of bombs fell away from the Mosquitoes into the bay below, further scattering the small boats that were racing for shelter. A few seconds later the delay-fused bombs began exploding like depth charges, throwing up columns of spray.

Out over the islands the battle began in earnest. The Focke-Wulfs, short-winged, vicious, pressed home their attacks savagely, but Grenville's defensive tactics frustrated them time and time again. The sky was like a great aquarium tank with dozens of red-nosed fish swarming round a huge, spinning jellyfish—darting, biting, tearing, but unable to get a decisive hold. The sky was laced with snapping tracer and the black threads from smoking exhausts.

A Mosquito was hit. Its starboard engine stopped, sending out a white cloud of glycol. Another burst of cannon hit the same wing and the white cloud turned

147

to black. Tendrils of flame appeared, curling round the wing like a claw. A violent explosion, and the Mosquito spun helplessly away. Another explosion, tearing away the other wing and the smoking fuselage plunged down like a dart into the sea. No one baled out. The remaining Mosquitoes closed the gap, the circle growing smaller.

A Focke-Wulf, too eager to make a kill, caught the full vengeful blast of two cannon and two machine-guns right in its main tanks beneath the cockpit floor. It exploded like a bomb, leaving only an oily black cloud and a mass of fluttering debris. A hoarse voice bellowed out exultantly over the R/T: "I got him! See that! I got the bastard. . . ."

Two other Focke-Wulfs, their pilots intent on the same Mosquito and drawn together by its climbing turn, collided and spun down in a tangled mass of flame and wreckage. The top-level reinforcements had arrived now, cluttering up the sky with enemy aircraft. Their very numbers were against them, causing them to get in each other's way. But Mosquito after Mosquito was hit; man after man wounded. . . .

"Tighten up. Keep formation. Nearly there now. . . ." Grenville's voice kept coming over the R/T, encouraging his men. Seeing the squadron's objective the 190's pressed home their attacks with increased ferocity, attacking in pairs now. Staccato flashes ran along their clipped wings from the firing of their cannon.

The dark clouds, heavy with rain, lay over to the west, shadowing the sea. They were no more than three miles away now, a sanctuary from the hell of flame and steel. But three miles could be eternity with forty plus Focke-Wulfs barring the way. They came snarling in again and the Mosquitoes shuddered under the impact.

18

Gillibrand rubbed his bloodshot eyes and stared through his windscreen again. It was the English coast and never before had he been so glad to see it. Green-couched, with patches of woods, it slid gently over the horizon to drive back the pitiless sea.

With his face-mask slippery with sweat, the Canadian leaned over Jimmie and touched his shoulder.

"Here's the coast now. . . . Stick it a bit longer, kid; we're nearly home. They'll fix you up—you'll be fine in a couple of weeks."

Morphia had kept the boy dozing most of the way back. He awoke now, his face drawn with pain. As he tried to follow Gillibrand's pointing finger, the Mosquito hit a bump, jerking his body against its straps. The abrupt movement forced fresh blood from his lips, sending it oozing out over the congealed crust round his mouth.

Gillibrand's big hands closed convulsively around his control stick. He stared round the shattered cockpit with hating eyes, damning the aircraft, whipping it on with every tensed muscle in his huge body. If there was another airfield nearer than Sutton Craddock he could put the kid down on it, but there was nothing around here. . . . His eyes strayed to the boy's slumped body and a wave of panic swept over him. The kid mustn't die. . . . D'you hear, God—he musn't die. . . . Sweat poured from him, draining his strength away until he felt weak and sick. That afternoon, for the first time in his life, Gillibrand knew fear.

Sutton Craddock came into sight at last, sliding upwards behind its belt of trees. They had got his message—the ambulance and the fire-tenders were standing by. Ignoring Control he came in cross-wind, working his way down on his one red-hot engine. In spite of his care, the Mosquito made two high bounces before settling down, and from the corner of his eye he saw Jimmie jerk in agony. Cursing, he braked, switched off his engine and turned to the boy.

After the roar of the Merlins, the silence had a muffled, heavy quality through which the distant wail of the ambulance sounded thin and unreal. Gillibrand unbuckled Jimmie's straps and caught his slumping body in his arms.

"We've made it, kid. We're home. You'll be O.K now."

The blood on the boy's face was like a smear of red ink across a sheet of parchment. He did not move or speak.

Gillibrand's voice rose hysterically. "Kid, say somethin' to me. D'you hear? Say something, kid."

Jimmie's eyes opened wearily. He stared upwards at Gillibrand, looking puzzled. Then his crusted lips moved, trying smile. Gillibrand lowered his head to listen.

The sounds were as faint as the flutter of a moth's wing. "It's all right, Gillie. Don't worry. . . ."

"Don't worry. . . . Listen, kid. I'm sorry. I don't know why I did it. There ain't a skirt in the world worth your little finger. . . . You can have 'em all, kid —honest to God. Only don't die. . . ."

Jimmie's head sagged back. Gillibrand glared down, willing him to live. "Don't die, kid. For God's sake don't die!"

The boy's lips moved again. "It's funny Gillie. . . . I'm not a bit afraid. Tell her, will you? Tell her I'm not afraid. . . ."

The wonder of it was still in his eyes when he died.

Adams saw him lurching down the tarmac, throwing off helpers as a wounded bear shakes off dogs. His helmet was pulled back exposing his yellow hair which was matted with sweat. There was a streak of oil down his face and a red stain down the front of his flying suit. But it was his eyes that drew Adams' gaze. They were glaring straight ahead with the look of a man who had been given a glimpse into hell and knew for the rest of his life he would be haunted by the memory.

150

Adams approached him. "What happened, Gillibrand?"

The glaring blue eyes never shifted their stare as the Canadian lurched on. Adams took a deep breath and caught hold of his arm.

"Gillibrand! What happened?"

The Canadian swung round, his face murderous. In spite of himself Adams drew back, expecting a blow. Two long seconds passed, then Gillibrand jerked his arm savagely away and lurched down the tarmac.

It was only contempt for himself that drove Adams on. He caught hold of the Canadian's arm again and forced a ring of authority into his voice.

"I want a report on what happened straight away. Not later—now, in my office. Come on!"

Discipline succeeded where sympathy had failed. Gillibrand turned to face him, his wild eyes puzzled now.

Adams gave him no time to recover. "Come on. This is important."

Feeling as if he had a savage animal on a leash, Adams led Gillibrand into his office and closed the door. He motioned the pilot into a chair alongside his desk, put a 'phone call through to the Naafi for tea, then took a seat himself. He threw a cigarette across the desk, then pulled out a large official questionnaire. He kept his voice authoritative and impersonal.

"The first thing is—did you get the photographs?"

The Canadian looked dazed now. He nodded like an automaton. "Yeah. We got 'em."

Adams filled in the standard details on the form, then looked up. "See anything unusual on the way out?"

"Nothin' but sea and sky."

"Apart from the convoy, was there any other activity in the fjord?"

"Didn't see any."

"Any opposition from it?"

"The usual flak from the ships. Nothin' else."

As Adams made notes on the form, the Canadian's dazed eyes wandered round the office. "Where's the skipper?" he muttered.

The question was understandable. In his rôle of Squadron Commander Grenville was usually present at interrogations. Adams explained briefly.

"While you were out, we were given an emergency job—a raid on a building in Bergen. They're due back any time now—they didn't leave long after you." Adams paused, looking at his watch. "All right. You took the photographs and got out. You were due back around about 1545. It's now 1640. What happened in that extra time?"

Gillibrand did not appear to hear the question. His square, oil-streaked face reminded Adams of a bemused schoolboy confronted with a simple yet baffling problem.

"Did you say Bergen?" the Canadian muttered.

Adams nodded. "They went out at low-level. Why? What's worrying you?"

Whatever had sparked the question in the Canadian's brain clearly eluded him now. His eyes turned dull and he shook his head mechanically. "Don't know. Nothin', I suppose."

It was not the first time Adams had interrogated men in the last stages of physical and nervous exhaustion, and he knew the symptoms well. He was relieved when the Naafi girl brought in tea and sandwiches. He shoved them in front of Gillibrand.

Gillibrand sipped at the hot sweet tea but pushed the sandwiches aside. The smell of his flying-suit came to Adams' nostrils, a mixture of oil, grease, cordite and a hundred other indefinable things. Even at that moment something in Adams stirred in envy. He motioned to the sandwiches.

"Don't you want anything to eat?"

Gillibrand shook his head. "No; I ain't hungry."

Adams inhaled deeply on his cigarette. The question had to be asked—he had deferred it as long as possible. "What happened after you left the fjord?" he asked. And very gently: "What happened to your observer?"

Fatigue had dulled Gillibrand's mind like an anaesthetic, but this sudden reminder brought both memory and agony back. The cup in his hand jerked sideways, spilling tea down his flying suit. His blue eyes blazed their protest.

"You ran into trouble somewhere," Adams went on, trying to conceal his apprehension. "What happened?"

Gillibrand's madness returned. He leapt to his feet with a curse. "What the hell is it to you? What's it matter now . . . ?"

"I must know," Adams said gently. "A man has been killed—I must know what happened."

Ignoring him, Gillibrand turned and lurched for the door. Words were falling from his lips like blood from a re-opened wound. "Yeah . . . I'd forgotten. The kid's dead. . . . The little feller. . . . Oh, my Christ . . ."

He flung open the door and stumbled out. At that moment a siren screamed. He stopped dead, his blood-shot eyes staring around, trying to understand. The fire-tenders started up again and the ambulance began to wail. Under and through the noise came a deep, irregular hum that grew louder as he listened. He turned his eyes upwards and saw the arrival home of the Mosquitoes. . . .

They were flying in an open, protective box, guarding the two planes in their centre. Now, under instructions from Control, they began to orbit the airfield while the two badly-hit planes were given priority down.

Adams joined Gillibrand outside the office, his eyes huge behind his thick spectacles. On the airfield ahead the ambulance, accompanied by the Medical Officer in his jeep, was speeding to the distant end of the runway. One of the fire-tenders was moving in the same direction, the firemen on its running-boards looking like men from another planet in their grotesque asbestos suits.

The first crippled Mosquito appeared over the boundary fence. Its approach was going to lead it right over the two watching men. Staring upwards they could see the blackened scars on its engine cowlings, the wingtip that was half torn away, the tail unit riddled and tattered. It looked like a toy plane that had been dragged through a thorn bush.

They felt the chill of its shadow as it passed over

153

them, the wind whining over its airfoils. Its starboard engine faltered for a second, the torn wing dipped, and Adams felt his breath lock in his throat. Somehow it skidded level again, both engines coughing like a man trying to clear his flooded lungs. It levelled off at least 100 feet above the airfield as if its pilot had decided to make a fresh approach. At that moment the starboard engine cut right out and the damaged wing dropped as though pulled down by wire. . . .

There was an agonized pause that seemed to last minutes. Then a rending crash that tore through nerves like a bulldozer through soil. The Mosquito struck wing first, cartwheeled over, and fell tail forward, furrowing the ground for at least fifty yards. There was a dull, couching explosion, a vivid streak of light, then an out-flung cloud of oil smoke shot through with avid tongues of fire.

A fire truck raced up and thrust its radiator almost into the flames, hurling carbonic foam through its high-pressure nozzles. Swinging their axes like madmen, the firemen leapt into the flames, ignoring the danger from white-hot wing tanks and unspent cannon shells. But nothing moved in the furnace that was the cockpit. The stench of burning rubber drifted across the airfield, making Adams retch.

The second Mosquito made its approach. It was flying on only one engine, its dead propeller as stiffly up-right as a tombstone. The broken spars and ragged cloth hanging under its fuselage made Adams think of the dragging entrails of a crippled bird. With half its control surfaces shot away, it was having the utmost difficulty in avoiding stalling as its flying speed dropped for the landing. Its wheels hit the runway with a thud that made Adams wince, there was a sharp crack as a tyre burst, and the plane leapt 20 feet into the air. It crashed down heavily, one wingtip digging into the ground and tearing off as if made of cardboard. The rest of the plane ground-looped to the accompaniment of snapping spars and tearing fabric. There was an ominous hissing as petrol came into contact with the white-hot engine, but this time a fire truck had a chance and used it well. The crew rammed their nozzles right on to the smoking engines, covering them in foam. The danger of fire passed. The observer staggered from the shattered fuselage, then went straight back for his comrade. But the pilot was beyond aid. The firemen brought him out, as limp and broken as a child's doll.

Gillibrand started forward and after a second's hesitation Adams followed him, trying to keep up with the half-crazed Canadian. Gillibrand ran out on the field, then halted, his eyes staring up wildly at the smoke-blackened sky. A thin streak of saliva was trickling from his mouth. A Mosquito, with two mechanics holding its wingtips protectingly, came taxi-ing in their direction, its battle-scarred fuselage jolting over the uneven ground. Gillibrand, massive in his flying suit, turned and ran towards it.

Two men tumbled out of the plane. One was Teddy Young, the A Flight commander. His powerful shoulders were sagging with exhaustion. His observer was one of the reserve crews, a youngster named Reynolds whose blue eyes were still stupefied with the fear of death. As Gillibrand and Adams approached, the boy caught hold of the trailing edge of the wing to steady himself. He leaned down, vomiting from reaction.

Young peered at them through swollen eyes. He moistened his dry lips and tried to grin. His voice was little more than a croak.

"Hiya. I guess there's no place like home, after all."

Gillibrand's voice was even thicker. "What happened?"

The Australian's lips twisted. "We only ran into half the Hun Air Force over Bergen, that's all."

"You mean they were waitin' for you?"

"Yeah. Some bastard must have alerted 'em. Don't ask me how any of us got back. What about a smoke, cobber? You got one?"

But Gillibrand was stumbling away, wild-eyed and haggard. Later Adams wondered why he had not understood the Canadian's torment over the news. But his mind at the time was full of the sight and sound of crashing aircraft, of dead and wounded friends. The Mosquitoes were still coming down and the ambulances

155

making trip after trip to the casualty station. The airfield was a chaos of shot-up aircraft, shouting men, and wailing sirens. Some panic-stricken member of the Control staff kept firing off red Very lights, making Adams' tight nerves jump each time they soared overhead. The fire crews were still busy among the wreckage of the crashed Mosquitoes, and the sullen smoke, stinking of melted rubber, was drifting like a pall across the field.

Adams turned his short-sighted gaze back to Young. The tension was working out of the Australian now, and he was gazing after Gillibrand resentfully.

"What's the matter with him? Can't he give a guy a smoke?"

Adams thrust a packet forward. "Here. Help yourself."

Young muttered his thanks and went over to his observer. "Have a fag, Danny. Make you feel better."

Reynolds shook his head. He tried to speak but failed. The whites of his eyes showed as he retched again, and Young caught hold of his arm.

"Give me a hand with him, will you?" he said to Adams.

Adams nodded and took Reynolds' other arm. The youngster tried to fight them off but the Australian quietened him. "Nothing to be ashamed of, kid. I've puked often enough myself. You'll be O.K. after a drink."

As Adams slung the observer's arm round his shoulder, he caught sight of two more men in flying clothes walking away from a battle-torn Mosquito. One was Grenville, the very immobility of his twisted face testifying to the pent-up emotions within him. His companion was Hoppy. Hoppy's right shoulder and arms were soaked in blood, and smears of it made a red and grey patchwork of his flying suit. His thin, pointed face was drawn with pain, but a grin was locked around the cigarette in his mouth. With his uninjured arm he waved aside the solicitous attention of a crowd of mechanics. His shrill Cockney laughed came echoing back to Adams.

"Those 190's put up a black today, skipper. Used a

shrimping net with an 'ole in the bottom . . . I'll bet they caught 'ell when they got back."

A shudder ran through Adams. The thing inside him was groaning at the waste and glorying at the courage. Fighting to keep his emotions under control, he helped the still-retching Reynolds off the field.

A thin thread of desperation ran through Davies' high-pitched authoritative voice.

"Grenville, this thing is so urgent that if there was enough daylight left, I'd order the lot of you back tonight. As it is, you take them back at 0415 hours so that you can attack at dawn. That's an order."

There was no compromise in Grenville's reply. "I'm not taking them back in a few hours' time. Those boys need rest—what's left of them. You'll have to send someone else."

Davies was fully aware of Grenville's fatigue and for one of his temperament showed commendable patience. "I kept telling you—there isn't anyone else to send. These Mosquitoes are still a new job—we've very few squadrons equipped with them and you're the only one with experience to do this job. Don't argue any more. Get some sleep now and you'll feel better in the morning."

Grenville leaned forward, an aggressive movement. "Jerry must have been alerted about something or he wouldn't have been there waiting for us. Whatever it was, now we've had a crack, he'll be doubly careful and keep a patrol up, certainly for twenty-four hours. If I take back what's left of my boys, in the state they and their kites are in, not one of them will get back. I'm not doing it, and that's final."

Davies eyes were bright with shame and anger. "You realize this is insubordination? That I can have you arrested for disobeying an order?"

Grenville's resentment went out of control. "You can do just what the hell you like; it won't maky any difference. I'm not taking those boys out again until they're fully rested and their kites are repaired. As they are, they'd never even get to Bergen in the dark, much less be able to fight half Jerry's Air Force. What's the matter with you? Do you want to murder them?"

Their eyes locked across the table. The silence reminded Adams of a time he had lain dazed alongside an unexploded bomb while the dust settled around him. He watched the tableau in fascination. The office was his own, the Intelligence Room. Alongside him was Grenville, still in his flying clothes, oil-smudged and battle-weary. Opposite him at the other side of the long table were Barrett, the Brigadier and Davies. All wore different expressions. Barrett had sweat on his forehead, and his heavy breathing betrayed his anguish. The Brigadier looked old and straight and very soldierly. Davies was quivering with anger now and two red spots glowed high upon his cheeks.

Each of them, according to his background, was feeling a slightly different reaction to Grenville's insubordination, yet each had a deep sympathy for it, knowing its cause. But, like Adams, they knew something that Grenville did not know, a thing so compelling it could not allow personal feelings to stand in the way.

Because of this Adams felt no resentment at Davies's threat, wince at it though he did. He knew the urgency, the desperate race against time.

The Brigadier, laying a restraining hand on Davies's arm, turned his grey eyes on Grenville's defiant face. His voice was almost fatherly in its tone.

"I know how inhuman it must sound to you, Grenville, but believe me we wouldn't ask you unless it was desperately important. Having to wait until dawn is a tragedy in itself"—the grief in his tone was unmistakable—"It may well mean it is too late. But we have to hope for the best, and that leaves us no option but to send you back."

"Why is it so important?" Grenville gritted. "Why is a building in Bergen more important than these boys' lives? What's in it?"

In the silence that returned to the room, Adams could hear the distant clang of metal on metal as mechanics worked feverishly on the engine of some damaged Mosquito. He saw from their expressions that both the Brigadier and Davies were tempted to answer, but neither spoke.

158

Receiving no reply, Grenville lurched to his feet, staring bitterly at Davies. "You can tell the guard they'll find me in my room."

He stood to attention a moment, then left the office. There was a short silence in which none of the remaining men met each other's eyes. Then Davies turned his ashamed face towards the Brigadier.

"He'll be court-martialled, of course. We'll put the squadron in charge of another commander. But I must warn you there may be only half-a-dozen planes serviceable by the morning."

The Brigadier was staring down at the table. He lifted his head at Davies's words, his eyes oddly bright.

"You can't arrest him, Davies. He is doing it for his men."

In spite of his anger, Davies looked relieved. He threw a glance at Barrett, who nodded and said gruffly:

"I'm afraid my sympathies are with Roy, sir. It will be pretty near suicide for the boys as things are." As he paused Barrett was dully aware of the irony. Here was a real chance for him to fly on operations again, and he didn't want to go—not on this job.

"I'll take 'em out," he said, nevertheless. "I'll scratch up all the kites I can and give it a bang."

Hope stirred on the Brigadier's face, but Davies shook his head regretfully.

"No, Barrett. It isn't everyone's kind of job. Grenville is one of the few men I know who might have pulled it off. That's the trouble. . . ."

"You've nothing to lose," Barrett argued, crushing down his relief. "Let me have a crack at it."

Desperate though the situation was, Davies knew this was no remedy. "Sorry," he said, trying not to wound too deeply. "You and I are a bit past this sort of thing. It wouldn't work out."

Barrett sat silent a moment, then reached for his cap. "Then let me go and talk to Roy. We've been together a long time. He might listen to me."

Davies hesitated, but the Brigadier gave an eager nod. "Yes. Let him go, please."

Barrett paused at the door. "You know, Grenville's a queer devil. Can I handle him my own way?"

159

"You mean tell him?" Davies asked, startled.

Barrett nodded. Davies turned inquiringly towards the Brigadier. The silence lasted perhaps five seconds —seconds which beat on the temples of the breathless Adams like leaden hammers. Then the Brigadier nodded slowly.

"All right. Do what you think best."

Barrett nodded. The door closed and he was gone.

19

"Now relax a minute and listen to me."

There was nothing subtle about Barrett, which in the circumstances was probably as well. He pushed Grenville back into his chair and lowered his own heavy body down on the bed, ignoring the spring that twanged its protest. This wasn't going to be a pleasant job, but if it wasn't done Grenville might easily get himself arrested. To prevent that happening, Barrett was prepared to go a long way. . . .

"Roy," he said bluntly, "you've got to take 'em back in the morning."

"You're wasting your time, Don. I meant what I said back there."

Barrett nodded absent-mindedly. He took a match from his pocket and began picking at a tooth with it. After the operation he paid detailed attention to his moustache before eyeing Grenville again.

"Roy," he said, "do you remember Charley, that big collie I had last year?"

Grenville stared at him as if he had gone crazy.

"Well, do you?"

"Of course I do."

Barrett nodded reflectively. "That was a fine dog—I liked him. I've got a soft spot for dogs—most of the time I prefer 'em to people. I did Charley. You remember what happened to him?"

"He was run over by a truck, wasn't he?"

"That's right. I thought at first he'd get over it, but he was in pain, Roy—something was bust in his back. I tried for a couple of weeks to fix him but he got worse and worse. I used to lie awake at nights listening to him whimpering, poor devil. I stuck it as long as I could, and then one morning I shot him. And I'll tell you this, Roy—I couldn't have felt it more if he'd been one of us."

Grenville's face was sullen, impatient. "What are you telling me this for?"

Barrett sat up a little straighter on the bed. "I'm trying to say that sometimes you have to be cruel to be kind. That sometimes you have to kill something you like to put it out of its misery."

"We all know that, don't we? What's the point?"

Barrett shook his head. "No, we don't. We know it applies to animals, but we don't think of it applying to people. It doesn't apply in peace-time, of course, except when there are doctors around. I've heard it said they sometimes do it—on the quiet, naturally. . . ."

Grenville's voice was tight. "What in hell are you trying to say?"

Barrett took a deep breath. "You know what the Gestapo are like, don't you, Roy? You know what they do to anyone who has information they want. Well, supposing a friend of yours was caught by them, and in pain, and you couldn't rescue him—what would you do, Roy? What would you do if you had a plane and some bombs to drop?"

Under the smudges of oil Grenville's face was chalk-white now. "For God's sake come out with it straight, Don. What has happened?"

Barrett rose from the bed and put a big, rough hand on Grenville's shoulder. "I'm sorry, Roy, because I know you and he became good friends. But that building in Bergen is occupied by the Gestapo and they've got Bergman and another poor devil inside it. They took Bergman in early this morning. . . ."

It was nearly seven o'clock and quite dark outside when Adams heard footsteps approaching his office. He was alone, sitting in the same chair he had occupied when Davies and the Brigadier had left him half-an-hour earlier. An ashtray, half full of cigarette butts, was at his side, and he had a freshly lit cigarette in his hand. He was staring into the haze of smoke before him, utterly lost in his thoughts when he heard the footsteps. Instantly a thrill of nervousness ran through him, and he felt his heart pounding in his throat

162

and temples. A second later the curtain across the door was flung aside.

It was Grenville, alone. He was still in his flying clothes, still grimy and reeking from the smoke of battle. He stood a moment at the door, and Adams could not find the courage to meet his eyes.

The silence, full of mute, tortured emotions, frightened Adams. He wanted to speak but could think of nothing to say. Panic swept over him: he wanted to jump up and run. He cleared his throat, agonizingly conscious of the inanity of his words.

"Helly, Roy. What can I do for you?"

The sound of his voice, cracked through it was, gave him back some of his moral courage. He lifted his eyes to Grenville's face and shuddered at what he saw. A man on the rack could have looked this way at his torturers. . . .

"Barrett has told you," he muttered, knowing the answer as he asked the question.

Grenville came forward like an automaton, reached the edge of the table, and stood looking down. His voice was like the snarl of an animal.

"Damn you, yes. The one honest man among the lot of you."

Adams made no attempt to excuse himself. "What are you going to do?" he muttered. "Are you going to take them out again?"

Grenville's swollen eyes blazed with fury. "By God; I'm not. I wouldn't take them now if they were a hundred per cent fit and had two serviceable kites apiece. There's a limit to filth, Adams, even in this war."

Adams wondered afterwards how he found the courage to argue. "This is an act of mercy, Roy. That's how we all see it."

Grenville's reply was vicious and unprintable. Adams hesitated, then asked the question that was puzzling him.

"If you're not going, Roy, then what have you come for?"

Grenville's hands were resting on the table in front of the Intelligence Officer. Adams watched them in fascination as they bunched up into tight fists, the knuck-

163

les standing out above the oil-blackened skin like white rocks. Grenville's reply came down on him like a whip.

"I never said *I* wasn't going, Adams. I've come to look over the photographs and maps again. I'm taking off at 0415 hours."

Adams looked up aghast, "Not alone?"

Grenville sneered. "How can I take someone along now that I know what the job is? Tell me that, Adams."

Adams knew what he meant. He sat silent.

"Come on, Adams. You all want the job doing. Get those maps and photographs out. I want to run over it all again. I want to do a good job—a nice, efficient execution."

The nightmare began. Adams opened a drawer and took out the relevant material. Grenville pulled one of the photographs from him and pointed at it.

"That's the building, isn't it?"

Adams nodded. "Yes; it's a sort of annexe to the main Gestapo Headquarters. As you can see, this building is on a piece of waste land quite near the railway station. You can pinpoint it on your way in from the docks by using the Nautical School in the Nordnes Parken as a marker. Straight on you come to the National Theatre, which is almost alongside the main Gestapo Headquarters at the top end of the Ole Bulls Plasse, a wide avenue with flower-beds and trees down the centre. At the other end of the Plasse is a tiny park, and then a small octagonal lake." He unfolded a large-scale map. "Here it is, the Lille Lungegardsvann. Right behind it is the waste land with the building, and beyond that is a lake or fjord called the Store Lungegardsvann. You'll have to be careful over there. Jerry has plenty of flak both alongside the station and over near this bridge, the Strombro. . . . Here are photographs of the Nautical School and the theatre. . . ."

Grenville studied the photographs a moment, then threw them aside. "I'm not planning to come in from the docks. They'll be guarding their approaches. I want a route in from the north." He pointed at the map. "What's this valley here, behind the city?"

Adams studied his notes. "That's the Isdalen Pass

between two of the surrounding mountains. There's a lake in it called the Svartediket with a reservoir—it provides Bergen with its fresh water. The pass comes out into the Store Lungegardsvann."

"It looks quite deep. How high are the mountains on either side?"

"Ulrikken on the east side is over 2,000 feet. The other one is about the same."

"Where does this Isdalen Pass lead from?"

"It comes from the Arna district, up here."

Grenville nodded, his eyes moving up the map, following the fjords out to the sea north of Bergen. "This is my way in," he said at last, tracing a route with his finger. "If I keep on the deck I'll have the islands or mountains covering me on both flanks most of the way. Wait a minute; where's Herdla? That's one of Jerry's airfields, isn't it?"

"You're all right. Herdla's farther south, down here. . . ."

Grenville's questions came for over twenty minutes. His final ones were about the building itself.

"You say it's wooden?"

"Yes. Until the Gestapo took it over it was used as a warehouse. It's three stories high and about fifty feet long—it shouldn't be difficult to destroy if you get through all right."

Grenville's lips twisted. "No; it shouldn't be a bit difficult to blow up a place like that."

Adams cracked then. "Take someone with you, Roy. For God's sake don't do it alone."

"Why not? I've a better chance of getting through that way."

"It isn't that. I know how things are between you and Hilde—I'm not blind. You're never going to forgive yourself if you do it alone. The Brigadier told us this sort of thing has had to be done before, but never by one man. . . . If you take a couple of planes with you, or even an observer, it won't seem so personal."

Grenville's eyes burned their contempt. "Share out the guilt a bit—is that it, Adams? No; let's rather keep all the filth in one place."

He looked down at his watch, and his tone suddenly changed. "Barrett said they took him inside early this morning. Is that what you heard?"

Adams nodded. "Yes; they were seen arriving with him just after dawn. They took in a second man called Ericson later in the day—the message about him came through when you were on the raid."

"So he's been in there all day. And I can't do anything for him before dawn. Ten more hours, Frank. . . . That's a long time. . . ."

His words and the agony in them came as a shock to Adams. He had to look away, his teeth sinking deeply into his lips. When he turned back, Grenville was standing at the door.

"Thanks for the gen, Frank," he said curtly. "If all goes well I'll drop in tomorrow and let you know how things have gone. Cheerio."

"Cheerio, Roy," Adams whispered. The door closed, and in the silence that followed Adams could hear the tick-tick of his watch as it whipped on the stumbling seconds.

Hilde came out of the sitting-room the instant Adams entered the hall. Although she smiled at him, he did not miss the deep disappointment in her eyes on recognizing him instead of Grenville. Her face was pale and there was a tremor of unsteadiness in her voice.

"We've all been wondering when someone would be coming over. What happened today, Frank? Are you able to tell me?"

Adams had hoped to avoid seeing her, and now her words sent a shock through him, stiffening his features. It was a few seconds before he realized she was talking about the squadron's homecoming that afternoon—a tragedy he had almost forgotten in the events that had followed it.

"They had a special job to do," he muttered. "Something went wrong and they ran into trouble. But Grenville's all right—he's quite safe. . . . I'd forgotten—you'd see it all from here."

Her eyes had closed thankfully on hearing of Grenville's safety. As they opened again Adams saw in

166

them the memory of that blood-drenched afternoon. "Yes," she said unsteadily. "We saw both the planes crash."

In spite of himself, his gaze was drawn to her face. She was lovely . . . lovely and young, too young to be mixed up in anything as hellish as this. Suddenly he felt trapped, felt her blue-grey eyes were getting right into his mind, reading the secret there. . . . The palms of his hands grew sticky. She mustn't find out—it could turn her mind. He had to get away. . . .

"Yes; I believe so."

Adams had been given two hours off duty in preparation for the sleepless night ahead. His thoughts had tormented him, making him feel like a conspirator in a murder, and he had fled the airfield in an effort to escape them. Desperately needing solace, he had made instinctively for the inn; and had he been asked why he would have given the answer that his wife was there. Now he knew he had not come to see Valerie, particularly if she was in the lounge. . . .

"Where's the landlord?" he asked.

Hilde pointed at the kitchen door, which was closed. "The bar has been very quiet tonight as there have been no airmen over. I believe he is making tea."

Adams thanked her and started down the hall. She made a fluttering motion of her hand, stopping him. "Please. Is the Canadian, Gillibrand, safe? Maisie has been worrying about him."

A vision of Gillibrand's frantic face came to Adams. He hesitated, then nodded. "Yes; he's back all right. But he lost his observer today, so naturally he's rather upset."

A spasm of pain crossed the girl's face. "Do you mean the young boy he called Jimmie?"

Adams nodded. "Gillie was pretty broken up about it when I saw him, so you might tip Maisie off. He might be a bit difficult to handle at first."

"I understand and I will tell her," the girl said. She hesitated, then went on quietly; "And Roy is all right? Nothing like that has happened to him?"

Adams felt trapped again. "No; he's quite safe."

"I thought he might have come over for a little

while. Do you know why he has not?" As soon as she had spoken, the girl flushed, then went pale.

"He's had a bad day," Adams muttered. "And he's on duty tonight. Most of us are. I've only come over for an hour myself."

He knew his voice was giving him away. He wanted to turn and run. She gave a helpless shake of her head.

"It is so difficult with Roy. He does not seem to realize how much one worries about him. And one is so helpless, sitting about here. Oh, *denne fryktelige ventingen. . . ."*

It was her breakdown into Norwegian that went through Adams' guard. In some odd way it lent intense expression to her loneliness. Under the shaded bulb of the hall she looked very young and clean and vulnerable, and Adams could bear it no longer. He stumbled away, feeling blindly for the kitchen door.

"I'm sorry. I must see . . . the landlord. Excuse me."

He lurched into the kitchen, closing the door to hide her from his sight. He remembered Grenville's words. Filthy!—even the knowledge made one feel that. Unclean and tainted. . . .

He tried to see round the kitchen. From a shapeless blur the familiar face of Kearns slowly took shape, eyeing him with concern.

"What's the matter, Frank? What's happened, lad?"

Adams tried to speak, but the sound that came from his throat alarmed him. He gritted his teeth and closed his eyes tightly.

"Frank, lad; what is it? Here, sit down."

Adams sat down, gripping the arms of the chair for support. He sat motionless for a full thirty seconds, breathing heavily. Then he looked up at the solicitious face of Kearns.

"You're right, Joe. War is vile. Dear God, it is. Unspeakably vile."

20

The last of the locals said good night to Maisie and closed the bar door. After the low hum of conversation the room seemed very silent. Maisie stared around it and suddenly shivered. She didn't want to be alone—not after what Miss Bergman had told her . . .

She latched the door, and mechanically began collecting up the empty glasses. How could the kid be dead? Why, he'd been in here drinking beer only a couple of nights ago, looking better than she'd seen him looking before. And two weeks before that she'd kissed him up there in her room, and felt his tears soaking through her dress. . . . He couldn't be dead, cold and grey in the soil. People couldn't go as quickly as that. It didn't make sense.

The shock was wearing off now, and dullness giving way to both grief and panic. How was Gillie taking it? Mr. Adams had promised to try to get him to come over, but he might be holding it against her more than ever now. Surely not—surely he could see now how unimportant it had been. Beside men's lives it was nothing . . . But some men didn't see it that way—not men like Gillie.

She put the empty glasses into the sink, turned on the cold water, and let it run over her hot wrists. She was worried about Gillie. He'd thought an awful lot about that boy—he might go right off the deep end if she didn't get a chance to talk to him first. Why couldn't he see she'd done it for him as well as for the kid? Why hadn't he come over already? She was frightened. . . .

Anxiety and hopelessness hung over her like a blanket, dulling her eyes and ears. She did not hear the stumbling footsteps on the drive outside: it was the sound of the latch being tried that awakened her. She looked up in unbelief, her heart pounding madly. Switching off the lights, she ran forward and unlatched the door.

Gillibrand staggered inside, swaying drunkenly in the darkness. Massie closed the door, switched on one of the lights, and led him to a chair. Tearing a scarf away from his throat he dropped into it, breathing heavily.

She knelt down beside him. His cap had fallen back, letting his tangled yellow hair fall over his forehead. Under the scarf his collar was undone, and there was a shadow of beard on his cheeks. He looked very drunk.

She threw her arms around him, pressing her wet face against his shoulder. "Thanks ever so much for comin'. . . . I didn't think you would. I'm sorry, darling. Miss Bergman told me. . . . The poor little kid. . . ."

His huge body suddenly writhed, pulling away from her. She misunderstood and became frantic. "Don't Gillie! It wasn't the way you thought. I did it for you as well as him—honest I did. I was scared for you both. Don't hate me for it, Gillie. Please don't hate me."

He lifted his face, and the agony in it made her catch her breath. She saw now that only his body was drunk, not his mind. He made a sound that could have come from a trapped animal.

"Yeah, the kid's dead. Passed out just after we landed. Can't get used to it, somehow. Seems all wrong. . . ."

She clutched hold of him again, talking as a woman talks to a distressed child, using words of comfort without meaning. Again he pulled away.

"They sent th' kid and me out on a recce job. We got the photos. O.K., but I was sore with him and went lookin' for trouble. Found a minelayer off Bergen and attacked it. An' the kid got hit. . . ."

She did not understand and went on trying to comfort him. He shook his head, ignoring her.

"I got him back, but he passed out a couple of minutes after we landed. He got a few words out—said I had to tell you something."

"Me?" she breathed, suddenly hushed.

"Yeah. He said I had to tell you he wasn't afraid any more.... That's why I came over."

Maisie's black eyes were huge with wonder. "He said that?"

"Yeah. I guess he was sayin' thanks. He was, too."

Tears rolled unchecked down her face at the miracle of it.

"Yeah.... And then I found out that the rest of the boys had gone out to prang some place in Bergen. Bergen, mind you. I saw 'em come back an' that finished me."

The spasm that ran through his body made Maisie apprehensive in spite of what she had just heard. "Why?" she asked.

Gillibrand's blue eyes filled with agony again. "Why? Don't you see—it was the minelayer I attacked that alerted those fighters and put 'em up. If I hadn't gone lookin' for trouble, the boys would have got though O.K."

Her voice sharpened with alarm. "You mustn't tell them, do you hear? You mustn't tell them or they'll court martial you."

He stared dully down at the table. "I ain't goin' to tell them, kid. I've thought about it and decided it wouldn't help them or me. No; that ain't the way out...."

"It wasn't your fault," she said, relieved. "It was just bad luck."

He gave a slow, drunken shake of his head. "You ain't got it yet. I went for that layer because I wanted to punish th' kid. I wanted to hear him squeal; I wanted to frighten and break him up again. Now do you get it?"

Suddenly she drew back as if struck with a whip. "You're drunk," she breathed. "That's why you're saying this." Her voice rose hysterically. "It is the drink, isn't it?"

He lifted his bleary face upwards. "No, honey. I ain't that drunk, although I've been tryin' hard enough. I killed that boy—killed him as sure as if I'd stuck a knife in him."

She shrank back as if from a leper. Her hushed

voice was incredulous. "You mean you killed that decent little kid because of that. . . ."

He saw her expression and lurched to his feet. "I know how you feel. And you're right, too. You helped him to live, an' I helped him to die, and nothin' can change that now. Nothin' at all, because he's dead. I'm gettin' along now, kid. S'long. . . ."

And he stumbled out into the darkness.

Five hours later a party of four men, huddled together for comfort, watched a lone Mosquito heading down the flare-path. With screaming engines, it hurled its bomb-packed fuselage over the airfield fence with an abandonment that made all four men wince. None of them met the other's eyes as they turned away, nor did they speak. Their ears were filled with the sound of those engines, now fading into the silence of the night sky.

21

The dawn broke grey and cold, and the wave-tops below the Mosquito snapped like the fangs of hungry animals. Grenville peered anxiously at the lightening horizon. He was ten minutes late to his E.T.A.—either he was off course or the meteorological forecast had underestimated the strength of the head winds. He hoped fervently it was the latter, although any delay, whatever the cause, would be serious enough if the Focke-Wulfs came up at dawn.

He was flying at just under 1,000 feet and as the light improved he dropped down to one hundred. He dared not go lower in his present condition. Strain and lack of sleep had slowed his reflexes: during the last hour he had kept turning his oxygen on every few minutes to keep himself awake.

It was another five minutes before he sighted land. At first it was a fog bank that appeared, clinging to the sea like a dusty cobweb. As he lifted the Mosquito over it, conical peaks rose from its flat surface like tiny islands. Instantly his eyes lifted to search the sky above. It appeared empty and he gazed down again. The fog patch passed below him, as did the islands it was shrouding, but he knew now that he was not far from the coast. The tiny peaks were part of the Oygarden group, the long fence of islands that lay outside Bergen and the Nordhordland district.

Another line of islands appeared, an unbroken chain this time with banks of fog swirling in their hollows. Grenville leapfrogged over them, banked steeply, and dropped down another fifty feet. He was flying south-south-east now, with the islands guarding his right flank.

Now that his target was drawing near his fatigue left him. Since leaving Sutton Craddock he had lived a nightmare, either fighting off sleep or fighting off thoughts that clawed his mind like torturer's hooks.

Now, with no observer to assist him, he was too busy to think, and was thankful for it. Increasing his boost, he dropped right down on the water, the black and grey islets of rock flashing by in a blur of speed. He caught sight of a fisherman's wooden house, half-a-dozen goats feeding on a patch of bright grass, a clump of shrub, a cluster of windswept trees. . . .

A larger island appeared . . . a small jetty . . . two fishing-boats at anchor . . . a hamlet . . . a woman waving an apron from the front door of a house. . . .

Two minutes more and land soared up on either side of him. Petrol tanks swept by . . . a group of large, camouflaged buildings . . . three tall, smoking chimneys. Not 200 yards from his port wing-tip a freighter was making her way up channel, her bow wash white against the shadowy sea. Grenville caught a glimpse of a brace of multiple pom-poms on her boat deck before his speed swept him by. No shots were fired and thirty seconds later a shoulder of land hid the ship from sight.

The channel broadened as a tributary flowed into it from the east, then narrowed again. The land on either side rose higher, became mountainous with denser vegetation of scrub and pines. Houses became more frequent, typical Norwegian country houses with wooden frames and high-sloping roofs. Grenville was in a fjord now and the water below him was calmer. His slipstream shivered a wake behind him as he streaked not 30 feet above it.

He drew back his stick and a town flashed below him. That would be Garnes. Garnes, and not a shot fired at him yet! He made a little altitude and scanned the sky above. Still no sign of fighters! He went down again, his eyes probing the green, birch-covered mountainside on his right.

He found the valley and banked steeply into it. Trees flashed under him, mountains towered on either side. The Isdalen Pass! Rocks . . . bright grass . . . trees . . . then a long sheet of water, Svartediket! The green-wooded mountain on his left was Ulrikken. A cold, sadistic voice inside his mind suddenly began to mock him. "Are you wondering what it feels like to be an executioner? Well, you'll soon know. You're nearly there now. Nearly there . . ." He tried to blank his mind to it. The woods and water of the pass flashed by. . . . "Nearly there," the voice mocked again. "Nearly there."

Quite abruptly he was there. The pass fell away and Bergen, beautiful in its cradle of seven mountains, lay below him. Opposite was Lovstakken, a long massive ridge that ran to the U-boat pens south of the city. Below was a broad lake—what had Adams called it? The Store Lungegardsvann. It was dotted with small boats of all types. On its far side was a bridge—that would be the Strombro. Watch that—there were flak posts on it! On this side of the lake were railway lines and the station. Flak there too, although none of it had started up yet. . . .

He had banked steeply to starboard on leaving the pass and was over the centre of the city before he got all his landmarks. Behind him he caught sight of the small octagonal lake Adams had mentioned. It was near the railway station, and behind it was a piece of waste ground. . . .

Gritting his teeth, he threw the Mosquito into a sharp 180-degree turn to port. Bergen, clean-looking in the early morning light, swam in a dizzy arc under his vertical wingtip. When he straightened out he was flying inland again along the Lovstakken range, with Bergen on his port side. From the corner of his eye he caught sight of other landmarks: the Nautical School in the Nordnes Parken, the green roof of the National Theatre, the wide tree-lined avenue of the Ole Bulls Plasse. . . . But he needed no markers now. His target was in sight, standing alone like a diseased thing on the waste land between the two lakes.

The first flak appeared, coming up from the docks, a red, yellow and green chain that seemed about to hit him between the eyes before curving away. As if it were a signal, flak opened up from all directions—not for nothing was Bergen considered to be one of the best defended ports in occupied Europe! Within seconds his Mosquito was bracketed by a cloud of bursting shells, making him take violent evasive action.

As he approached the Strombro Bridge, a fan-shaped cluster of white bursts opened out dead ahead. How could he make a run-in across the lake with all this stuff lined up. . . ? With these flak posts on the bridge and the others on the railway opposite, they'd be able to catch him in a cross-fire. He wouldn't have a chance. . . .

He made a split-second decision. Switching on his gun-sight, he dived straight at the bridge, opening fire with both cannon and machine-guns. Tracer came upwards in blinding sheets—he felt he was flying right into the barrels of the murderous guns. Just as he believed himself finished, panic-stricken grey shapes rose from the gun-pits and fled before the fury of his attack. His shells burst among them, mowing them down. Three men, seeing the flame-spitting thunder-bolt howling down on them, leaped straight from the bridge into the water below.

Drenched in sweat, Grenville pulled the Mosquito out of her dive and sent her rocketing up the slopes of Ulrikken. The ferocity of the fire from the bridge had now greatly diminished: he had to press home his attack before the crews were rallied.

The Mosquito rolled over on the top of her climb and came plunging down again, the tight skin on her wings and fuselage drumming with speed. Behind Grenville the green slopes of Ulrikken streamed dizzily away. He was travelling at well over 400 m.p.h. when he pulled out over the lake, lowering the Mosquito down until her belly nearly touched the water. He opened his bomb doors, clicked down his selector switches, and fixed the building at the far end of the lake dead in the center of his gunsight. Then he had nothing to do but wait. In the few endless seconds that his Mosquito took to flash over the shivering water, the voice in his mind began torturing him again.

"It won't be long now. Just a few more seconds—if you get through, of course. . . . I wonder if he'll guess it's you that is killing him. . . ."

The accuracy of the guns alongside the railway was terrifying. Three posts got Grenville's range at once.

176

The water below him seethed as shells tore it into spray, blurring his windshield and hissing into steam on his red-hot engines. White puffs enveloped him, interspersed by black ones as the murderous 37 mms. joined in. A shell went clean through his bomb hatch without exploding, ricochetting off a 500-lb. bomb. Another one burst near the starboard engine, making the Mosquito wince as shrapnel tore through its wing. A blinding flash came from the instrument panel, followed by an explosion that almost shattered Grenville's eardrums. There was the smell of cordite and burning rubber . . . sparks spluttering from a damaged contact box. Outside, tracer soared through the smoke like coloured streamers, graceful to watch and death to touch.

Grenville was hunched down in his seat to gain what protection he could from his armour plating. His legs were affected by an intense nervous convulsion and his toes clenched up inside his flying boots. He had to get through . . . he had to get through. . . . He gritted the words over and over as the flak thunder increased around him. "Of course you must," the devil voice jeered back. "An executioner shouldn't be late for his appointment. . . ."

The building was huge in Grenville's gunsight when a party of black-uniformed figures began pouring out from it. Instantly loathing drove all other emotions from Grenville's mind. Here were the bullies he had always hated: here were Bergman's torturers, running for their lives! He kicked the rudder bar, brought them into his sights, and fired a long vicious burst, his thumb tight down on the button. The Mosquito shuddered under the tremendous kicking recoil. Grenville sawed on the rudder bar, hosing the stream of shells and bullets among the screaming men. The effect was murderous. The earth itself was churned into furrows and men were thrown into shapeless heaps of bloody flesh and charred rags.

The building swung back into Grenville's sights again. His 20mm. shells smashed through its wooden walls, doing enormous damage. Two hundred yards . . .

one-fifty yards . . . the lake fell away, he was over the waste land now. One hundred yards . . . fifty. . . . Now! He pressed the bomb release and jerked back on the stick. The Mosquito screamed upwards, missing the roof of the building by less than ten feet.

The four bombs, tail-fused and falling horizontally, hit the ground and bounded forward like flat stones on water. They smashed through the wall of the wooden building as if it had been cardboard and disappeared within.

The wide avenue of the Ole Bulls Plasse streamed under Grenville like a green ribbon, ignoring the vengeful flak that was still following him, he banked steeply to look back. He was counting to himself . . . seven . . . eight . . . nine . . . ten. . . .

At eleven there were four simultaneous explosions that disintegrated the building, hurled it upwards in a mushroom of red-cored smoke and splintered wood.

Although the flak by the bridge would be reorganized now, Grenville was prepared to make a second attack for Bergman's sake if anything was left standing. But there was nothing on the waste ground but four blackened craters and a blazing pile of debris. No one could have survived that holocaust.

Reaction hit him as he stared down. His stomach retched, jerking his body against his harness. His eyes felt as if nails were being driven through them into his brain. The physical pain he welcomed; it was an ally against the worse pain within.

It was the instinct of self-preservation plus his innate flying habits that saved him at that moment. Before making his attack he had noticed patches of fog hanging round the southern slopes of Lovstakken and among the fjords and islands beyond. Now, without conscious thought, he flew over Lovstakken, dived down among these patches, and worked his way round their fringes towards the coast.

He was only just in time. The hundreds of flak bursts that pock-marked the sky had barely lost their separate identity before the first flight of Focke-Wulfs came howling in. With snarling engines they darted

178

over the city like dogs sniffing for a scent. Then, at a given signal, they hurled themselves over Lovstakken and into the chase. The vengeful roar of their engines followed the Mosquito out to sea and faded with it.

22

It came again, and in some odd way Grenville knew it was a nightmare. Yet the knowledge only heightened his feeling of trapped terror. He was coming in to land after his raid on Bergen. His undercarriage would not lock down, the hydraulic mechanism had been damaged by shrapnel. Nor would it fully retract, which meant the crooked wheels were a menace to a belly landing.

He thought for a moment of doing some steep dives in an effort to force the undercart down, but his tired mind rejected the idea at once. The shattered Mosquito might disintegrate and in any case he was weary . . . weary. . . . He had to get down before the black cloud floating at the corners of his eyes closed over and blinded him. There wasn't much time left.

He heard his tired voice speaking to Control, "I'm coming in for a belly landing. Please stand by. Switching off. . . ."

The field swam dizzily before his eyes as he banked up-wind. The Mosquito answered sluggishly; shrapnel had sprung a hinge in the starboard aileron, making lateral control difficult. To make certain he would not be trapped in a flaming coffin, he reached out to jettison the escape hatch but it would not budge. He tugged again but it was tightly jammed and he was tired. . . .

A vision flashed in front of him as he dropped lower. Priestman piling up yesterday morning—the blackened scars in the grass lay dead ahead. From the corner of his eye he saw the crash wagon and ambulance following his shadow along the runway.

God, the field seemed to be coming up fast! His reactions were slow, deceiving him. He switched off both engines and pulled the stick back. Easy, easy, don't let her stall. Hold it. . . . Hold it. . . . Now!

The Mosquito bounced a full fifteen feet, nearly snapping Grenville's neck with shock. The wooden fuselage buckled and splintered like a bamboo cane, the wings crumpled like papier mâché. Another tremendous jerk and this time Grenville was flung forward, his harness snapping with the strain. He managed to half-cover his face with his hands before it was smashed into the gunsight. There was a sickening pain in his lower jaw . . . the taste of blood . . . the feel of a broken tooth on his tongue. . . .

Then only pain and silence. No, not silence. The hiss of petrol vapourizing on the white-hot engines. Get me out! For God's sake, get me out!

Frantic hands suddenly pulled at him, bringing a shock of pain through his head. Blackness for a moment, then a vague, confused picture of the shattered Mosquito twenty yards away with firemen playing pumps and extinguishers on her. His last impression before unconsciousness was that of a thin black column of smoke rising from the disembowelled port engine. . . .

He knew what the nightmare was going to do to him, and tried desperately to awake. But the thing held him tightly, forcing him to watch. The column of smoke belched and burst into a red-cored explosion. Now he was over Bergen, looking down on the thing he had done, seeing the four smoking craters and the heap of flaming wreckage. The fire seemed to reach up and burn every corner of his cringing mind.

He awoke then, and soaked in cold sweat lay trying to identify his surroundings. But his mind was still too dazed: the figures in the grey mist that swirled around him were out of focus and unreal. He tried to call to them, but his lips were still and would not move. A few minutes later darkness and the nightmare swooped down on him again.

Just after 1600 hours that same Thursday Davies entered the Intelligence Room. There was a peaked look about his sharp face, and the usual briskness was absent from his movements. He motioned to Adams to remain seated, and tossing his cap on the table, sat down opposite him.

"I've just come from seeing Grenville," he said, catching the anxious question in Adams' eyes. "They've put him in Stanhope Hospital in Highgate. He'll be all right in a few days. He got a nasty crack on the head and face when his harness snapped, and a wrenched shoulder in the bargain. The head injury is the worst—there was slight concussion and he's been a bit delirious—but they say none of it is serious. Anyway, I told them to keep him there a few days. The rest won't do him any harm."

Adams nodded his relief. "He was lucky. I never thought he'd come out of it alive."

"His type are hard to kill," Davies said with some pride.

"Particularly when they don't much care about living." Adams had not meant to say it—the words slipped out—and his plump face turned crimson when Davies's eyes fixed themselves resentfully on him.

"I didn't know the rest of the story when I ordered him out. And it might have been better if you hadn't told it to us last night. I felt enough of a murderer as things were."

"I should have kept it to myself, I know," Adams muttered.

The aggressiveness left Davies's voice at once. "I don't blame you. Some things are better shared. I don't suppose I'd have been able to keep it quiet myself." His tone changed, became awed. "My God: the guts of the man. He'll get a bar to his D.S.O. If I've got any say in it."

Adams winced at the suggestion. "It might be better to leave that for a while, sir. I'm pretty certain he wouldn't want it—not for this."

Davies nodded reluctantly. "I suppose you're right. But it seems damnable there isn't some reward one can give him."

"Have you seen the camera films yet?" Adams asked.

Davies showed some of his old spirit. "They were the first thing I went to see when I got back. God, man, aren't they terrific? The way he slaughtered those devils as they came running out. . . ."

Adams nodded. He had seen the films as soon as they were developed. Grenville's hate had come out through them, holding him in horrified fascination.

182

"It's a pity he had no way of photographing the destruction of the target," he said.

Davies lowered his voice. "The Brigadier got confirmation two hours ago. That's what I came to tell you."

Adams knew his face had paled. He tried to keep his voice steady. "Was it completely successful?"

Davies held his eyes grimly. "Yes. Completely."

"Does everything go on as before, then? Or don't you know yet?"

Davies hesitated a moment before replying. "The Brigadier seems optimistic again. None of the patriots has been arrested yet, so it doesn't look as if anybody talked, God bless 'em. Yes; if nothing else happens we shall go on as planned. We must; we've no option."

"Isn't all this damage to our planes going to delay us?"

Davies picked up his cap and rose to his feet. "It's been a blow, but we've got to get over it somehow. Barrett must keep everyone working until they're airworthy again. I don't know the exact date we're supposed to go, but for some reason or other it has to be before the end of May." His voice was grave. "After that the Brigadier reckons our chances of success are greatly reduced, perhaps gone altogether. So we've no choice but to be ready."

Grenville awoke from his doze and stared round the room. The walls were cream-washed, sterile and blank. A small cabinet stood alongside his bed, its glass surface littered with bottles. A polished electric stove stood near the half-open door. The air held the faint smell of antiseptics.

He lifted a hand to his head. They had removed some of the bandages, but his jaw and mouth were still bound up, making it impossible to have a smoke. He shifted restlessly. Three days of this was more than enough. He'd have another go at that confounded doctor when he came tonight. . . .

Something tapped on the window, and his eyes moved sharply towards it. At first nothing was visible but a rectangular patch of sunlit blue sky. Then, as he

183

watched, the bough of a flowering almond moved across the glass, tapping gently as it passed by. It had no leaves, just a thin branch and a cluster of pink blossoms that waved like a magic wand in front of the blue sky.

Grenville watched it in fascination. The ward sister's voice outside the door made him start. "Yes; you can go in; he is awake. But only ten minutes, please. And don't expect him to talk to you—his face is still bandaged up."

"Thank you."

Grenville's breath stopped at the sound of the second voice. His head jerked sidewards, then he lay motionless, only his eyes moving as she approached his bedside. She was wearing a grey, slim-fitting coat with a blue scarf at her throat, and was carrying a large leather bag. A sunbeam made her uncovered hair shine with golden light. A faint perfume came from her, driving back the smell of the antiseptics.

His panic-stricken mind searched desperately for comfort. Her appearance, her smile . . . she could not know yet. Thank God for that. . . .

"I had to come to see you," she said, as the door closed, leaving them alone. "Frank told me where you were."

Damn Adams. He wanted to close his eyes to save himself looking at her, but could not. She took three packets of twenty cigarettes from the bag she was carrying and laid them on the cabinet alongside him.

"It is very little," she said apologetically, "but they were all I could buy."

To get them she would have had to queue up at half the tobacconists in Highgate. Don't make it worse, please! Don't do things for me. . . ! Grenville wanted to beg her to leave, but could force nothing from his bandaged mouth. His eyes, the only part of his face visible, stared up at her mutely. She misunderstood their expression and looked anxious.

"Frank said you were not seriously injured—I had not expected to see you so bandaged. Are you in much pain?"

He shook his head. Her grave, blue-grey eyes did

not lighten. "For a while I almost hoped you were more seriously hurt, because then you would not have had to fly for a long, long time. . . ." She smiled at him sadly. "Why could you not have broken an arm or a leg, Roy? It would have made me very happy."

As if ashamed of her seriousness, she flushed and took a large bunch of daffodils from the bag at her feet. She went over to a water bowl on the window-ledge and began arranging them.

"They brighten a room," she said defensively. "I picked them this morning from Mr. Kearns' garden. You should see his fruit trees—the sun has brought out all the blossom."

He caught sight of the pink almond blossom again, nodding above her shining head, and emotion struck him like a blow. He lay half-dazed as she told him more about the innkeeper's garden.

She finished arranging the flowers and turned back to his bedside, smiling. "You know, Roy, it is rather nice for me to do all the talking and to know that you cannot argue with me. It makes the words come easier, somehow."

The ward sister tapped on the door at that moment. Hilde's face saddened at the reminder. She hesitated, then laid a hand on his forehead. Grenville lay motionless, hardly breathing, not daring to think.

"I'm coming to see you again as soon as I can," she said. "They say I may come on Tuesday."

Grenville moved his head sidewards, like a dazed boxer trying to avoid a blow. Three more days—she would know by then! Her voice came from far away, yet with the purity of a bronze bell.

"Somehow it is easier to ask you now. Roy, when you are better, please do not be long in coming to see me. It is so very lonely without you. Good-bye. *Gud velsigne deg.*"

She kissed his forehead, then ran quickly from the room. Grenville closed his eyes. Something like acid was running into them, blinding him.

23

Two mornings later the Dispersal Hut alongside the Southern perimeter of the airfield was unusually quiet —only one Mosquito standing ready for take-off with filled tanks and loaded guns. She was the outcome of an order from Group for 633 to provide a plane for meteorological duties.

With the rest of the squadron still feverishly licking its wounds, Barrett had had no option but to cancel the dawn training flights. Six of his aircraft were undergoing major repairs in the hangars (where ground crews had been working day and night since the battle over Bergen), and the rest were dispersed around the field with cowled engines, waiting for daylight to bring another swarm of mechanics to attend to their repairs. Nevertheless, Barrett was hoping to resume training in four days' time. Townsend, the Maintenance Officer, thought his mind had gone.

Shortly before dawn a five-hundredweight truck from the Transport Section pulled up outside the hut with a grunt of brakes. Two men, Gillibrand and his new observer, leapt from the tailboard, sparks showering from their cigarettes as they landed on the tarmac. Both were wearing flying suits and harness. They pulled down their parachutes, then Gillibrand thumped a huge hand against the tin side of the truck. "O.K., Mac. Take it away."

The yawning driver threw in his gear and the five-hundredweight lumbered away. Gillibrand made for the hut without a word. The observer shivered and followed him. A cold, gusty wind was blowing, rocking the Mosquito's wings. It was growing lighter and objects began appearing out of the darkness: the sandbagged shelter near the hut, the nearby gun-post, the shadowy outline of the Control Tower.

A chink of yellow light shone under the door of the

hut. Gillibrand pushed his way inside. It was warmer in there: someone had lit the stove which was giving off clouds of sulphurous smoke. Above it hung a naked electric bulb, which was shining down on a group of mechanics who were warming their hands round mugs of tea. They looked around at the newcomers and muttered their greetings, their sleep-encrusted eyes a little wary of Gillibrand. Once Gillie had been one of the boys but since he had lost his observer he wanted watching. . . .

The Canadian tossed his parachute on a chair, then turned to the mechanics. "Well; what about some char?"

The diminutive corporal in charge of the fitters jumped up, took two mugs down from a shelf, and filled them with black tea. He slopped in condensed milk from a half-opened tin and handed the mugs to the two men.

"Chilly out 'ere this mornin', sir," he offered Gillibrand.

Gillibrand nodded without speaking, lifted the mug to his lips and drained it. The naked light, with its uncompromising shadows, made him look a grim and formidable figure. His heavy brows shadowed his eyes, sinking them into his skull. Lines showed round his nose and mouth, and a bristle of beard on his massive jaw added to the grim-visaged effect. His young sergeant observer, just posted to the squadron, looked subdued and unhappy alongside him.

Gillibrand handed the mug back to the corporal, then jerked a thumb towards the door. "You'd better be gettin' her started up, hadn't you?"

The corporal looked surprised and glanced down at his watch. "She's been warmed up, sir. I thought you wasn't due off for another quarter of an hour."

"Never mind. Get her runnin' now. I want an early start."

The corporal nodded and gave an order to two of his men. They put their mugs down and went out sullenly. The corporal handed the D.I. to Gillibrand.

"She's O.K., sir. We've given her a good check."

Gillibrand barely glanced at the form before shoving

it back. He dropped on a bench, his eyes brooding on the smoking stove. The observer, looking embarrassed, began fishing inside his flying suit for cigarettes. The corporal offered him one in sympathy before going out to his men. As he left the hut the first of the Mosquito's Merlins coughed and fired.

The sergeant hesitated, then followed him outside. It was almost daylight now. The eastern horizon was a blaze of red fire, shot with the black smoke of clouds. At the distant end of the field a row of poplars stood out against it in dark relief. The second engine fired, throwing mud and pebbles against the side of the hut. The cold blast made the sergeant shiver again.

Gillibrand came out of the hut, carrying both parachutes. He tossed one at the sergeant and jerked his thumb at the Mosquito. The sergeant stamped on his cigarette and followed him. He was half-way to the plane when the Canadian halted, lifting his head like a Great Dane sniffling danger.

The next moment the sergeant saw them himself— Messerschmidt 110's, two lines of them, one line coming straight down the airfield perimeter towards the dispersal hut. . . . As his eyes froze on them, the nose of the leading plane lit up with stabbing flashes.

A huge hand grabbed his arm, he was almost lifted off his feet, and a moment later found himself slumped inside the sand-bagged shelter with Gillibrand alongside him. Another second and the startled mechanics tumbled over the parapet and dropped beside them.

The noise of the engines and cannon fire came in brutal waves, hammering the men down among the sandbags. Tracer whiplashed over them and smashed into the nearby gun-post. A thin scream sounded over the din. Gillibrand's face was murderous as he glared over the parapet.

The strategy of the 110's was already clear. Their first target was not the planes or the airfield, but the gun-posts on its perimeter. They were making their attack in two lines astern, one line strafing the south boundary posts, the other line attacking the north ones. The unfortunate gun crews, with a year's immunity from attack behind them, were caught completely napping.

Only one Hispano opened up, and its gunner died not five seconds later with a bullet in his throat.

With the skill of rehearsal behind the manoeuvre, the two lines of 110's completed their attack on the two boundaries, swung in a tight arc, and made for the remaining east and west posts. Here, with a few seconds of warning to prepare them, the gunners put up more resistance, and one 110 sheered off, trailing black smoke. But lack of battle practice was all too evident, and the tough 110's were allowed to press their attacks right into the muzzles of the guns. Post after post was blasted and destroyed.

Gillibrand saw the outcome. With all flak cover gone, the airfield would be wide open. And the Messerschmidts were carrying more than long-range tanks under their slim bellies. . . . It would be good-bye Mr. Chipps—planes, crews, erks, the lot. . . .

He leapt over the sandbagged parapet, bent double, and ran for the Mosquito. Running under its wings he snatched away the chocks, then heaved himself up into the fuselage and into his seat. No time to turn upwind, no time to use the runway. . . . With over 3,000 revs, full boost, and flaps right down, he released the brakes and gave the Mosquito her head. She bucked and reared like a maddened horse, but somehow he kept her nose straight. Through his windshield he saw the 110's were making another attack on two gunposts that were holding out stubbornly. His tight lips moved. Just a few seconds more, boys. . . . That's all I want. A chance to pay back. Give it to me, boys. . . .

The Mosquito's tail was up now and her controls lightening. But a Messerschmidt saw him, banked steeply, and came in like a winged devil. There was nothing Gillibrand could do but hold on and pray. The 110's height saved him: its pilot had no air space to jockey into position. He could only take a split-second, full-radius deflection in the hope his cone of fire would take care of any error.

It nearly did. The Mosquito's tailplanes were riddled like a sieve, only a miracle saving the control wires. Baffled, the 110's pilot gave the alarm over his R/T and went into a climbing turn for another attack. The rest of the bandits, their job on the flak posts completed, turned to blast the lone Mosquito from their path.

But Gillibrand was airborne now, back in his element. With one wing-tip clipping the grass he turned into the astonished 110's, scattering them right and left to avoid collision. In the confusion he settled on the tail of one of them and opened fire with both cannon and machine guns. At point-blank range his fire did terrible damage, shattering the tail planes and ripping open the fuselage like a tin-can. The 110 rolled over and plunged into a clump of trees. Blazing petrol swept over them, setting them aflame like giant torches.

Putting his weight on his stick, Gillibrand reversed his turn, his Mosquito skidding round like a car on ice. The pale-blue underbelly of a 110 appeared from nowhere in his sights. He was close enough to see the blue oxide flames from its exhausts and the patched scar from some earlier encounter under one wing. Everything seemed to slow down for a second, the 110's propellers waving like arms as it struggled to escape. The luminous graticule of Gillibrand's sight moved deliberately to a spot between its wings. He steadied his controls—then pressed his gun button exultantly.

The clear picture blurred and disintegrated before his eyes. Only a violent jerk on his stick saved him from collision. As he plunged through the cloud of oily smoke interspersed with flaming wreckage, the acrid smell of it came to his nostrils. He glanced sidewards, saw the attack had led him some distance from the airfield and that one or two of the 110's were steadying themselves to make a bombing run. With a growl he rolled the Mosquito over and went plunging back.

Down below all was confusion. Men were crouched behind shelters, lying under beds, gaping from windows. Others were bawling orders no one could hear for the tremendous racket of engines and cannon fire. Over in the inn all its inhabitants in various stages of undress, had invaded Hilde's bedroom; and, blind to their own danger, were standing alongside her; craning their necks to follow Gillibrand's fantastic manoeuvres.

There was even more confusion among the Messerschmidt's. The R/T channel was swamped by cursing voices. The Squadron Commander was growing frantic with anxiety. The attack had been timed to seconds; already his planes should have dropped their bombs and been heading back for home. Spitfires would have been alerted minutes ago. . . . But no one could make a bombing run for this madman: he broke up every attack before it could be made. The Commander shouted his call sign above the din and gave his orders. . . .

Messerschmidts closed in on either side of Gillibrand, trying to box him in. The Canadian's answer was simply to turn into the plane outside his starboard wing. Its terrified pilot broke away, almost crashing into a telegraph pole. His nerves were further shattered by the burst of shells Gillibrand sent after him which missed his port engine by inches.

The battle raged on for another thirty seconds with 110 after 110 trying to make a run-in on its target, and Gillibrand foiling each attempt with complete disregard for his life. Some bombs did fall, but they were released without aim and did little damage. The very madness of Gillibrand's manoeuvres made them successful, bewildering the enemy pilots. Yet the odds were so great there could have been only one outcome had a different noise not made itself heard through the colossal din. A small, shark-like body leapt over the distant poplars and fastened itself with incredible venom to the tail of one of the Messerschmidts. Another followed it, and yet another. Spitfires! Hundreds of watching eyes below glowed their relief.

The German Squadron Commander gave orders to break off the action. But he was a brave man, and goaded with the knowledge that only one plane had stood between him and success. He at least could make some atonement. Snatching his opportunity in the confusion, he dived over the poplars and headed straight for the distant hangars.

Gillibrand, watching for nothing else, turned on a wing-tip and dived after him. The slim body of the 110 grew in his gunsight—500 yards . . . 400 . . .

350. . . . He pressed his gun button and heard only the clank of breechblocks and the whine of compressed air. He pressed again. No use! His ammunition was finished.

The 110 had levelled out and was making her run-in. Gillibrand was not fifty feet above her. He could see the pilot clearly, looking like a huge insect in his goggles as he stared backwards. In the nose his observer would be lying over his bombsight, waiting with his thumb on the button. . . .

Everything slowed down once more for Gillibrand, and in the early morning light everything became very clear. The plane, with its huge black crosses and turning propellers, the hangars beyond it, and the Nissen huts of the airmen. . . . And beyond them the familiar road leading to the inn with its flowers, its white apple trees, with Maisie. . . . Spring below . . . bittersweet at that moment beyond all understanding.

One last look, and then Gillibrand pushed his stick forward. He hit the 110 between the tailplane and cockpit, cutting its fuselage almost in two. Locked together, both planes spun into the ground not seventy yards from the Control Tower. There was a sheet of flame, followed by an explosion that showered bricks and mud as far as the men's billets by the road. No court martial was needed for Gillibrand now.

24

Davies could not wait a minute longer to ask his question. "Before you go on, sir—doesn't this attack mean they've found out everything?"

The Brigadier's grey eyes rose from his table. "No. Not by any means."

"But surely it must. There hasn't been an attack of that strength on one of our British airfields for over a year. And this was no hit-or-miss affair. It had been carefully rehearsed beforehand."

It was at moments like these that the different temperaments of the two men, so often complementary, fell out of step. Davies was wishing the Brigadier wouldn't be so damned tight-lipped and stoical, and the Brigadier was regretting Davies's dramatic instinct that could never resist discussing all the possibilities of a rich situation aloud—a habit doubly irritating on occasions such as this when he might possibly be right.

"I agree the attack was planned and that it was no coincidence 633 received it," the Brigadier conceded. "But that doesn't mean the enemy knows very much. Look at it this way—they saw you try to raid Bergen and would recognize your squadron markings. If they didn't know then what your target was, they would know the next morning when Grenville went in alone. After that they would guess you had some connection with Bergman. But if Bergman and Ericson didn't talk —and we've no reason to believe they did—how would they learn any details? Their suspicions are aroused, that is all, and the stakes are so high that they've played safe by trying to wipe you out."

Davies shifted uneasily in his chair. "I'm not sure they don't know more. I can't see them risking a whole squadron of 110's just on a vague suspicion."

The Brigadier was silent for a moment. "There is a possibility they may know more, of course," he said quietly. "But what are we to do—you know the impor-

193

tance of the target as well as I. So far none of the patriots has been arrested, and they've got a leader to take Bergman's place. So what alternative have we got but to carry on as before?"

Davies snapped his fingers, impatient with himself. "I'd forgotten about the patriots. Of course, that's proof enough Jerry doesn't know very much." His tone became brisk as he tried to destroy any impression of pessimism he might have created. "As long as they are there to silence those flak posts, we'll prang the thing all right. Sorry—I see your point now."

"What is the latest news from the squadron?" the Brigadier asked.

"Barrett's hoping to have the kites serviceable by the weekend. Crew replacements are his biggest headache because altogether he lost more in killed and wounded than he had in reserve. Obviously we can't give any new men the training the others have had, but we'll do our best with them. I've organized it with Barrett that where a replacement comes into a plane he has a trained man alongside him. And as fast as the kites become serviceable the new men will be taken up to Scotland and put through the drill. By Monday at the latest we hope to start the full squadron flights again."

"Have replacements arrived yet for the planes you have lost?"

"A.T.A. tell me they'll be along at any time. That top priority order did the trick, of course."

The Brigadier leaned forward. "And what about Grenville? How is he getting along?"

"He'll be there all right," Davies told him. "He's back with the squadron now."

The Brigadier showed his surprise. "Already? But I thought you'd given orders for him to remain a week in hospital."

"I did," Davies muttered, shifting uneasily again. "But it seemed Miss Bergman went to the hospital to visit him." He saw a shocked look appear in the Brigadier's eyes. "She didn't know about her brother at the time—as you know, the wire only arrived yesterday—but apparently she told Grenville she was going to pay

194

him another visit shortly. He couldn't stand it, I suppose, and returned to camp. In the circumstances I thought it better for the Station M.O. to attend to him. He's got the bandages off now, in any case."

The Brigadier nodded slowly. "How is he taking it?"

Davies shrugged. "It's difficult to tell—you know Grenville. But Adams thinks it has hit him hard."

"Hard enough to affect his morale?"

The sharpness of Davies's reply betrayed his resentment of a war in which courage had to be evaluated as coldly as this. "I shouldn't worry about his morale. He'll attack the bloody thing because it is his duty to attack it. After what he has done already, I don't think anyone should have any doubts about that."

The strain was telling on all of them, the Brigadier thought. It was as well there was not much longer to wait. . . .

"No one could admire Grenville and his boys more than I," he said quietly. "His raid on Bergen, that magnificent sacrifice of Gillibrand's yesterday: everything is quite beyond any praise of mine. But you know the importance of this raid—at the risk of appearing soulless we can't afford to overlook anything, particularly the morale of the man who is going to lead it."

Davies was quite disarmed by this reply. "I don't think you've anything to worry about on that score. He'll probably try all the harder to prang it for all the misery it has caused. I know I would."

Satisfied, the Brigadier drew Davies towards a large contour model of the Svartfjord and district that lay on the end of his table.

"This model has been built up from photographs received from your men and from patriots on the other side. Here is exactly what I want your lads to do. . . ."

Less than an hour later the Brigadier shoved aside a pile of papers and looked up at Davies. "Well, that's everything. The contour model and the photographs will be sent to Adams under armed escort this afternoon. Let Barrett and Grenville see them, and tell them and Adams all I have just told you. But not a word to another soul until the briefing. Tell Adams to keep this model out of sight and to have a security guard round his office day and night. I think, to make quite certain no one gets a look at it, the four of you should take turns in sleeping there."

Davies nodded. "What about these special bombs? When do we get them?"

"We can't give them to you yet, because the moment they go into your bomb-store your armourers will become curious and start talking. They'll arrive the night before the raid and go straight on to your aircraft. It won't matter then who talks, because, in addition to your own security safeguards, we shall send a crowd of our men down for the night."

"And you want us to commence our full squadron training flights again as soon as all the kites are serviceable, and to keep them up every dawn until the day of the raid?"

"That's right. Then no one outside the airfield can guess which morning is zero hour."

Davies felt his heart thumping excitedly in his wrists and ankles. He took a deep breath. "And when is zero hour? That's the one thing you haven't told me?"

"They'll go in on the 14th," the Brigadier said quietly. "At 0645 hours to be precise. That will give the patriots just enough daylight to do their job first. If all goes well, the gunposts will be in their hands by 0645. The rest of it will be up to your boys. For all our sakes, let's hope they do a good job."

Davies stared around for a calendar. He eventually found one on the wall directly opposite him. The high-pitched sound of his own voice startled him. "The 14th! But that's only nine days off!"

"We can't afford to leave it a day longer." The Brigadier paused, not for effect but to compose his own anxious voice. "Well, can you give your new men enough training in that time? Are you going to be ready?"

Anticipation of the battle drove away Davies's doubts. He was quivering now like an aggressive bantam cock. "Don't worry, sir. One way or another, we'll make it!"

"Hey; you up there! McTyre!"

McTyre, the old sweat, wedged on the wing along-side the stripped-down engine of a Mosquito, poked his long, sharp nose cautiously over the leading edge. He saw the bow-legged, unwelcome figure of Corporal Martin, one of the S.W.O.'s underlings, leaning on his bicycle below, and instantly his mind, allergic to M.P.'s, began searching for a reason. Unable to find one, he replied truculently.

"Whatcha want?"

"You! You've got to report to the S.W.O.'s office at 1400 hours sharp. That's in fifteen minutes."

"What for? Can't yer see I'm busy?"

The Corporal grinned sardonically. "Not 'alf as busy as you'll be after Bert's seen you. You're in trouble, mate."

"What've I done this time?"

"Bert made an inspection of the billets this mornin'. He found your bed not made up, fag-ends all over the floor, and half a bottle of beer in your locker."

McTyre gaped down incredulously. "Yer mean he's been snoopin' round the billets at a time like this. . . ."

"Gotta keep discipline," the corporal pointed out.

"Discipline!" McTyre nearly choked. He waved a scandalized arm round the perimeters of the airfield where other Mosquitoes were being repaired. "Look at 'em all! Shot to 'ell! How many of 'em would ever fly again if it wasn't for us? Here we are, workin' day and night, workin' ourselves to skin and bone, and he goes worryin' about a fag-end and an empty beer bottle. . . ."

"Half empty," the corporal insisted.

"Here we are, riskin' our lives out 'ere, never knowing when them 110's are coming again, and he goes muckin' about in our billets. . . . It's terrible. Ain't it terrible?" McTyre demanded of the young, chubby face that suddenly popped up at the other side of the fuselage.

The young erk swallowed, nodded, saw the corporal frown, and popped down out of sight again. McTyre shook his head in bitter disgust.

"It's terrible! Makes yer wonder what yer're fightin' for. Snoopin' about while men are riskin' their lives, crawlin' around looking for fag-ends. . . . What's the matter with you all? Can't yer find anythin' better to do?"

The corporal saw the dignity of his own office was now coming under fire and took swift retaliatory action.

"That's enough of that. It ain't my fault you've got dirty habits. You mind what you're sayin', see."

"Dirty habits," McTyre growled, wiping his oily hands down the legs of his overalls. "You wouldn't 'ave the guts to say that if you didn't have two tapes on your arm."

But the corporal was not staying any longer to argue. He threw his bow legs over his bicycle and started away. "1400 hours," he shouted back. "And don't be late."

McTyre slid down the wing and rolled off. He was joined a few seconds later by the young A.C.2. "Well; what d'you think of that?" McTyre demanded. "See what I mean now about Bert?"

The erk nodded. McTyre pulled a blackened fag-end from the top pocket of his overalls, looked round furtively, then lit it. "A bastard through and through," he grunted. "I ain't ever told you about him and the duck, 'ave I?"

"Duck?" the A.C.2 asked curiously. "What duck?"

McTyre gave a bitter laugh and motioned the erk nearer. "Listen to this, kid, and you'll see what you're up against. Fair frightens yer, it does, to think a man can be so low. . . . It happened at our last station—before your time. About a quarter of a mile down the road there was a small wood; and as me and my mate was courtin' a couple of local girls, we used to nip into it on the summer nights for a cuddle or two. Behind the wood was a field that didn't seem to belong to nobody, and right in the middle of the field was a pond.

"Well, the four of us were in there one evenin' in August when Jim suddenly nudges my arm. I look around and of all the people in the world I see Bert walkin' across the field towards the pond. He was alone and whistlin' to some one or other. We couldn't catch on, an' were beginning to think maybe his conscience had

198

driven him that way when a little duck came waddlin' out of a clump of grass straight towards him. An' Bert leans down and gives it some food from his pocket."

McTyre shook his head at the memory. "You could've knocked me down with a feather if I hadn't been lyin' down already. We don't say nothin'; we just watch him. He puts some more food on the grass, pats the duck for a while, then after about ten minutes goes back the way he came. . . .

"Jim, who was a bit of a Bible-puncher, said it proved what he'd always believed—that every man had some good in him somewhere. He said Bert must be lonely in the camp, an' this was an outlet for his feelings. Jim said it made him feel better towards Bert now, more sympathetic, like. Me, I didn't know what to think.

"Anyway, this duck business went on for months. It must've been a nightly routine because every time we took the girls in the wood we saw Bert about the same time, round about eight o'clock. He'd feed the blooming thing, pat it, even play with it the way you'd play with a dog. Jim was real sorry for him by this time, and I was startin' to get that way myself. The girls thought he was a nice man and must have a very kind heart to come all this way at night to feed a lonely little duck. Can y' imagine it. . . ?

"Well, the months went by and it got a bit too cold for us in the woods at night, so we didn't see so much of Bert. But every now and then I'd have a squint, and sure enough, rain or snow, he kept goin' to that pond every night. I began to think Jim must be right—any man who went to all that trouble for a little duck must have a heart tucked away somewhere. Not that it was a little 'en now, mind you. It was gettin' as fat as a pig with all the food he'd been stuffin' into it.

"Christmas came, an' it was as cold as the clappers with everything frozen up. Do you know what duty Bert gave me on Christmas Eve, kid?"

The youngster shook his head.

"Goin' round the camp pulling W.C. chains to keep 'em working! Yeah, that was Bert!" McTyre took a deep breath, and blew smoke out through his long nose at the memory. "And even that didn't convince me. Every time I pulled a chain I'd think about the duck and forgive 'im.

"Christmas morning I was off duty at eight. At a minute past eight I was gettin' my pass from the Guard Room. As I went out of the gate I saw Bert goin' down the road ahead of me. My bus stop was down that way, so I followed him. When he reached the wood he turned off into the field and, curious now because he was off schedule, I hid behind some bushes and watched him. He looked around, didn't see anybody, then walked across the snow towards the pond. He let out a whistle, and sure enough that duck came waddlin' up just like a dog glad to see 'im; so 'elp me, you could see the trust on the bloomin' thing's face. I stood there watching, thinking maybe Bert had come over early to give it a Christmas present or something. But I was wrong, kid. By the centre I was wrong! Do you know what he did?"

The erk shook his young, puzzled face.

For one moment McTyre paused, as if reluctant to destroy such cherubic innocence. Then he gave a cynical grin and hitched up his overalls. "All right; then I'll tell yer, kid. I'll tell yer how I know Bert's a bastard through an' through."

And tell McTyre did before slouching away to see the villain of the piece in person. The shocked expression on the young erk's face left him in no doubt that he had proved his point.

25

Adams closed the door of Grenville's billet with some attention to detail, painfully aware of his procrastination. He turned slowly, inwardly wincing at the unfriendly stare that met him.

"What do you want?"

Adams was not completely certain what he wanted —that was part of the trouble—and having had too much to drink did not help matters. His eyes, distressed and slightly puzzled, began wandering round the billet as if soliciting aid. None came from the tallboy in the opposite corner, none from the few photographs of planes and crews on the walls, and the flying suit hanging from a peg near the bed seemed positively contemptuous. The photograph on the top of Grenville's locker gave him great hopes until his shortsighted eyes discovered it to be of an elderly, white-haired woman. Adams felt a sense of injustice at the odds. It was going to be very, very difficult. . . .

"What's the matter with you? What do you want?"

Adams glanced hastily back at the bed on which Grenville, fully-clothed but for his tunic, had risen on one elbow to stare at him. A heavy shadow from the reading-lamp on the locker lay over the pilot's forehead and eyes, giving his severely bruised face an almost satanic expression. Adams discovered the words he had so carefully memorized on the way over from the inn had all fled in dismay, leaving him sorely tempted to follow them. He cleared his dry throat and blurted out the first thing that came to him.

"I've come to you about Hilde, Roy."

The sudden silence hurt his ears. Then Grenville rose higher on his pillow. "What do you mean?"

Adams braced himself. This was it, now or never. He took three jerky steps forward. "Roy; I like that girl. She's the nicest kid I've known in years." His own words brought a shock to Adams, confirming the suspicion that so far he had avoided meeting face to face. But there was no time to consider himself and Valerie now. That would have to wait until later. Ignoring the regret that lay like a heavy bruise in his mind, he went on: "I can't bear seeing her being hurt like this. There's a limit to anything. . . ."

"Go on," Grenville said, watching him with that devil's face from the shadows.

"As you know, the poor kid got the news about her brother last week. She took it well—too well, somehow. She doesn't talk about it, doesn't cry, doesn't say anything—but you can feel how bad it is underneath. And we can't do anything: not a damned thing. That's why I'm here tonight—to ask you to come over to see her."

Grenville was sitting upright on his bed now. Adams saw his expression and went on with a rush:

"You're making it ten times worse for her, Roy. She must know you've heard about Finn—it's over a week now—and yet you haven't been to see her. To her it must seem as if the whole world has let her down. That's the look she gets in her eyes sometimes and I can't stand it. . . ." Tears suddenly blinded Adams. He blinked them back, cursing the treachery of the drink that was making him maudlin. "She's never said a word about you, but I know what she's thinking. For God's sake go over and help her, Roy, before it's too late. You're the one person that can. You don't have to tell her what happened. . . ."

"Get out of here, you drunken sot!" Grenville said, with sudden viciousness.

Adams waved a plump hand in a half-protest, then let it fall to his side. "Call me what you like, Roy, but do me this one favour."

Grenville was on his feet now and moving threateningly forward. "I said get out, damn you!"

Adams drew back one step, then stood his ground, dazed at his courage. As if in reward memory returned to him, bringing back some of his prepared arguments. He snatched gratefully at one. "What about Bergman?

You and he were good friends. How would he feel if he knew you'd never gone to see her?"

Grenville halted. The sound of his breathing came to Adams, harsh and uneven.

"You know what he'd want," Adams went on with renewed hope. "He'd want you to comfort his sister. Any man would."

The purple and yellow bruises stood out evilly against the pale background of Grenville's face. His swollen lips sneered at Adams.

"You fool. What comfort can *I* bring her? I killed Bergman, remember?"

Adams caught the despair as well as the derision in Grenville's voice, and relief brought weakness to his legs. The worse was over: now he had a chance. He motioned to a chair and sank into it without opposition from Grenville.

"Roy; you've got to look at it differently." As he spoke Adams realized how sober he had become. "You were ordered to destroy that building. That alone excuses you from blame . . ."

Contempt blazed in Grenville's eyes. "Don't tell me that, Adams."

"But it's true."

"True be damned. If it were true there wouldn't be a guilty man in this war. Every Nazi who tortures his prisoners could be excused: every S.A. devil who throws children into gas-chambers could plead innocence. A man has a greater moral duty to himself than to the State, and you know it. I didn't kill Bergman because of an order, damn you."

Adams wetted his dry lips. "All right. But you did kill him to save him from torture. You can't deny that."

Grenville's laugh was not pleasant to hear. "And is that what you want me to tell Hilde—that he was being tortured? Or has the telegram already given her those little details?"

Adams was silent. Grenville jeered at him. "You want me to go over and console her! I'm to tell her that everything's all right, that her brother didn't die in action as she thinks, but was put into a torture chamber where half a dozen sadists went to work on him. That we didn't like this at all in case he talked, and so I, being the squadron's best murderer, was sent out to finish him off. Well; is that what you want?"

The arguments Adams had prepared earlier had covered no more ground than this, and he felt defeat close at hand. And the intense hunger of Grenville's eyes made him miserably aware that it was not only the girl he was failing. . . .

"Get out, you fat fool!" Grenville suddenly gritted. "Get out and leave me alone!"

In his desperation, Adams' words stumbled over themselves like a small child's running feet. "I didn't want you to tell her anything of your part in his death. . . . But if you can't see her without doing it, then even that's better than not seeing her at all. Her brother's dead, but you're alive, Roy. You're the one thing she has left. . . . It'll be a shock for her to hear it, I know, but later on she'll be more proud of him than ever. And she'll understand why you did it and think even more of you too."

"What a fool you are," Grenville sneered.

"But can't you see—it's better for her to know the truth than to think the whole world has let her down. Her brother's loss she can understand now—she knows he is dead—but she will never understand why she has lost you. Why haven't you bothered to go over—you, the one person in the world who can comfort her? She'll wonder that for the rest of her life. It's enough to break the kid's faith in everything. Can't you see that?"

Grenville's face was very pale. "Why should I matter so much to her?"

"Why? How can anybody answer that? Why do people care for one another—God knows why. But she's got you deep in her system and unless she knows why you're acting this way, it's going to ruin the kid. Think of her feelings"—Adams was shouting now. "Damn it, if you'd ever been in love you wouldn't need telling all this. She doesn't know the job is coming off tomorrow night, but she must know it's coming off soon. She knows you might not come back from it, and yet the precious minutes are ticking by without her

204

seeing you. . . . It's enough to turn her mind. Blast you; you've got to see her. If you don't, I'll tell her the whole story myself. I will; I mean it."

Grenville's reply was not the vicious one Adams had expected. Low, with all anger gone, it caught him completely by surprise.

"There's something you don't know, Frank. When I first took Finn up with me, she thought I was exposing him to unnecessary danger and told me so. Now you're trying to tell me she'll forgive me for deliberately killing him. You're wrong. She'll get the shock of finding out the truth, she'll loathe me, and she'll discover what happened to Finn in the bargain. How is any of that going to help her?"

"Better loathe you and get you out of her system than go on fretting about you for the rest of her life," Adams said, the sweat trickling down his face. "But she won't loathe you. She'll understand. Go and find out, for God's sake."

At his words Grenville's expression had suddenly changed. He stared at Adams for a long moment with an indefinable look in his eyes. Then, without speaking, he eased his stiff shoulder into his tunic and picked up his cap.

"Are you going over?" Adams breathed.

Grenville turned back at the door, his lips twisting. "Yes; I'll go and put things right. I don't like being a disease in anyone's system." A second later the door slammed behind him.

Adams sank weakly back into the chair, not certain from Grenville's expression whether to feel relief or anxiety.

26

Grenville waited in the hall while the innkeeper went upstairs to call her.

"Miss Bergman! There's Squadron-Leader Grenville to see you. . . ."

She came running breathlessly down the stairs, pausing on the bottom step. Her face was pale, and Grenville saw the glisten of crushed tears under her lashes. With an impatient movement of her hand, she brushed them away. She gave a smile, and the courage of it pierced him like a knife.

"Hello, Roy. How good it is to see you again."

"Hello, Hilde. Sorry I've been so long in coming over."

As he stepped forward, the shaded hall-light fell on his face, revealing its heavy bruises. She let out a low exclamation of concern.

"Your face—does it hurt you very much?"

He shook his head, glancing towards the sitting-room door. "No; I'm all right now."

Her face clouded as she followed his eyes. "Valerie is in there—listening to a radio play. It will be difficult to talk. . . . Shall we go upstairs to my room? It will be quiet there."

He did not want that, but could think of no suitable protest. In silence he followed her up the stairs and into her room. As he had feared, its atmosphere caught him at once. She had not lived long in the room, but it had already taken her personality for its own. It lay all around him, in the restful murmur of a clock, the graceful fold of a curtain, the white shoulder of a pillow. He felt trapped and afraid.

"I came to talk about Finn," he muttered. "I should have come before, but somehow . . ."

"You had not fully recovered from your wounds," she said quickly. Relief came into her eyes, and he

realized she had already found an excuse for his behaviour.

"It wasn't that," he protested, but she cut off his
words with a fluttering gesture of her hand.

"There's no need to apologize. I quite understand.
You were not fully recovered, and the news came as a
shock to you. I had forgotten what good friends you
and he were."

There was a ring of self-condemnation in her voice.
Grenville realized she would always find an excuse for
him if an excuse could be found. This was what
Adams had meant by saying he was deep in her system. That look in her eyes on coming down the stairs
had been another sympton of it.

He knew the feeling himself. It was like having
another life inside one, crying for the birth his raid had
made impossible. Adams had been right: it must not be
left to torture her throughout the years. One way or
another it had to be killed. The truth would do that,
but would also hurt her too deeply. There was another
and better way. . . .

Her voice was like the sweet chiming of a clock
heard through the grip of a nightmare.

"What is it, Roy? What are you thinking?"

She was standing no more than a yard from him, her
eyes fixed with concern on his face. He noticed for the
first time that she was wearing a simple black frock that
unintentionally set off the whiteness of her skin and the
bright gold of her hair. The faint perfume that always
clung around her drifted towards him, evoking a
thought-image as clear as the one given by his eyes. The
one image superimposed on the other made her more
real than reality.

"Why are you looking at me like that?" she asked
again, uncertainly.

His mind answered her. Why? Because this is the last
time I shall see you like this. In a few seconds the thing
that makes your eyes warm when you look at me will
be dead, and you will never be the same again, not to
me. . . .

Another moment and he knew he could never find

207

the strength to do it. He dragged his eyes from her and looked down at his watch.

"I haven't got long," he muttered. "I only dropped in for a few minutes."

"You are going—so soon . . .?"

He nodded, not meeting her eyes. "I'm afraid I must. The boys are throwing a party in Highgate, and I've promised to take a friend of mine along. I'm late as it is —she's already been waiting over half-an-hour." His voice was deliberate with meaning. "It's as well we're old friends or there'd be trouble."

She looked dazed, unable to understand. He went on quickly:

"She moved up here a couple of weeks ago. Got herself a room in Highgate."

He saw the delayed action of the shock strike her now. Her words were as involuntarily as a cry of pain.

"A girl! But I had no idea. . . . You have never spoken of her before."

Grenville forced a sheepish grin, believing the bruised skin round his lips would split with the effort. "I should have mentioned it, I suppose. Sorry if you got any wrong ideas."

"But the things you said that day in the car. . . . You said you did not want anyone worrying about you. You made it sound——"

"I made it sound simpler than it was," he broke in roughly.

Her voice had a dead sound. "So when you said that after the war things might be different, you were talking of . . ." She suddenly turned away, moving as if blinded. Her hand moved in the fluttering gesture he knew so well, then fell helplessly to her side. It was a few seconds before she turned back to face him. Her face appeared frozen with shock, but tears were falling down her cheeks like the beads from a broken necklace. She made no sound with them, and the silence was like a tightening cord round Grenville's temples. He had to speak to break it.

"After all, I've never pretended to be over-keen. You can't say that I have."

Her eyes closed to hide her shame. "That is true. But I misunderstood the reason. . . . I see now. . . . The fault has been mine, not yours."

Grenville had been praying for anger, not forgiveness. He turned quickly to pick up his cap, hiding his face. He heard her voice again, still bewildered.

"But it is so hard to believe. . . . You have never been unkind before. Why have you chosen this time to tell me? Why not before, or . . . or even a little later? I would so much like to know that."

Grenville knew now that there was no gentle way of killing anything. He lifted the knife and struck. "Surely that's obvious enough. I didn't tell you before because it was quite pleasant and I was enjoying it. I'm telling you now because she has come here, and it has to end at once. That's why. Sorry."

He dared not hold out his hand, dared not to touch her. At the door he paused and turned back, with the excuse he was making certain of his murder. But his eyes failed him: he saw nothing but the white blur of her face and the misted brightness of her hair. Then he was outside, with the black fields and pitiless stars a part of the agony that racked him.

27

The briefing-room was packed to capacity. At one side of the table on the platform, a group of men were confering quietly. Among them were Davies, Barrett, and Grenville. The silence was aggravated by the shuffle of feet, the whispers of conversation, and the scratching of matches. In the centre of the table stood the contour model of the Svartfjord, covered with a cloth. Nervous eyes pulled away from it, examined the empty blackboard alongside it, then wandered round the walls, which were covered with diagrams of German aircraft set in gun-sights with the correct aiming deflections. Battle slogans were everywhere, giving such admonitions as: "It's the One you don't see who gets You," "Always watch the Hun in the Sun," "Remember your Cockpit Drill," as well as the ubiquitous "Careless Talk costs Lives." From the ceiling dangled scale models of Focke-Wulfs, Dorniers, and Messerschmidts, as well as Allied aircraft, all of them turning uneasily in the rising smoke from over thirty cigarettes. Eyes wandered back to the covered model on the table. The tension could be felt, catching at the throat.

The group on the platform reached agreement, and Davies moved forward to face his young audience. The low mutters among the air crews ceased abruptly. There was a red spot on each of Davies's high cheekbones and a bright glint in his eyes. His sharp, high-pitched voice added to the tension.

"Well, chaps; here it is—the big show you've been waiting for. You've had a lousy time training for it—all this getting up before dawn and stoodging around in the dark over Scotland must have made you fed up to the back teeth. And your having to throw your bombs into a corrie in the side of a valley must have made it seem an ever bigger muck-up. Well; now I'm going to try to fit all the pieces together. Here we go...."

Davies stepped back alongside the covered model of the Svartfjord. "In a few minutes I'm going to let you all come up here to take a closer look at this thing. But for the moment you'll have to be content with a long-range view while I explain what it's all about."

He pulled the cloth away. The young faces before him craned forward, both curious and apprehensive. Someone coughed loudly, relieving his tension. Davies picked up a pointer.

"This is the scale model of a certain fjord in Norway. It's very deep and narrow, over 20 miles long, and ends as a *cul-de-sac* at its eastern end. It is this end, the far one, that we're chiefly concerned with. A high waterfall drops down here and gives power to a hydro-electric plant at the bottom of the fjord. Built around this plant is another building the Germans have put up, a massive affair with walls nearly as thick as U-boat pens. This is our target. Keep it in mind while I explain the rest of the scenery."

His pointer moved to a mountain on the side of the fjord, directly alongside the hydro-electric plant. "This mountain is called the Trollfjell. It rises steeply to over 2,500 feet, retreats into a corrie a couple of hundred feet deep, then bulges out again into a massive, over-hanging summit. On this summit is a glacier called the Trollisen. The whole thing resembles a man's chest, neck, and head. Like this. . . ."

Davies made a quick sketch on the blackboard. "Here you are! The chest is the side of the fjord, the neck the corrie, and the head the overhanging summit. Add the glacier on the top and that gives you a crop of white hair. That's how the mountain and glacier got their names—Troll is a kind of Norwegian gremlin." Davies paused, giving a puckish smile that made him look more than ever like a gremlin himself. "This job gives you a chance to get your own back on one of the little beggars."

He moved forward to the front of the platform again. "Later on you'll be given all your wireless, navigational, and bombing gen in detail, and after that Squadron-Leader Grenville will give you his personal orders. But

211

I'm going to explain the job to you first so you know all the whys and wherefores, and know what is expected of you. So listen carefully.

"Tomorrow morning you are going to take off before dawn just as you have been doing throughout your training. You're even going to fly north on the same track for ten minutes. After that you start playing a different game. Instead of going to Scotland, you're going to Norway, and instead of carrying dummies, you'll each have a special bomb apiece in your bomb bays. These bombs arrived five minutes ago and will be loaded straight on to your kites.

"Right—you're on your way and scheduled to reach the mouth of the fjord at 0645 hours, from now known as Z hour. Meanwhile, at Z hour minus thirty, a very brave band of Norwegian patriots will be clearing the way for you." Davies went on to explain the task of the underground forces. "If all goes well they will have the guns out of action by the time you arrive. You fly straight in and make for the other end of the fjord. Once there the fun starts.

"I don't think I need stress by this time that you don't drop your bombs on the target. As I've told you, it has massive walls, and a very thick roof. You're flying low, and it would be impossible to achieve sufficient penetration to do any damage even if your bombs were designed for that sort of job, which they are not. Instead, we have quite a different scheme. . . ."

Davies went back to the blackboard and made another sketch. "As you've heard, this summit overhangs the fjord. Naturally, before the Germans built their project, they sent geologists up to check on it. Their reports were that it was safe enough and there were no risks of accidents. That was enough for the Germans —they needed this site badly because of the hydro-electric plant. So the project was built—a top priority job. Now I'm not allowed to tell you much, but I can say this: As you know, German scientists are working just as hard as our own to discover new weapons, and, like ourselves, hope to find something that will end the war quickly. Well, in this building, using some of the energy and by-products of the hydro-electric plant alongside, the Germans are on something big. Something so big, in fact, that it might have a far-reaching effect on the outcome of the war if it isn't destroyed."

Davies' sharp eyes travelled slowly round the arc of breathless crews, letting the point sink home. His voice became brisk once more. "All right. Back to the old gremlin's head again. The German geologists passed it as safe, but we heard an interesting story through Intelligence channels. A Norwegian geologist, who examined it before the hydro-electric plant was built, says there is a fissure at the back of it. Normally this fissure is completely covered by snow and ice, but every summer the ice retreats a little, and apparently the summer he made his examination was an exceptionally warm one. He was able to study the fissure in detail and found that the perennial dripping of water had hollowed it out inside to a considerable depth. However, after very careful study, it was decided there was no danger of the overhang falling through natural causes, and the Norwegians went on to build their hydro-electric plant."

Davies eyed the puzzled faces before him with grim amusement. "I know! You're all wondering what the devil all this geology has to do with your prang tomorrow. The answer to that is everything! Because you're going to use this knowledge to chop off old Trollfjell's head and drop it right on top of the target."

There was a sudden buzz of amazement among the pilots and observers. Davies gave them a few moments to recover before holding up his hand.

"Here is a non-scientific explanation. You know the way you've been dropping—a better word is hurling —your bombs into a corrie in the side of a valley. Well, tomorrow morning you're going to hurl these special bombs into the corrie under old Trollfjell's head. These bombs have been specially designed to give maximum blast effect, or, to put it another way, to start severe shock waves.

"Now shock waves are greatly magnified in effect when they enter solids like earth or rock—they become tremendously destructive. Normally the blast from a surface bomb goes upwards into the air where

213

it is wasted. But in this case the shock waves from your bombs will go upwards into this overhang, and shiver up to the fissure like a seismic disturbance.

"Our scientists haven't been able to calculate exactly how many bombs it will take, but they are confident that a succession of explosions will fracture that fissure more and more until the front part of the overhang comes crashing down. To put it inaccurately but graphically, the shock punch from your bombs will throw old Trollfjell's head backwards, his neck will snap like a carrot, and another redskin will bite the dust. . . ."

The excitement among the crews was intense now. Davies held up his hand again for silence. "You'll guess now that everything has been most carefully worked out. The date, for example, is most important. At this time in May the snow and ice on the summit is ideal for an avalanche. It is beginning to thaw, but still has lost nothing of its mass and weight. If part of the overhang goes, the ice and snow goes with it, and that'll be curtains for anything in the fjord below."

He laid down his chalk and dusted his hands. "Just to tuck in all the loose ends, I'll add that this scheme has the full approval of the Norwegian Government. The loss of the power plant will be a serious one to them, but the alternative is too grim to consider. Right—now you'd all better come up and take a closer look at your gremlin."

Pilots and observers clustered round the contour model, taking notes and drawing sketches. When all were satisfied Davies waved them back into their seats. "All right—now for the technical details. Don't miss anything. We can't afford a single boob."

Detailed instructions were given by the Senior Signals officer, the Navigational Officer, and the Armament Officer, the crews again making careful notes. Barrett made a short address. Then they were all taken into the Operations Room, where photographs of the fjord were projected on to a screen. Maps were scrutinized and E.T.A.'s chalked up on a blackboard. Before the crews returned to the Briefing Room Adams presented each observer with his wallet, making him check that it contained the full complement of maps and charts.

It was well over an hour before Grenville himself came to the front of the platform. Immediately there was a subtle change in the atmosphere. Previously an onlooker might have gained the impression that the crews had given their attention more to the duties and office of the speakers than to the speakers themselves. Now the man facing them was their battle leader: the pilot who was always the first to fly into danger, the pilot more accomplished than themselves, the pilot on whose judgement their lives depended. Their attention now was born of both a personal and a professional respect.

Grenville's cultured. if forceful, voice was at odd variance with his battered appearance. If the usual touch of devil-may-care humour he used before an operation was less marked this evening, none of his listeners thought his tone unfitting to the occasion.

"We shall be using our full strength of fifteen Mosquitoes and will fly in battle formation, sections of three, line abreast. It shouldn't be difficult to keep visual contact because the Met. forecast is good, and, in case you don't know, the sky in those latitudes is always luminous at this time of the year.

"The essence of this raid is strategy and surprise. For that reason it is not considered expedient to have a fighter escort on the way out. Coming back is a different matter and, as you have already been told, we have a rendezvous with long-range Spitfires over the sea.

"All signals on the way out are to be visual only—there must be strict R/T silence. Keep close contact until I fire one green Very light. That means you fall back in line astern. I shall make that signal just before we enter the fjord and we shall enter it at forty-second intervals. The reason is that your bombs will have eleven seconds delays—if you make your attacks too soon after the other bloke you might find the mountain falling on top of you. So remember—forty-second intervals!

"Watch out near the mouth of the Svartfjord. There's an enemy naval base on the island of Utvik, and I don't want any fool going close to have a look what those funny-looking trees are. They aren't trees—they're 88 mms., so keep away!

"We're not expecting too much flak, but if there are any posts still in enemy hands, the Green sections from each flight will engage them. Watch out for the target itself—it might pack a few guns on its roof and of course the patriots won't be able to silence them.

"When you drop your bomb, remember all you have practised. Get as far inside the corrie and as much underneath the overhang as you can—we want to give it the maximum shock possible. Once you've dropped your bomb, beat it straight out of the east end of the fjord or you'll clutter up air space, and that's one of the things we shall be short of.

"When you come out of the fjord, keep a sharp look out for enemy fighters. We're hoping to have finished before they arrive, but you never know. If they are there, form a defensive circle directly south of the fjord. If they aren't, head straight for the kelk factory on the island south of Utvik. You shouldn't be able to miss it—the Intelligence Boys say it has a smoking chimney and stands out white against the black rocks. We shall reform over it.

"The Code word I shall send back to base when old Trollfjell's head falls will be "Sneeze". When you hear that you can start getting ready for a party.

"Every navigator will keep an individual log so that he can bring his plane home alone if necessary, and everyone will synchronize his watch before take-off. The squadron call sign will be 'Vesuvius' and the station call-sign 'Dudley.' Any questions?"

There were three. Grenville answered them, then threw a glance at Davies. The slow shake of the Air Commodore's head said everything. Nothing more could be done now but send them out and pray. All that had gone before, the courage of Bergman and his men in discovering the building, their sufferings, the frantic efforts to discover a way of destroying it, the scheming, planning, designing, the race against time: all had led to this. A single squadron; a handful of boys. More depended on their skill and courage than one dared consider.

Grenville turned back to his men, his voice curt. "There is just one more thing. Some brave men have already died in making this raid possible. For their sakes, and for more than their sakes, it has to succeed. We've been specially chosen to do it, and that means if it is humanly possible, we shall do it." His uncompromising eyes travelled slowly round the arc of hushed men. "We pull it off whatever happens. Is that quite clear?"

Nods, a pause, then Grenville's voice again on a more cheerful note. "Right, chaps; that's all. Off you go to bed. You'll be called at 0330 hours sharp. Good luck."

28

It was cold in the Operations Room the following morning, and no amount of attention could coax any heat from the radiators. Nevertheless, none of the four waiting men could pull himself away to make enquiries about the heating plant. They were scattered all over the room. Adams was sitting huddled in a chair near to one of the dead radiators. Davies was at the foot of the huge operational map that almost covered one wall, the Brigadier was seated at the end of the long table, and Marsden, the Chief Signals Officer, with headphones at his ears and a message-pad before him, was hunched over a small table at the opposite side of the room.

Adams shivered and shrugged himself deeper into his greatcoat. It seemed to be growing colder, and the bluish-white light from the fluorescent tubes did nothing to improve matters. Adams tried to close his weary eyes but they opened immediately as if on springs. The stark, shimmering light, merciless to his fatigue, gave the room and its occupants a touch of unreality. The Brigadier looked like a pale, waxen statue as he stared unblinkingly at Marsden. He was wearing no greatcoat, but the intensity of his concentration appeared to make him unaware of physical discomfort. In complete contrast Davies, sitting under the huge map on which had been pencilled the track lines of the squadron, was fidgeting about like a schoolboy in church. He too was watching Marsden, whose earphones and transmitter key were connected to Signals. Marsden had been listening-in for over ninety minutes, but as yet no message had come through.

Another ten minutes passed by. In the silence the tapping of Davies's fingers on the arm of his chair was like a monotonous jungle drum. Adams would have shouted at him to stop if one shouted such things at Air

Commodores. As it was he hunched down farther in his seat and tried again to close his eyes.

A sudden metallic crackle sounded in the earphones, amplified by the silent room. All four men jerked upright as if pulled by the same string. The crackle grew louder, then died away. Marsden stared round apologetically. "Static," he muttered, lowering his head again.

Davies swore. Another minute, then he jumped to his feet. "It's confounded cold," he said, looking around for agreement. No one answered, leaving Adams with an immediate sense of guilt. The Signals Officer wasn't expected to reply, the Brigadier was above coercion—didn't that leave him with the baby? But it was too late to answer now. Davies frowned peevishly, began pacing up and down in front of the map, and Adams suppressed a groan. This was going to be worse than the chair tapping.

At the end of his tenth oscillation, Davies halted and turned his sharp, resentful eyes on Adams. "I wonder how Barrett is getting on."

The testiness in his voice told Adams this was his last chance. "Yes; I wonder," he muttered.

Davies did not appear to notice the inadequacy of his reply. "I shouldn't have been fool enough to let him go," he said resentfully. "But he'd worked himself a pretty cast-iron case."

In spite of the reserve crews and the replacements that had been rushed to the squadron after the disaster at Bergen, 633 had found itself one trained pilot short. As Davies had previously said he wanted every serviceable plane in the air, this had been Barrett's chance. He had offered to fly without a command; and when Davies had reminded him about his weakened chest, he had pointed out that the raid was to be carried out at low-level throughout, which should mean no undue strain on him. Davies had had his doubts, but in the circumstances had felt forced to agree. Now he was regretting his decision.

"The idiot will probably go and kill himself. He'll probably ram his kite into the side of the mountain."

219

Adams was inclined to agree, but knew better than to say so. He nodded uncomfortably, shuffling in his chair to avoid Davies's stare.

Davies looked at his watch, then up at the wall map. "If everything's going all right, they should be coming up to the coast in less than fifteen minutes. Hear that, Marsden?"

The Signals Officer turned his head briefly and nodded. The Brigadier showed signs of life. He looked down at his own watch, then took a handkerchief from his pocket and dabbed at his moustache with meticulous care. Adams tried to visualize the scene out there—the dawn sky and sea, the roar of lifting engines, the approaching enemy coast; but his imagination, usually so reliable, refused to help him this morning. The blue-white glare of the fluorescent lamps, the waiting figures, the tense, anxious *safety* of the room: he could not escape from any of it. He felt betrayed and his sense of inferiority deepened.

The telephone alongside Marsden gave a sudden buzz, an urgent sound that made Adams jump. A second later the Brigadier was at the table, taking the receiver from Marsden. As he leaned forward to take the message, a premonition of disaster shot through Adams like the stab from a decayed tooth.

"Hello," the Brigadier called. "Hedgerow speaking. . . ." Adams guessed this was a password. "Hello, Graham, what is it? What's that . . . ?" The Brigadier's clipped voice was suddenly tense, shocked. In the hush the metallic rasp of the voice on the 'phone could be heard clearly. The words were not distinct but their urgency was unmistakable.

Davies drew near, his bright eyes and jerky movements reminding Adams, even at that moment, of a nervous cockerel. The Brigadier let out a sudden gasp of dismay, an event of such significance that Davies turned pale. Adams jumped to his feet, waiting anxiously alongside the Air Commodore.

The Brigadier dropped the receiver and turned towards Davies. His face was grey and drawn, with a look about his eyes that shocked the others.

"Get in touch with Grenville at once! Tell him to turn back. Quickly! There's no time to lose."

Davies started. "Why? What's happened?"

It was clearly an effort for the Brigadier to speak. "We've just had a message from one of our Norwegian agents over there. He was wounded, but managed to escape and reach his transmitter. . . ."

Davies's voice was suddenly shrill. "Don't tell me they haven't managed to capture the flak posts!"

The Brigadier shook his head heavily. "Worse than that, I'm afraid. They haven't even had the chance to try. The Gestapo rounded up every man during the night."

Davies stared at the Brigadier in horror. "Rounded them up? But how? How could they know . . . ?" His voice trailed off as he remembered.

"Torture will get anything from a man if he suffers it long enough," the Brigadier said wearily. "We've always known that. It wasn't Bergman who talked—it was Ericson, the poor devil they captured later that day. The Gestapo must have passed on the news before Grenville destroyed the place. . . ." His voice sharpened. "Hurry, man, and warn him. Can't you see, the whole thing is a trap. After failing in their attack on your airfield, they've deliberately delayed capturing the patriots until the last minute. If it wasn't for this message the squadron would fly into a death trap."

"My God, you're right," Davies muttered. He nodded to Marsden, who immediately sent out the Station call sign to the squadron. While they were waiting for a reply, Davies turned back to the Brigadier.

"There'll be everything waiting for them—fighters, the lot. For all we know they might be among them now. We can't receive their R/T at this range."

The Brigadier had himself under control again. "I don't think that's likely, not yet. Remember—they don't know we have been warned. I think they will let the squadron fly right into the fjord before showing their hand. Once they're inside Jerry can close the net and they haven't a chance."

Davies shuddered at the mental picture of the Mosquitoes trapped among a hundred guns. The buzz of morse in Marsden's earphones came as a welcome relief. It was Grenville, acknowledging their call.

"Thank God," Davies muttered, snatching a pencil from Adams' pocket. "Here, send this." He wrote on the pad. *Dudley calling. Patriots captured. Guns still in enemy hands. Return to base immediately.*

Marsden tapped out the message.

"Send it again," Davies ordered, taking no chances.

Marsden obeyed, the transmitter key jerking up and down under his practised fingers.

There was a pause of perhaps fifteen seconds, then Marsden's earphones buzzed again. Three pairs of eyes followed his pencil as it traced out words on the pad.

Vesuvius leader calling. Request permission to attack alone.

Adams felt sick. Davies turned towards the Brigadier, his eyes unnaturally bright. "Grenville's offering to go in alone. What shall I tell him?"

For a moment a wild flicker of hope had sprung into the Brigadier's eyes. It died as he shook his head. "No; it would be suicide. And even if he got through it's most unlikely one bomb would bring it down. Tell him to come back."

One bomb useless, Davies wrote on the pad. *Return to base. Dudley.*

Silence followed this transmission. All four men looked at one another uneasily. "What's happened now?" Davies muttered. "Don't say the Focke-Wulfs have got them." He was just about to order Marsden to transmit again when the ear-phones began buzzing afresh. Words grew on the pad.

Vesuvius leader here. Have called for volunteers. Squadron will go in with me. Believe we have chance. Request permission. . . .

Nothing, not even the magnitude of the disaster, could keep the glowing pride from Davies's voice now. "They've all volunteered to go in with him, sir—every man jack of 'em. What do you want now?"

Adams' imagination came back when he wanted it least. Mosquitoes entering that black fjord . . . running the gauntlet of a hundred guns that could weave an unbreakable web of steel from wall to wall . . . the vision brought the sweat out of him, cold though the morning was. He wanted to shout his protests to the Brigadier: instead he stared at him mutely, pleading with his eyes.

The Brigadier, overcome by emotion at the news, had swung abruptly away. The few words he spoke, when he could speak at all, were the outward expression of the conflict raging inside him.

"There'll never be another chance! After this they'll make it impossible to get near the place. And it's so desperately important. . . ."

So are those lives, Adams wanted to shout. You can't send them in there now. It's murder. Plain bloody murder. . . .

It was full thirty seconds before the Brigadier faced them again. "If they have volunteered, then I must say yes." He paused, then went on quietly, "I'm very sorry —please believe that."

He walked over to the long table and stood stiffly before it, his back towards them. Davies's voice had a dry, proud sob in it as he looked down at Marsden.

Permission granted. God bless you all. Dudley.

God help you, you mean, Adams thought bitterly.

29

The Mosquitoes were riding as tight as a troop of horsemen, stirrup to stirrup, nose to tail. Every man was aware of an odd kinship between himself and his machine that morning. The powerful engines seemed to merge their vitality into his own, the speeding wings to be an extension of his young, powerful arms. It was a madly intoxicating feeling.

Even Grenville felt it, and his mind, coldly analytical, dissected the reasons. One was the morning. White columns of cumulus towering into a blue sky . . . sea-washed islands with patches of dazzling green . . . grey-blue sea streaming under their wings. Spring always had the magic quality that made a man feel godlike.

There were other factors bound up in it too. One of them he had often felt before, in the spring before a raid. To walk out to one's plane with the smell of spring in one's nostrils and the knowledge that impossibly soon one would be flying into a sky stinking of death—to do that was to know the real bitter-sweetness of life.

Then there was the spirit of sacrifice. It gave men a feeling of unity and purpose that was near ecstasy. It might well be the greatest ecstasy a man could experience. The trouble was that to sustain it one had to fight shoulder to shoulder with one's comrades, or it had a way of betraying one and letting in the fear of death. And in the air one had always to fight alone.

"Five minutes more to the coast, sir. And Utvik at two o'clock."

Grenville's mind returned from the abstract. That was Phillips, his new observer, playing safe. He glanced at him briefly. Phillips had a sallow complexion, a pencil-thin moustache, and dark, intense eyes. He looked the keen, earnest type. He wasn't new to operational flying, of course, or he would not have been sent to them at this time, but he'd had little training for this job. Grenville had managed to take him three times up to Scotland, and that was all. He must be feeling more than nervous, particularly after the news from base. . . . At the same time Grenville was glad Hoppy was tucked away safely in hospital.

He took a long, careful look at the dazzling white clouds ahead, but could see nothing. They'd be up there, all right, waiting for the trap to close before coming down. His job was to keep them there as long as he could.

Telling Phillips to keep his eyes open, Grenville swung nearer the rocky island of Utvik. He passed close enough to catch a glimpse of a harbour, the camouflaged shapes of oil tanks, and a couple of destroyers, but no flak opposed them as they swept by. His lips pressed tightly together. No doubt now that the trap was laid.

He swung five degrees to port and the high mountains flanking the Svartfjord lay dead ahead. He fired a Very light and his crews began falling back in line astern as if preparing to enter the fjord. He had given them their new orders during the last ten minutes—enemy R/T would have picked them up, of course, but he was hoping there had been no time to put out a general alarm. If the Focke-Wulfs received advance warning of their intentions they wouldn't have a chance.

As he watched the rapidly approaching mountains, a vision of the waiting gun crews came to him. They had everything in that fjord: batteries of 20 mm. in both double and quadruple mountings, at least three dozen 37 mms., an unknown number of 88 mms. near the target, and all with predictors. . . . The gun muzzles would be swinging about like the heads of waiting cobras as the Mosquitoes drew nearer the trap.

Phillips stabbed a finger upwards. Fearful that the Focke-Wulfs had been told his new plan and were making a swift counter attack, Grenville glanced upwards, only to see a black speck dodging back into the towering cumulus north of the Svartfjord. He nodded his relief. Better they were hiding on that side than the south, although there might be more than one squadron up there. . . .

The entrance of the Svartfjord was taking detailed shape now, the grim, soaring rocks, the dense clumps of birch, the seagulls cluttered around some object in the water. . . . Beyond the entrance he could see the twisting, shadowy fjord beckoning them in.

Out of the sun now, into the shadow of the mountains, the entrance only 200 yards away. . . . A seagull smacked right into his windscreen, sliding off in a mass of blood and feathers. A second more, the arms of the fjord were almost around him—then Grenville suddenly flung his Mosquito into a tight, ninety-degree turn. The right flank of the fjord reeled under his vertical port wing, not fifty yards away. Another ninety-degree turn a few seconds later, to port this time, and the line of Mosquitoes were now speeding inland parallel to the fjord, with its own flanking mountains protecting them.

Grenville knew the alarm would be up now. The fox had dodged the trap: now the hounds would come baying down. But as yet he could not see the 190's; the mountains on either side hid them from view.

Birch, patches of scrub, rocks, flashed beneath them. They were in a wide valley. A stream ran under them for half a mile, its clear water reflecting back their racing shadows. A bridge shot by, a white-painted house, a clump of fruit trees laden with blossom. . . . Then the land began rising again, black rocks showing through the grass, patches of snow appearing.

Grenville's eyes were intent upon the steep mountain range on his left, the one flanking the Svartfjord. The responsibility made his whole body clammy with sweat. One mistake on his part now and the mission was a hopeless failure. It would fail anyway, he reminded himself, without the X factor, luck. . . .

He ordered the planes behind him to throttle back and increase further the distance between themselves. He forced his memory alert as his eyes probed the unfolding mountain range. A minute gone, a minute and a half. . . . Nearly half the range covered and still no break in it. Had he missed it? He fought back panic, gritting his teeth. The ground below was shelving steeply upwards now, there were thick patches of snow on the mountain-tops above him. Two minutes . . . two min-

226

utes and a quarter . . . the Focke-Wulfs were now overdue. Where was it?

Then he caught sight of the blacker rift among the early morning shadows. His voice snapped out over the R/T.

"Attention, all Vesuvius aircraft. Follow me at twenty second intervals. Repeat time alteration—*twenty* seconds! Notify me the moment you enter the main fjord. Green sections one and two go over and attack flak posts. Going in now. . . ."

He banked steeply, saw the massive rocks leaping towards him, and for one ghastly moment thought he had made a mistake. Then, with a deafening roar, the walls of the gorge closed around the shuddering plane.

It was a little easier this time than the last because now the gorge was falling away from him. He shot over the waterfall into which the Focke-Wulf had crashed and plunged on, followed by the rushing water. The noise of his engines, reverberating from the steep walls of rock, made the Mosquito tremble. Trees and bushes, growing precariously from crevices, reached out and seemed to touch his wingtips.

Relaxing for a few seconds, Grenville reviewed his plan while his body flew the plane instinctively. The six members of his Green sections, who had jettisoned their bombs to make their planes more manoeuverable, should emerge over the fjord at approximately the same time as he entered it. Their job was to harass the guns, to make things a little easier for the squadron following behind. They would provide only a slight diversion: Grenville had no illusions regarding the nightmare ahead. By entering the fjord *via* the gorge they had avoided Innvik and twelve miles of the fjord, which meant they had by-passed perhaps half of the waiting guns. Theoretically that doubled their chances. But a devil voice in his mind reminded him that double zero was still naught. . . .

The thoughts blazed in his mind with the clarity and suddenness of a photoflash. Then they changed, fixing themselves on Phillips again. Poor devil; what an introduction to a new squadron! Wonder what he was thinking. . . .

The gorge widened, then quite suddenly fell away, its stream plunging a sheer 700 feet to the bottom of the Svartfjord.

The sensation was like walking over a cliff edge. Instinctively Phillips gasped and drew back. Grenville banked steeply, gave his engines full boost, and waited for the inferno to begin. . . .

In the split-second before the gun crews recovered from their surprise, he had an unmolested view of the Svartfjord from the inside. Here, barely eight miles from its eastern end, it was a grim and savage place. From the black water that looked like oil, the mountains shelved steeply upwards, their lower slopes covered in birch and scrub, their upper slopes rising as sheer as the walls of some enormous prison. Impressions registered themselves indelibly on Grenville's mind in that final moment before hell broke loose. The grey clefts among the black rocks caused by melting snow . . . the rockfalls that had left inverted funnels of scree . . . the wisps of snow in crevices . . . the golden ledge of sunlight far above . . . a waterfall up there, bursting into a rainbow. . . .

Then it came. A huge eye suddenly winked from the shadowy mountainside and a glowing chain of shells came swirling towards them. Two more guns opened out on the opposite side of the fjord, then one from above. A line of red-cored white puffs burst dead ahead, making both men flinch back. A vicious explosion made the Mosquito rear like a frightened horse.

Now every gun within range had opened out, vieing with one another for the kill; 20 mm. parabolas made dazzling white bridges under which the Mosquito tried to dive. Tracer squirted out from clumps of trees and from rocky eyries, lacing the fjord with a deadly net of steel. Shells came reaching out, slowly at first, then with diabolical speed, clawing for their eyes. A succession of black explosions rocked the Mosquito, and shrapnel gashed her port wing; 37 mm. now, trying to bracket her. . . .

Grenville had never seen flak like this before. Thank God his Green sections were up there, ready to attack.

If only there was an escort to help them. . . . He spoke, into his microphone.

"Vesuvius leader calling Green sections. Attack now, Go."

The distraction they caused could not help him. They could not pin-point the guns until they opened fire on him, and before they could make their attack he would be either past or shot down. But it should afford some relief to those behind. His earphones crackled a moment later.

"M Mother calling, Skipper. Am in fjord now."

That was Milner, twenty seconds behind him. One half of Grenville's mind was on his mission, checking, calculating, deducing: the other half was engrossed with the business of keeping alive. A massive rock face, black-bearded with trees, thrust itself at him from out of the smoke. He hugged it closely, trying to find cover from the flak, and nearly impaled himself on a double-pronged fork of tracer that stabbed upwards from a clump of trees. He saw the shuddering flashes open up and instinctively slammed his stick forward, kicking the rudder bar at the same time. The Mosquito skidded away, a whiplash of steel snapping two feet above its fuselage. The twin barrels swung down viciously, but Grenville had banked into the cliff again and his speed carried him to safety behind a rock shoulder.

Sweat poured into his eyes, almost blinding him. That was one flak post that had to be destroyed. . . . He gave orders to his Green sections, inwardly cursing the shakiness of his voice.

He found himself counting and realized that some cell of his mind had been doing so ever since hearing Milner enter the fjord. Twenty seconds then . . . now thirty-one, thirty-two, thirty-three. . . . In distance covered about two and a half miles. At least five more to the target.

The lichen-stained rocky walls of the fjord streamed by, their shadows lit up by the rapid flashes of automatic guns. Another mountain spur deflected the fjord from its course. Grenville took this one wide, kicking his rudder bar left and right as he went by. The fire this time came from two posts on the rock face above them. Dazzled by the tracer, Grenville and Phillips crouched down. Coloured lights flashed by the perspex windshield, deadly white puffs cast a hail of shrapnel in all directions. There was a sharp metallic crack, a jerk, and the smell of burnt rubber and cordite. A hollow voice echoed round Grenville's mind as if his skull were a cavern. This is it! Here it comes. . . !

But miraculously they were past and still alive. The fjord widened as the spur fell behind them and the fury of the flak lessened for a moment.

"F Freddy calling, skipper. Have just entered fjord."

That was his number 3, Ayliffe. He listened again to the monotonous voice still counting in his mind. Only forty-five seconds since he had entered hell! He glanced back. The fjord appeared blocked with an impenetrable curtain of smoke trails and bursting shells. Six lines of tracer were converging on an invisible point, probably Milner. Nearer, looking frail and tiny against the massive rocks, a Mosquito was diving on a flak post with all four guns ablaze. Far above he saw a black speck soaring over the jagged rim of the fjord—either another of his Mosquitoes or a Focke-Wulf, he did not know which. His lips drew back painfully as he remembered the Focke-Wulfs. They would not venture into this hell of flame and shrapnel, but they would be waiting up there to pick off any survivors. They were a problem to which he had found no answer. But they could wait: they were a full minute away.

As his Number 4 announced his successful entry into the fjord, the mountains closed in. A row of flashes appeared above an approaching treeline. God; how many guns were there in this place . . . ? Grenville threw a sidelong glance at Phillips. The observer's sallow face was shiny with sweat and a white spot of saliva hung at one corner of his mouth. He was sitting with his knees bunched up and his body strained forward as if he were in an electric chair. He caught Grenville's eyes and tried to smile. The poor devil . . . sitting there helpless . . . waiting for it. What a filthy job!

The fjord straightened out again, and at last Grenville could see Trollfjell. It was at eleven o'clock, a mountain that from this angle looked oddly like a man, with a woolly chest of trees, a gaunt grey neck, and high above a massive bulging head with a cap of ice. Alongside it, at the extreme end of the fjord, was the high waterfall that fed power into the hydro-electric plant below, and built round this plant was the huge concrete building that was their target. On the banks of the fjord, half-hidden by birch and firs, were dozens of small huts which Grenville guessed to be living quarters.

But there was no time for curiosity. At this last line of defence the flak posts were more numerous than ever, and their gunners no longer exultant but desperate. The tiger had broken through its trap and its prize lay dead ahead. The entire area around the building lit up with the flash of guns, and their stunning thunder brought minor avalanches down from the surrounding heights. Luminous balls of tracer criss-crossed the sky around the weaving plane, the coloured glow from their shells reflecting back from the dark water below. The Mosquito shuddered and rocked like a cockleshell caught in a typhoon.

Grenville heard his Number 5 calling, but now his whole attention was focused on the mountain that was leaping forward at nearly five miles a minute. It loomed nearer, crushingly near—so near that he could see the flak shells hitting it and sending rock splinters flying like shrapnel.

Phillips had opened his bomb doors and he could feel them quivering in the airflow. The red light on his bomb distributor panel was glowing, and Phillips had fused the bomb. Airspeed was right, everything was ready. . . .

The Mosquito flashed into the rock-strewn corrie. Below it were the wooded slopes that led down to the water, above it was the massive overhang with its millions of tons of rock and ice. Oblivious now to the raging flak, Grenville pin-pointed his aiming mark—a huge boulder where the neck curved outwards. He watched the red paint-mark on his port nacelle, speaking slowly into his intercom.

"Coming up now . . . easy . . . easy." The Mosquito was on her side now, her wings vertical with the cliff. The red mark was almost in line with the boulder. "Ready . . . ready. . . ." With all his strength Grenville pulled the Mosquito away. "Now!" he shouted, and Phillips pressed the bomb release.

30

The Mosquito shot away as if ricochetting from the rocks. The huge bomb, released in the steep turn, cata-pulted away to crash among the debris of loose rocks at the foot of the overhang.

Grenville felt himself rammed into his seat by the g. Invisible fingers clawed at his eyes and cheeks, and for a few seconds everything turned grey before him. Then he found himself shooting across the fjord like a rocket with the vengeful flak following him. The imperturb-able voice in his mind was counting again. Three . . . four . . . five. . . . He pulled back on the stick, going into a steep climbing turn that lifted him towards the blue sky above.

Six . . . seven . . . eight. . . . The flak was following him up. A blinding flash burst dead ahead, and long gashes appeared near the port wing root. Not a second later another shell burst in the nose, shrapnel ripping through pneumatic pipes and electric cables. The cock-pit filled with the stink of cordite and fumes from the escaping hydraulic fluid. Air screamed through the shattered nose, adding a banshee wail to the sound of the engines.

Nine . . . ten . . . The Mosquito suddenly burst into the clean morning sunlight. Flak still followed it like lava being tossed up from the bowels of a vol-cano. Grenville should have taken cover over the rim of the ridge, but instead he turned back. Eleven . . . his mind chanted.

Half a second later the bomb went off. Every detail below became etched in brilliant light. The volcanic ap-pearance of the fjord was increased by the cloud of stones and rubble thrown upwards by the tremendous explosion. The Mosquito reared and almost turned over in the blast. Still dazed from the flak, Grenville fought the controls, his eyes on Trollfjell.

But the massive overhang had not moved, although

small falls of rock and ice were still sprinkling from it. Milner came over the radio. "Am going in now, skipper."

Twenty seconds was a perilous margin between attacks. Grenville had known it, but because of the waiting Focke-Wulfs it had been imperative to get the planes into the fjord as quickly as possible. He had gambled on the mountain spurs protecting the attacking plane from the explosion ahead and it seemed he had been right. Of course, there was danger from rock falls, but that was nothing compared with the flak.

From above, Milner's tiny Mosquito looked like a dragonfly being pierced by a dozen brightly-coloured pins. Somehow it got through and vanished for a breathless moment into the deep shadows under Trollfjell. Then it came shooting out and began corkscrewing upwards.

"O.K., skipper. Bomb gone."

Grenville was just congratulating Milner when a row of eight black bursts cut the climbing Mosquito in two. Her right wing tore off at the root, fluttering away like a leaf. The asymmetrical fuselage spun down, trailing black smoke and a shred of flame from its port engine. The flame lengthened, brightened, there was a sudden brilliant flash, then nothing but a glowing ball of fire that dropped like a plummet into the dark mass of trees below.

As if in revenge, the bomb Milner had planted burst two seconds later. This time a heavy sheet of snow cascaded from the summit and fell among the shrubs on its lower slopes. But the massive head of Trollfjell still towered over the smoke and falling debris.

A medley of shouts over the R/T brought Grenville's stunned mind back to the present.

"Focke-Wulfs at eight o'clock. . . !"

"Look out, Green two! Break port!"

Grenville realized the Focke-Wulfs were among his Green sections and remembered his own danger. His tight turn came just in time—red tracer snapping by his port wing-tip. A green and black Focke-Wulf dived by: he was about to attack it in turn when he remembered his own orders. Every plane that survived

234

the attack on the mountain had to go back to help the others through. As another 190 came snarling at him, he dived away into the shadows of the fjord. The Focke-Wulf did not follow him.

Flying as he now was in the opposite direction to Trollfjell, the flak did not pay him much attention for the moment. He turned to Phillips and saw with a shock that the observer was slumped forward in his harness. As Grenville pulled him back his head lolled sideways, showing the front of his flying suit to be sticky with blood. Grenville had no way of knowing how seriously he was hurt, and could do nothing for him at the moment. He checked his controls. It seemed nothing vital had been hit, although his trimmer controls appeared to have gone.

He stared down. Far below Ayliffe was commencing his run-in on Trollfjell. The flak caught him the moment he stopped weaving. A thin stream of burning glycol from his starboard exhaust showed white against the shadows. It turned black a second later . . . a thin tongue of fire licked back . . . lengthened . . . a bright explosion among the rocks. Gone.

Not three seconds later, far up the fjord, flak got his Number 4. The curving plume of flame and smoke, the pathetic shower of sparks against the rock face, they could mean nothing else.

Whatever the cost, they had to get more bombs on Trollfjell! Grenville called up his Green sections, only to hear Young's Australian drawl come back wearily:

"We're doing our best, skipper. But there's only Archer and me left. . . ."

And not ten seconds later Archer went, caught by a 190 as he came up blinded after attacking a 20 mm. post on a rock shelf.

Two spitting barrels came into Grenville's gunsight. He pressed his attack so close he was able to see the discarded shell cases leaping out from the recoiling breeches, and the crouching loaders with their clips of ammunition. He opened fire and his shells cut down men, splintered trees, ricochetted off rocks. Only his two cannon were firing, the shell that had burst in the nose must have cut the pneumatic leads to his Brownings. He pulled away, looking for another post. Through the animal fury that was shaking his body, a cool untouched part of his brain was analysing the reports that were coming over the radio, and giving orders both to himself and his crews. Number 5 had planted his bomb successfully, had turned back up the fjord, then gone silent—probably shot down. Number 6 had also got through to Trollfjell, but appeared to have crashed into it after planting its bomb. Seven, eight, and nine were still on their way.

Trollfjell was still there—Grenville could see its ugly head in the distance as he raged over a mountain shoulder. Bitterness was swilling about inside him like acid. What fool had thought of this idea? Throwing men against a mountain in the hope of bringing it down. . . .

The Focke-Wulfs above were buzzing about like flies over a jam-pot. Occasionally one of them would screw up enough courage to venture down over the rim of the inferno, only to draw back hastily a few seconds later. But they were ready, waiting like hawks for any survivors.

"I've had it skipper. Sorry. . . ." That was young Parsons—Parsons who was so proud of his baby. He was hit as he cleared the last mountain spur. His smoking Mosquito tried to pancake into the fjord, crashed in a cloud of steam, and turned over. Only one yellow Mae West showed among the bubbling black water.

The loss of his crews was driving Grenville frantic. He called down Young, the last survivor of his Green sections, and ordered him to escort Number 9 while he flew ahead of Number 8. Perhaps by flying in pairs, with fifty yards between each pair, they might thin out the intensity of the fire.

Number 8 was Barrett. As Grenville dived over him to take up position, he saw the Wing Commander's squirrel-brown moustache clearly as Barrett leaned back and waved at him. His gruff voice came cheerfully over the radio.

"Quite a party, Roy. Everything but the dancing girls."

Grenville tried to remember the sites of the flak posts as he led Barrett by them. The fire from them was thinned a little, but only relatively. Not a mile behind them Young followed, leading his Number 9.

The smell of leaking hydraulic fluid was severe now. Grenville pulled up his oxygen-mask, somehow managed to do the same for Phillips, and turned the taps on to emergency. His heart was hammering both from the tension and the sheer physical effort of throwing the Mosquito about in the narrow fjord.

The last mountain spur approached, and with it the flak post that had got Parsons. Its multiple pom-pom gave Grenville a burst, then, as if knowing who was carrying the bomb, turned its full fury on Barrett. A flash on his port engine, and a piece of cowling was torn away. Another flash, and a leg of his undercarriage dropped like a broken claw. Then they were past.

Grenvill's mouth was dry. "You all right, Don?"

"Still around, Roy. Now where's that gremlin?"

The massed flak posts round the building opened up like the roll of drums before an execution. Two shells went right through Grenvill's tailplane without exploding. Barrett's voice came longingly over the radio.

"Hell, Roy; wouldn't it be just the job to drop the bloody thing right on top of em?"

Grenville led him almost under the massive overhang before turning away. He was unable to see Barrett drop his bomb, but heard his excited voice a few seconds later.

"Right on the button, Roy, or as near as damn it, anyway. Now let's get out of here."

Doubting Barrett's skill, Grenville could only hope he had been as accurate as he believed. He fought for height through the thundering flak, Barrett following him. As they climbed higher the flak lessened as the gun-posts, knowing now they carried only one bomb apiece, concentrated on the planes yet to come in.

Just under the lip of the fjord Grenville levelled out and waited for Barrett's B Bobby, with its dangling undercarriage, to come alongside him.

237

"Any second now, Roy. Watch for it," Barrett called.

Grenville held little hope of bringing down Trollfjell now, and was busy watching the sky for fighters. Barrett was staring intently down. The familiar blinding flash came, the upflung shower of rocks, the blast, and then Barrett's hysterical voice.

"Roy! It's going! The bloody thing's going. Look!"

Startled, Grenville looked down. The massive head of Trollfjell appeared to be wobbling drunkenly. Then, as if split by some enormous mason's chisel, the front section of it slipped away and toppled into the void below.

The noise could be heard over the roar of the engines, an earth-shaking thunder as thousands of tons of rock, followed by the dislodged mass of the glacier, plunged 3,000 feet into the fjord. An irresistible force, terrifying to watch. . . .

It hit the lower slopes and bounded forward like a tidal wave. It swept over trees, huts, flak posts, hydroelectric plant and concrete buildings, grinding them and crushing them as a steamroller flattens an ant heap. It set off enormous echoes that reverberated across the fjord for minutes.

"God!" Barrett said, awestruck.

All the firing had stopped. Even the Focke-Wulfs had broken off their vigilance to stare down aghast. But one flak post commander, more phlegmatic or perhaps more revengeful than the rest that had survived, saw the Mosquitoes approaching and snapped out orders that pulled his shocked crew together.

Grenville had just finished transmitting the code word that would send Davies delirious with pride when he saw the red flashes open up dead ahead of them. He yelled a warning to Barrett and swung sharply away. But Barrett's reflexes had lost their edge through lack of combat flying and he turned too late. Tracer stitched a line of holes the full length of his fuselage. . . .

Even then it seemed no harm had been done. His Mosquito flew over the post and swept on along the range.

Grenville's voice was sharp with anxiety. "Don; are you all right?"

No answer. Grenville flew closer until he was right alongside.

"Don! How bad is it?"

He could see through B Bobby's transparent hood now. The observer was lolling sideward against his harness and Barrett was huddled over the stick.

"Don! For God's sake. . . . Get the hatch away. Try to bale out!"

A ghost voice answered, a million miles away. "No . . . good, Roy. No . . . good."

The whisper died away and the Mosquito's nose dropped wearily. Steeper . . . steeper . . . one wing dipping as she went. Down . . . down . . . out of sight A red glow straining the shadows of the fjord. . . .

Grenville went back to look for the gun-post. His face was that of a devil. With the target destroyed and his crews virtually wiped out, he was at last able to give full vent to his bitterness. He set the flak post with exquisite care in his gunsight as he came back along the ridge. It was not enough to blast it with shells, however; pure hate is never satisfied with long-range killing. He was going to hurl the Mosquito's white-hot engines on the crew, to impale them on the struts of its fuselage, to smash them to pulp with the impact of his own flesh. They were to be killed for many things, not least for letting him live when so many others had died.

The crew were inside his luminous sight now, warmly dressed, crouching behind the quadruple 20 mm. with a mountain hut behind them. The four automatic guns were already firing, doing mortal damage to his Mosquito, but he noticed the shells no more than a berserk fighter notices the blows of his opponent. A white-faced loader carrying ammunition clips halted, staring upwards in terrified fascination. Grenville's pressure on the gun button was as savage as if it had been on the windpipe of an enemy. The loader was flung away, unrecognizable now as anything human. Grenville swung his rudder bar, mowing men down with meticulous care. . . . Crouched behind his gunsight he urged his plane on to destruction. A gunner lost his nerve and began running. That won't help you. . . . Nothing can help you now. Faster. . . . Faster, you bitch. . . .

It was a small thing that prevented the final tragedy. A shell bursting under the starboard wing, that made the Mosquito lurch sideways. . . . Grenville corrected the movement immediately, but its suddenness had thrown the unconscious Phillips towards him and the observer's head nudged his arm. . . .

The contact pierced the mist of hate round Grenville's mind. It was as if the unconscious man were pleading for his life. One could sacrifice a conscious man, a nod from him and the thing was done. But not this. . . .

With a curse he jerked back on the stick. The shell-torn smoking Mosquito pulled away not ten feet above the stricken gunpost. Grenville's duty now was to get Phillips home—he knew it, and his bitterness was complete. Duty lay on him like the curse of Cain.

With one engine feathered and his starboard aileron dragging loose, he struggled painfully to clear the snow-topped mountains. But the Focke-Wulfs were waiting. Crippled, with the last of his ammunition gone, he was helpless against them. A burst of 7 mm. sent a stab of agony through his legs, smashing them from the rudder bar. He managed to side-slip away, but he was tired . . . tired. . . . A Focke-Wulf came weaving in for the kill, its pilots eyes cold behind his gunsight. He fired at point-blank range.

One burst was enough. The Mosquito's weakened tailplane broke away and its surviving engine choked and died. It struck the mountain-top, skidded forward under its speed, then suddenly vanished in an enormous flurry of snow. A few seconds later all that showed to the circling aircraft was a pathetic tangle of spars and the flaming mass of a broken-off engine. The battle of the Svartfjord was over.

31

The innkeeper slowly closed the folder. "Every man who took part in that action was decorated, and Grenville got the V.C." His eyes lifted upwards. "And there you are. That's the whole story."

The two young airmen were spellbound, too awed for the moment to speak. The innkeeper took a glance round the lounge while he waited for the questions he knew must come. The fire was burning red now, deepening the glow from the shaded lamps. No one else was present but the car driver, who was still sitting in the corner among the shadows. The room was hushed, and the atmosphere even more intense than it had been earlier. An odd shudder ran through the innkeeper as again the reflections from the photographs swam in his vision. . . .

The English boy found his voice first, stealing the question from his friend's lips. "What about the girls? What happened to them?"

The innkeeper nodded. "Maisie stayed on here for another eighteen months, then got herself married to another Canadian airman. This one came through all right, and she went back with him in 1945. She has two children now, a boy and a girl. I think she's happy."

The American found his voice now. "That's good to know," he said huskily. "And what about Hilde?"

"She didn't stay here long after the raid. Like everyone else she thought Grenville had been killed. She went into the Services and stayed in uniform for the rest of the war."

Daly was opening his mouth to ask another question when his friend again interrupted him. "Just what did happen to Grenville? How was it he escaped? I've never been sure of that."

"Rocks tore off both wings, so keeping the burning

engines away from the fuselage. The deep snow did the rest by cushioning the effects of the crash."

"Grenville must have been convinced he wasn't meant to die after that."

"He must indeed. Of course, like Phillips he was badly wounded and in prison hospital for a long time."

"They thought over here he was dead, didn't they?"

"Yes. They believed it for over two months."

The American could not be withheld any longer. "Hilde—that's the girl I want to hear more about? What happened? Surely she met Grenville when he got back?"

The innkeeper shook his head heavily. "She has never seen him since that last night before the raid."

Daly looked shocked. Then he exploded. "But why? Why the hell didn't someone tell her the truth? Why didn't this guy Adams have the guts to tell her?"

"He did tell her," the innkeeper said quietly. "But it was two days before he found out what Grenville had said. He knew Grenville had no girl friend, he knew the whole thing was a pack of lies and told her so. He told her everything. . . ."

Daly's voice was hushed. "How did she take it?"

"It was a shock to her, but she took it as he'd always believed she would. But then it was too late."

"But it wasn't too late! Grenville came back. Couldn't something have been done then?"

"It wasn't her fault; it was Grenville's. You're forgetting his state of mind. It was he who had always believed there was an impassable barrier between himself and Hilde, and two years brooding in a prison camp did nothing to change his mind."

"But if someone had told him she understood!"

"Someone did tell him, but he would not believe it. He was too bitter."

"But in time he would have come round if they'd kept at him. . . ."

"There was no way of keeping at him. Once he had given his story to Intelligence he was discharged, and then everyone lost touch with him. Letters came back undelivered; nobody knew if he was alive or dead. And to my knowledge nobody knows to this day."

The silence had a finality about it that brought a sudden chill to the room.

"It's a long time ago," the innkeeper said wearily. "And yet at times it seems only yesterday. Nothing has ever seemed as real since."

"What about Adams and his wife? How did they get on?" The American's tone betrayed little interest; like the innkeeper he was only talking now to drive off the silence.

"Yes; I can even tell you that. They were divorced in 1948."

One question had been in Daly's mind ever since the innkeeper had laid down the manuscript, but it had had to take second place until more urgent ones were answered. Now he leaned forward curiously.

"There's one thing I can't make out, Pop. You say that Kearns was a man in his fifties. O.K.; I guess you're in your fifties too. But you weren't ten years ago. And there's something else, too. How did you find out all the details—all that happened in the Intelligence Room, the Operations Room, and in the house in the country? And how did you find out all the technical stuff? You tell it as if you'd been one of the boys."

The innkeeper took off his thick glasses and wiped them. "I realized some time ago that you hadn't been told my name, and was rather hoping you wouldn't ask." His weak eyes looked at them almost apologetically. "It's quite simple, really. You see, I'm Adams. . . ."

There is always a shock in discovering that in real life characters have a way of living on beyond the final curtain. Both airmen felt it now.

"You're Adams?" the American muttered.

"Yes. I bought the pub just after the war. The old man and I had become good friends and he gave me first option when he sold." The years had weathered away Adams' bitterness; there was barely a trace of it in his voice as he went on: "It was one of the things Valerie and I quarrelled about. She didn't like the idea of being a country publican's wife, and perhaps one can't blame her—it can be quiet here in the winter."

"Why did you buy it?" the English pilot asked curiously.

Adams hesitated. "I don't really know." Then he smiled. "Perhaps because I'm a bit of a sentimentalist. Perhaps that was it."

"Was it you who told Grenville?"

"Yes; it was me. I wrote him in prison camp, telling him everything, and I had another go at him when he was ordered to give us the full story of the raid. But he wouldn't discuss her at all. I wrote him quite a few times afterwards, too, but all my letters were returned address unknown."

The American moved unhappily in his chair. "It's a waste," he muttered. "Two people kept apart like that—I don't like it."

Adams gave a faint smile. It was not difficult to recognize another sentimentalist.

"Where is Hilde now?" Daly asked. "Back in Norway?"

"Yes. She lives with a cousin in Bergen." Adams tapped the manuscript in front of him, smiling ruefully. "It wasn't easy to get her permission to include her in this book. Of course, I haven't used any of the girls' true Christian names—theirs are the only fictional names in the book—but she was still very hesitant. I think only one thing changed her mind."

"What was that?"

"I pointed out that if it were published, Grenville might read it and realize how wrong he had been. I'm pretty certain that was the only reason she gave in."

Daly winced. "The poor kid," he muttered. Then he looked at Adams eagerly. "But you're right. It could bring him back—even after all these years. When is it to be published?"

Adams' reply startled him. "It's already published. It came out on the sixth of this month."

"And you've heard nothing from him yet?"

Adams shook his head.

"Maybe he wouldn't know where to find you," Daly suggested.

"Oh, he knows I am here. I had already bought the pub when I last saw him in 1945."

Daly was young. He refused to give up hope. "There's still plenty of time. Supposing he did come back—could you get hold of Hilde easily?"

"Oh, yes. We keep in touch. In fact, she comes over here every spring to stay with me."

"Here?" Daly said hoarsely. "Every spring? Why?"

Adams smiled quietly. "Why? Why do people keep their memories alive? Why do they keep souvenirs and photographs? Tell me that and I'll tell you why she comes over here every spring."

The young American did not need telling. He was staring at the huge bowl of daffodils on the counter with an awed, almost frightened look in his eyes.

Adams nodded. "Yes. This year as well. She has been here over a week now. Of course"—this is a trifle wistfully—"we have become good friends over the years. I like to think that has a little to do with her coming." He glanced at his watch. "She went into town this afternoon. The bus is late; she should have been back over ten minutes ago."

None of them had noticed how emotion had been clawing at the face of the man in the corner. Nor did they notice how he started now at Adams' words. He only drew their attention five minutes later when light, hurrying footsteps on the gravel outside brought him sharply to his feet. Adams caught the abrupt movement, heard his harsh, expectant breathing, and peered at him curiously. Slowly the white, intent face swam into focus. Adams gave one incredulous gasp, and then the lounge door opened. . . .

Half an hour later they had all gone from the lounge, and Adams stood alone behind the bar. Something inside him was still trembling, still glorying, still weeping a little. In the glistening blur before his eyes, the lights from the photographs had diffused and became his ghosts again. They were as gay now as they had been in the old days—laughing, joking, congratulating one another. Then, one by one, they waved to him and slipped out. They were the dead who wanted the living to live, and for years their leader's loneliness had been their sorrow. They had joined him this night with a long-held wish, and at last they had seen that wish granted.

They could all rest well now.

THE END

ABOUT THE AUTHOR

FREDERICK E. SMITH joined the R.A.F. in 1939 as a wireless operator/air gunner and commenced service in early 1940, serving in Britain, Africa and finally the Far East. At the end of the war he married and worked for several years in South Africa before returning to England to fulfill his life-long ambition to write. Two years later, his first play was produced and his first novel published. Since then, he has written twenty-four novels, about eighty short stories and two plays. Two novels, *633 Squadron* and *The Devil Doll*, have been made into films and one, *A Killing for the Hawks,* has won the Mark Twain Literary Award.

JOIN THE 633 SQUADRON

The original 633 SQUADRON, written a number of years ago, has become a classic of air literature, translated into many languages. The British author, Frederick E. Smith, had not planned any further books until he was deluged with reader inquiries from all over the world asking for more information about the members of this Yorkshire-based Special Service Unit. He finally was persuaded to continue the series of books about this legendary Mosquire Squadron of the RAF. The results are rousing, action-filled stories which are now being published in the United States for the first time.

633 SQUADRON

(now available)
The mission was called Vesuvius, and the invasion of Europe depended on it. The squadron's target was a Norwegian fiord where Germans were developing something so secret that even the RAF crews were told nothing about it. But everyone knew this was a dangerous, almost suicidal, mission. Caught between the attacking German aircraft and the grim mountain walls, the 633 Squadron plunged into the howling valley of death.

633 SQUADRON: OPERATION RHINE MAIDEN

(available April 1st)
Under the young, brilliant, new Commander Ian Moore, the squadron flew a mission to thwart the new German anti-aircraft rocket which posed the

most deadly threat to Allied invasion plans. The squadron had to come in on a daylight bombing run to wipe out the rocket factory and strike an underground target buried deep in a Bavarian valley.

633 SQUADRON: OPERATION CRUCIBLE

(available May 1st)
Autumn 1943. To restore world confidence in the RAF, which had been blamed by a British correspondent for heavy U.S. losses over Europe, the RAF and the 8th Air Force top brass chose the 633 Squadron to perform their most hazardous mission yet—giving ground support to American troops going in on a daring Dieppe-style landing against totally unforseen odds.

633 SQUADRON: OPERATION VALKYRIE

(available June 1st)
February 1944. The squadron was called on to destroy a large consignment of heavy water being smuggled out of Norway to Germany. To succeed in this mission seemed impossible until Intelligence Officer Frank Adams came up with a bizarre scheme—the only hitch was that it would put the entire squadron in great peril.

633 SQUADRON books are published by Bantam, to be available wherever paperbacks are sold.

BANTAM WAR BOOKS

These action-packed books recount the most important events of World War II. They take you into battle and present portraits of brave men and true stories of gallantry in action. All books have special maps, diagrams, and illustrations.

☐	12657	**AS EAGLES SCREAMED** Burgett	$2.25
☐	12658	**THE BIG SHOW** Clostermann	$2.25
☐	11812	**BRAZEN CHARIOTS** Crisp	$1.95
☐	12666	**THE COAST WATCHERS** Feldt	$2.25
☐	*12664	**COCKLESHELL HEROES** Lucas-Phillips	$2.25
☐	12141	**COMPANY COMMANDER** MacDonald	$1.95
☐	12578	**THE DIVINE WIND** Pineau & Inoguchi	$2.25
☐	*12669	**ENEMY COAST AHEAD** Gibson	$2.25
☐	*12667	**ESCORT COMMANDER** Robertson	$2.25
☐	*11709	**THE FIRST AND THE LAST** Galland	$1.95
☐	*11642	**FLY FOR YOUR LIFE** Forrester	$1.95
☐	12665	**HELMET FOR MY PILLOW** Leckie	$2.25
☐	12663	**HORRIDO!** Toliver & Constable	$2.25
☐	12670	**THE HUNDRED DAYS OF LT. MACHORTON** Machorton	$2.25
☐	*12668	**I FLEW FOR THE FURHER** Knoke	$2.25
☐	12290	**IRON COFFINS** Werner	$2.25
☐	12671	**QUEEN OF THE FLAT-TOPS** Johnston	$2.25
☐	*11822	**REACH FOR THE SKY** Brickhill	$1.95
☐	12662	**THE ROAD PAST MANDALAY** Masters	$2.25
☐	12523	**SAMURAI** Sakai with Caidin & Saito	$2.25
☐	12659	**U-BOAT KILLER** Macintyre	$2.25
☐	12660	**V-2** Dornberger	$2.25
☐	*12661	**THE WHITE RABBIT** Marshall	$2.25
☐	*12150	**WE DIE ALONE** Howarth	$1.95

*Cannot be sold to Canadian Residents.

Buy them at your local bookstore or use this handy coupon:

Bantam Books, Inc., Dept. WW2, 414 East Golf Road, Des Plaines, Ill. 60016

Please send me the books I have checked above. I am enclosing $_____ (please add 75¢ to cover postage and handling). Send check or money order —no cash or C.O.D.'s please.

Mr/Mrs/Miss _____

Address _____

City _____ State/Zip _____

WW2—2/79

Please allow four weeks for delivery. This offer expires 8/79.